The Highwayman and the Spy

Daniel Carlson

Published by Daniel Carlson, 2022.

THE HIGHWAYMAN AND THE SPY

First edition. November 2, 2022.

Copyright © 2022 Daniel Carlson.

ISBN: 979-8215356142

Written by Daniel Carlson.

Chapter 1

Blyton, The South Riding, England 1745.

Jem Rose gulped down the last sip off his Graves Bordeaux, the Baroness's favourite wine and moved away from the table to cleverly gain him a few more valuable seconds of thinking time.

He probed deep into his addled mind to search for an explanation, but stunned by this sudden and unexpected discovery there was none to be found.

He lent his elbow upon the mantel of the Cippolino marble fire surround and swivelled around at his waist to respond to the beautiful women's accusations in the only way he could.

"How could you imagine such a thing?"

The flickering shadows of flame distorted and disguised the anguish that fractured his countenance as he continued.

"Me a robber, a vagrant and an imposter. Think of what you are saying. Even the thought of it is an insult to my integrity."

Swallowing the last remnants of her wine, she opened her vermillion covered, glistening lips to relay her anger.

"I don't just think that it is true." The Bordeaux shook her head suddenly left an unpleasant taste in her mouth, which could only be equalled by the way she felt.

"I know it's true, all of it!"

Distress and disappointment could be detected in her tones and anger raged in her water filled eyes.

Jem avoiding her piercing glare turned himself back towards the blazing fire. He remained silent as he watched the Baron of Walden's widow, his secret lover for the last two years in the reflection of the mirror, which hung purposefully above the mammoth fireplace.

Swinging out her legs from under the table and gathering with both hands her finest mantra, the Baroness almost seemed to glide her way through the cast of his giant shadow until the orange glow of flame softened her features and hued her white powdered wig and the accompanying entwined ribbons of lace.

She angled her face in the reflection to force the handsome and imposing man into direct eye contact.

"I feel as though I don't know you anymore Jem." She referred to her recently acquired knowledge of her lover's duel existence.

"Claudia please, this is ridiculous."

"You're right. This is ridiculous. You've played this game with me for the last two years and I've been so love blind and stupid that I couldn't see it."

"No, no. Please don't say that. It's not true."

For the first time in his life, this normally confident, quick thinking and voluble man was struggling to find some convincing words of denial.

"How can you distress and pain me beyond what you already have by standing there and openly lying to my face?"

"Claudia please believe me," He tilted his head slightly in a contrite way and turned away from the mantelpiece, "my love for you is no lie."

"Believe you. The master of deceit, scourge of the Ridings, king of the night and the ruler of the highways."

Her accusation triggered a shuddered to splice his spine. He now knew that it had to be over between them and he did not want to over expose himself or divulge any extra information which she may not already know.

"I don't know what to believe anymore"

Finally, her cool, calm and controlled barrier collapsed and tears began to brim over her eye lids.

"Claudia don't do this to yourself by believing this nonsense."

He was faked the sincerity flawlessly and he tried to console her in his arms, but she resisted his advance and held him off with her flat palm.

"I feel as though I only know half of you. For the last two years I've found myself loving only half a man whilst secretly the other half is gallivanting around the shadows of the countryside reigning terror upon the innocent."

A furrow formed on his forehead as he speculated and waited for her to reveal what else she knew but averting his gaze she lowered her head and sobbed inconsolably into her hands.

There was a lengthy pause as neither of them spoke until after a long moment she broke the silence and raised her face from her wet hands.

"Oh, how I wished I had listened to General Preeceton"

General Algeron Preeceton was a tall skeletal man who looked far more aged than he was. He had been a neighbour and a close friend of the Baroness's late husband and since his death seven years ago he had plagued her affairs with his persistent interference.

Jem, being astute as he was devious, was not oblivious to note the financial rewards gained by claiming the Baroness's hand in marriage and he more than suspected the General, himself a widower was planning to acquire this security.

The General and Jem despised each other, mainly because of the rivalry with both of them vying to gain the affections of the Baroness.

Jem knew the General did not trust him and he knew one day he would have to manoeuvre the General into the distance and beyond the reach if he was to have a successful relationship with the Baroness.

Firstly, after the Baron of Walden died the General offered his loyalty and friendship to the bereaved widow, he gradually turned the friendship into trust then admiration. His aim was to substitute the admiration for affection and then the matrimony was sure to follow.

Jem intervened at the admiration part, sweeping the Baroness off her feet with his advantageous good looks and articulate tongue and it was he who nurtured the admiration into affection.

A deep hatred had regained ever since and now the mere mention of Algeron Preeceton turned Jem's stomach and ignited his fierce temper.

"Just what the hell has that piteous bastard got to do with this?" He closed the distance between them.

"Nothing." Realising her error she shied away from the confrontation.

"What do you mean nothing? Tell me. What has he been telling you this time?"

"Nothing" Jem reached out his hand and clasping it around the woman's forearm, he spun her around to face him.

"I don't believe you. One minute everything is fine and I'm sitting eating my supper before I begin my night journey for the Beverly market and then suddenly I am being accused of God knows what."

He gestured annoyance with the dismissive wave of his arm. "Then you let it slip that the old jealous weasel has been around here again interfering. Now tell me just what kind of a story he has got you believing this time."

She drew breath, braced herself and began.

"He followed you Jem. Last month when you said you were going to Lincoln, he followed you all the way up the North Road to Wentbridge." She sighed. "Isn't that near to where the Pontefract night carriage was held up and robber?"

"And you believe him. This is ridiculous. That man is twisted. He just wants me out your life so he can worm his way back in."

"Your right this is ridiculous and General Preeceton is twisted, but he is not half as twisted as you."

"I can't believe you are prepared to believe his word against mine. I'm telling you Claudia while you allow him to come around here he will continue to interfere with your life until your life is nothing but a misery just as his own is."

"I did not believe a word," She struggled to contained the noticeable quiver in her words, "not at first."

"What?" He scowled wondering to what she was going to say next and hoping she had said nothing to the local constables.

"So I paid Henry Mason's son, to follow you last Tuesday. Do you remember last Tuesday Jem?"

He said nothing and his face revealed nothing.

"You told me you were going to the Nottingham horse market, quite away from Wentbridge .... isn't it Jem. Do I need say anymore?"

He sighed with relief knowing that she only knew part of the ruse and she had not discovered his other home in Badsworth.

He felt safe with the knowledge that both General Preeceton and young Mason hadn't the calibre of riding skills that it would take to follow him down the dark and secluded ravines of the Ridings which he knew like no other man on earth. He knew for certain that neither the man nor the boy would have been able to keep up with him after the hold up and his escape from the scene with the speed and elusiveness of a demon.

"We'll talk about this when I return." He tried to dismiss calmly.

"There will be no more talking Jem. It's over."

"Claudia I'm already late and you know I need to be there when the market opens."

"Market? Liar! You're a liar Jem Rose." She bellowed in recrimination.

"I haven't got time for this nonsense."

"No you haven't. You're like the jewel of the Azure."

Jem didn't reply to her comparison, he simply waited for her to continue.

"You too are a fake."

"We'll continue this discussion when I get back." He angles himself towards the table and checked his glass was empty then he straightened to glance at his gold pocket watch, a gift from the Baroness.

"No we will not Jem, because if you leave this house tonight you will never come back." The Baroness insisted, her eyes diverted to the shimmering reminder of happier times.

That was Jem's exact intention, but he feared his mistress had a different view of the outcome.

"What do you mean Claudia? What are you saying?"

Although she didn't reach his shoulder in height and he could barely feel the grip of the detaining hand she had placed around his solid arm he feared for the moment to move.

"I'm saying leave me tonight and you'll never live to see me again." Her eyes were no longer wet and her voice no longer contained the nervous quiver.

Speculation danced in their dark, flame reflecting eyes as they brooded intensely into each other's soul.

The creaking of a floor board beyond the dining room door brought a premature halt to the quarrelling and it shattered the scrutiny.

Leaving the Baroness by the fireside, Jem soundlessly moved across to the door. Unbeknownst to the Baroness, he slid out from beneath his waistcoat a dagger and then with instantaneous speed he twisted the brass door handle to pull the door open.

His alarm immediately decreased as before him stooped the aged and fragile head servant.

"Sorry to disturb." He began.

"Ah, just the man," Jem cut in, "is she ready Blackyard?"

"Y.... Y.... Yes sir." Came the flustered response. "I was just coming to tell you, sir," he felt the need to prattle as a necessity, "I gave her a good feed and rub down earlier, just as you always like her sir."

"Good man. Saddle her up and I'll be down in a moment."

Jem did not know what Blackyard was up to nor did he care. In a few minutes he would be well on his way out of Blyton and with partial regret, out of the Baroness life forever.

He watched Blackyard drag his stiffened limbs down the corridor and satisfied they were alone once more he turned to draw nearer the Baroness.

He had been on this stage many times before and he knew exactly how the script would read, word for word.

"It's time for me to leave." He announced feigning sincerity.

"Of course it is," she replied with hardened sarcasm. "We don't want you to break from your routine, do we?"

"Claudia please don't." He forced their eyes to once more collide. "Don't let us end the night on bad terms."

He leant forward, closing nearer and nearer to her face, but just as his mouth reached hers, for the first time ever, she resisted and pulled back turning her face to evade his advancing lips.

However, he had anticipated her action and so he calmly continued the motion landing one long and tender kiss upon her cheek.

"I must go now. I'm late."

"Oh yes! You're late." She scorned now raising a venomous tone. "Late for the Halifax to York and you don't want to be late for that, do you."

Once more she turned to hide her pain and the trembling of her hands. She felt betrayed and suddenly fragile. A chill but, not from the cold, tormented her neck and fluttered in her chest.

Jem could find no immediate answer without admitting his guilt and thankful that she didn't know the entire truth, he turned to close the door behind him fixing his eyes upon the Baroness, for what he knew would be the last time.

Beautiful and elegant, she had retained her position in the radiance of the fire, watching Jem's movements through the reflection in the mirror.

"Goodbye my love." She tearfully said to herself as Jem disappeared behind the closing door.

"It's going to be a cold one tonight, sir." Blackyard said leading into the star lit courtyard a huge gelding.

"It is that Blackyard." Jem agreed with the servants forecast as he mounted his treasured English grey barb.

He pulled around tight and fastened up the collar on his long frock coat delaying his leave as he sensed by the way Backyard was taking his time and being extra particular that he had something he wanted to say.

"Well, I'll see you tomorrow night Blackyard." He prompted as he turned the horse to face his exit.

"Please be careful, sir." The old man wheezed.

"Oh, I'll be careful Blackyard. I've had enough experience to know how to deal with those wily horse traders." He purposely associated the advice to his horse trading guise.

"No sir, it's not that what I mean." He slowly uttered raising to the sky one finger. "It's just that where I came from they say it is bad luck to travel when there is a blood moon."

"You know I'm not a superstitious man Blackyard." Jem countered looking upwards to see the emergence of the huge carmine sphere above the stable roof.

Hoping to discover the real reason behind Blackyard's nervousness he continued to slowly urge the horse forward.

"No sir, but tonight your destiny is controlled by more than just superstition."

Jem halted the horse. He knew Blackyard caution contained a hidden warning and that the old man knew something sinister, but it was too late, he had vanished into the darkness of the estate.

Any ordinary man would consider it foolhardy to continue with the plan especially when they suspected a trap awaited them, but Jem Rose was no ordinary man. He was fearless, supremely confident and he considered it a challenge to outwit his would be captors and return to his secret life which was waiting for him in the sleepy refuge village of Badsworth.

Without any further hesitation, he heeled his horse into motion and cantered off into the darkness towards the North Road.

The darkened sky was a clear mass without a cloud in sight and there was no getting away from it, the sheer blackness above was a continual reminder of the Baronesses deep, dark eyes and without the cloud cover it was sure to be as Blackyard predicted, a cold night.

The elements were not in Jem's favour, the cold would fatigue his horse and in the absence of any cold the bright red moon would hinder his cover.

Two hours later, Jem awaited his prey. Tucked discretely between trees and thick undergrowth on a secluded and notorious section of the North Road near to Aberford he sat motionless with only the call of an owl and the rustling breeze in the trees to accompany him and his trusty thoroughbred.

His mind pondered the future and his thoughts delivered a smile to his face, what he would give to see General Preeceton's face when the old nuisance heard the news of the successful robbery and the villain's escape.

After the holdup he intended to sell off the stolen items to his contacts in Beeston and then return home for a few days before travelling down to Nottingham to see his two sons just as he always did.

He had no morals, scruples or principles and cared little for those he hurt or from whom he stole. He had grown up hungry and deprived and there was no way his own family would suffer the pain and anguish of destitution.

His victim's coaches were chosen after hours of painful research and weeks of meticulous planning to ensure a plentiful bounty.

Sometimes it would humour him to give a prospective victim a reprieve at the last moment, especially if the robbery had resulted in a prosperous haul. If, when he held up a coach there was someone there that he took a liking to and for that reason only, never pity, he would tease them with words of humour before he volunteered a reprieve.

Standing alongside them with their hands held and legs quivering might be someone of equal pedigree and of similar stature who he would rob of every valuable and treasure of which they had in their possession.

He revelled with the feeling of power, he felt no guilt and his conscience remained unnerved and clear.

His craving for excitement fuelled his appetite and his desire for adventure was insatiable. He was supported by the knowledge that his home and financial situation were secure and free from suspicion.

His every breath oozed confidence and his every thought was of success. Even with the cryptic warning from Blackyard and the knowledge that a possible trap lay ahead, he considered himself free from peril. He was sure that his credentials in endurance riding and his skill with a pistol would guarantee him a safe exit.

At last, after what seemed an extraordinary and suspicious long wait the first signs that the coach was approaching became apparent.

He had done this so often that he could interpret all the telling signs of nature. The disturbance in the tress, the unrest in the undergrowth and the increased attention from his mount.

It was now in these final seconds that he pulled his Tricorne down firmly to shroud his eyes and fastened his black handkerchief securely to veil across his face. Once disguised he then prepared his flintlock to half cock and held it out at arms level in direct aim at the coach driver. He took in a few deep breaths and heeled the barb out into the path of the approaching carriage.

"Stand and deliver!"

The carriage horse's heads arched painfully back as the driver struggled to pull the coach to an immediate halt with all his might.

"It's the Yorkshire Raider!" The coachman screamed through his thick grey mass of a moustache jolting the travellers within suddenly out of their slumber.

By now Jem was well accustomed to the driver's reactions and he remained perfectly calm and still, his voice loud and menacing.

"Hold still your tongue and throw down your musket."

"I have nothing for vermin like you."

"I said be quiet!" The raised tone silenced the frightened man and Jem spurned him to cast down his musket by motioning with his pistol. "My interest with you lies only with your shooter."

After watching the dark red silhouette slowly raise then throw to a muddy thud the blunderbuss a slight nod signalled Jem's delight.

"Good. Now climb down here."

As Jem spoke a carriage window slid open and a fat face emerged. Alert to the danger he took aim at the huge round target and stiffened his arm.

"Damn all these interruptions. I've got to be in York by the morning." Fury reddened the man's saggy cheeks as he protested at the unscheduled stoppage without considering the consequences. "What in damnation is it this time driver?"

"I assure you sir, this will not take long and you will soon be again on your way." Jem presented himself out of the darkness and mirth crinkled his eyes.

Shock and fear immediately blanched the round face as now he understood the reason for the unscheduled stoppage, and as quick as he could he withdrew his head back into the carriage and out of Jem's view.

Cautiously Jem manoeuvred his horse alongside the carriage stopping at the open window, then shielding himself behind the horse's head and neck he slid his pistol through the curtains. Opening the smallest of partings with his pistol he glimpsed the fat man forcing his purse upon an old woman seated opposite to him and he saw eight eyes widen with fear and terror in unison as together they noticed the highwayman stalking them.

Briefly he scanned across the four terrified faces and he concluded that was there was no danger to be feared from within.

"Do exactly as I say and you will come to no harm." Nobody moved as he continued, "However, interfere with proceedings and I will not hesitate to blow you apart. Now slowly one by one make your way out of this door so I can unburden you from your valuables. " He then gritted. "Gentlemen first."

The first to appear was an elderly, weak man whose penetrative gaze scorned resentment, but he did as instructed without a word.

After a lengthy pause and a stern prompter from Jem the obese man showed himself. Dressed ostentatiously, his clothes indicated he was a man of wealth, but he looked pale and distressed as he gingerly took up a position of resignation beside the old man and the driver.

Next came the hoary women who was travelling with the old man, her cloak concealed her frailty whilst her hood to Jem's relief shadowed her hideous features.

Then finally to Jem's pleasant surprise there followed a much younger women. She too wore a cloak and a hood, but that's where the similarities ended, for she possessed a natural beauty that was beyond any comparison. For a slight moment he concerned himself that he had not noticed her charming looks when he first glanced inside the coach, but this was only a passing thought and he dismissed it with the notion he was not losing his keen eye for the appealing, but rather he hadn't seen her because he was too preoccupied with the element of danger that might have laid in store for him.

Wherever and whenever there was an opportunity to impress women of such magnificent attraction Jem always obliged to amuse himself with gallantry compliments and even in these circumstances when he knew he was being baited, he still could not resist the urging inclination to flirt and so he had the audacity and confidence to dismount.

He was not too lost in his thoughts however to notice how each one of the travellers made their exits deliberate and slow and this confirmed to him, that with no trap or unpleasant surprises to be found inside the carriage he knew the local constables would be following discretely behind. Still, he did not fear the consequences, he was confident that he could not be caught.

Flintlock held in one hand, reins firmly in the other he instructed the driver to remove the collections sack from his saddle and re-join him alongside the line of travellers.

"What delights do you have to offer me old man." Jem inquired, but implying the question as a demand.

"For a scoundrel like you I have nothing." The old man's face remained firm and he showed no hint of fear as he spoke with unexpected and unwavering defiance.

"I like a man with courage."

The old man's reply humoured Jem, but he knew he didn't have time for banter.

"And I like a man who will stand up for what he believes in but I won't let that stop me from getting what I want." With his comment Jem pushed the cold barrel of the flintlock hard against the old man's bulbous nose. "Now think again before I give you another eye socket."

The threat cracked the old man's brief resistance, his bottom lip began to quiver and his body tremble.

"Here... here take it. Take the lot."

With shaky hands he opened his overcoat and began to reach inside.

"Slowly... very....... very slowly." Jem cut in prodding so hard with the pistol that it twisted his nose and forced him to turn his head sideways.

"T.....T... Take my watch, it is all I possess." He finally stammered out.

Jem balanced the timepiece in the flat of his palm and inspected it the best he could in the ruddy moonlight.

"It's worth nothing to me, you may as well keep it."

This was out of character for Jem as he knew full well the watch was of value, but he felt as though he could relate to the old man in some strange manner. It was possibly his stubbornness and in any case he knew the fat man's bounty would more than make up for the lost value of an old battered watch. He lowered his gun and took a step to his right.

"And now good sir, I hope for your sake you have more to offer than just a worthless old watch."

Encouraged by the old man's fortitude and by the way the thief seemed gullible he retort.

"Go to hell! I have nothing for a scoundrel."

"Oh, I do admire men of courage. There seems so few of them about these days." Jem was affluent with language, conversations and ripostes came quickly and naturally to him.

The fat man liked what he was hearing, his chest expanded and his head raised as his confidence and his bold affront began to increase.

Jem had noticed the portly man's eyes flickering from left to right as though he was searching for something in the distance.

"But, there you go. I suppose that's just how things go sometimes when you are down on your luck. One minute there is not a man of courage to be found in the whole of England and the next thing you know there are two to be found in the same damn coach."

Jem could read his intentions perfectly and he knew that being conversable he had lured him into a false sense of security.

"However, I do like coincidences." He then raised his tone to emphasis. "Then again, I do not like liars and you sir by saying you have nothing are a liar!"

"Indeed sir, but I tell you this. I am a made man as is obvious to the eye and I stand by my principles and I'll tell you this you'll get nothing from me whilst I have a breath in my body!" Their eyes locked in a brief moment's battle of nerve.

"Then so be it. I have no desire to kill, but if you cause me any hindrance then I will take your last breathe as well as you for fortune."

"Damned bandits. You are nothing but leeches."

Jem normally enjoyed this type revelry, however he suspected he did not have the usual privilege of time and he had not yet attended to the two women, especially the younger women.

He levelled his pistol to within an inch of the man's forehead and he began to squeeze on the trigger. The prey clenched his teeth and bit down on them hard to hold firm his ill judge courage then flicking his eyes left and right he screamed.

"Hold it! Stop, stop." Pustules glistened his forehead, droplets of sweat ran cheeks and his jaw sagged to quiver. "Please do not shoot."

"You've got less than one second." Jem warned ominously looking to all as though he fully intending to blow open the man's head.

"Do you know your threatening the Mayor of Halifax and the member of parliament for Calderdale?" He cowered hoping the assertion would lead to privileged leniency.

"Then you'll soon be the deceased Mayor of Halifax and they will be an empty seat in parliament."

Jem forced the cold metal of his pistol hard against the stubborn man's forehead and the creek of the hammer broke his momentary resistance.

"No! No stop. Take my gold. Have my rings and my watch, my clothes, anything, but please, please spare my life."

Blubbering incessantly he crumpled to his knees with steam rising from his crotch begging for his life just as Jem anticipated.

Watching the Mayor's items disappearing into his bag and content with his takings Jem moved across to the old woman who was next in line.

"I trust old women that you will be more cooperative."

"You can see I have nothing of worth to give you." She croaked.

He would have believed her if he hadn't seen the fat man's bulging purse disappear into the fold of her cloak so with unexpected speed he slid his hand inside her cloak and felt beneath her warm clothing until his fingers clutched around the wealth.

"Then tell me, if you value this purse as nothing you will not object to trading it with me." Jem pondered purposely, "for let's say."

Holding the purse between his thumb and his palm he flicked through his fingers to dangle by it's chain the newly acquired gold watch by it's chain.

Furtive glances were exchanged between the decrepit women and the anxious looking fat man, but no words were relayed and she snatched without hesitation to hide away from prying eyes the valuable piece.

Jem nodded and side stepped to his left stopping directly in front of his final victim.

At last he finally stood face to face with the young women. He arched forward slightly so that his eye levelled with hers.

Her beauty stunned him in a pleasant way and he felt himself uncontrollably leaning nearer and nearer to her face. He wanted to feel her breath upon his cold skin and he wanted to fill his nostrils with her womanly fragrances, just as his ego always demands when he is in the presence of astounding beauty.

Without even realising what he was doing his hand moved forward to lower her hood and then it settled upon the back of her neck cupping her long soft locks. He wanted time to absorb her every feature, he glared at her unashamedly into her glistening eyes.

Her skin was pale and unblemished whilst her hair in contrast was as dark as the blackest night and it reflected the moons soft glow in a shine of health and vitality.

He felt a tingle in his thighs at the thought of her naked and he held the stare intensely like a mystic probing deep for a response.

It came, but not in the form Jem wanted. After releasing a self-conscious expression she averted her eyes from his inspection and lowered her head in the direction of the floor.

"Do not fear." He said sliding his fingers around from the back of her head to support and raise her chin, "I will not harm you."

The old women grunted something inaudible at the effrontery of Jem's flattery as with his other hand he lowered down his black neckerchief.

He knew the unveiling of the shroud would be a temptation far too great for her to resist and so once again he looked into her eyes, only this time his own handsome features were exposed.

"Damn your insolence man!" The Mayor's outburst shattered the eye contact and enraged the highwayman.

Scalding his fierce glare in unison with aiming his flintlock upon the coward Jem growled with fury. "Get back to your knees and pray to the Lord."

"Yes, I will pray to the Lord and I'll pray that I will never forget your face."

Jem's expression still portrayed a controlled smile as he replied pleasantly. "And nor the Lady I hope."

Then after bowing his head slightly to curtsy at the young women he swivelled at the waist and shook his head with an anger which equalled as he threatened. "Now pray for your life."

The fat man coward into a submissive ball, clamp shut his eyes and quaffed out the words of the Lord's Prayer as he waited for his life to end with a blast of lead.

However surprising everyone Jem raised his pistol to the sky and turned his attention back upon the women determining that she intrigued him more than the nuisance.

Tenderly he placed his palm under her chin again raising her face towards him, he felt her tremble, but he did not know it wasn't from fear of personal safety, but from the exhilaration of being touched by England's most wanted man.

"Be calm my Lady. It is well known the Yorkshire Raider does not steal from ladies or men of the cloth." He lied. "I will not harm you, although I must admit I have never laid my eyes upon anything that has enticed me in such a manner before. Your beauty and virtue are your assets so perhaps before I take my leave may I steal just one thing?"

Leaning slowly forward until their faces touched he rested his lips upon her mouth. She did not resist his kiss nor try and pull away for at that moment as she looked into his face and felt his tender warmth she easily denied he was the notorious Yorkshire Raider.

Jem's horse stepped back and pulled the reins taught. The animal was becoming agitated and it's unnatural savvy alarmed him that something was not right.

Parting from the kiss had seemed premature and all too brief for the couple, yet for the onlookers around the moment seemed to last for an eternity.

"I fear my beguile may have burdened you." She warned in answer to Jem's lusty petition.

Her eyes and face, mostly hidden by the shadows remained expressionless and she secretly concealed the pleasure she enjoyed by being kissed by England's most notorious highwayman.

"That may be true only for the fact that a man with my desire could hunt this country forever and not find such a beauty that to equal yours." Jem replied, holding firmly the reins and squinting out into the distant darkness towards a galloping advancement of horse and riders.

"It seems you have outstayed your welcome." The coach driver gleefully scorned.

Jem replied with just a smile cast at an angle. Even now when capture was closing around him he remained calm and his thoughts clear. He was supremely confident, safe in the knowledge that he could navigate the landscape at speed even in near darkness. Matching this with his daring prowess, his horse riding skills and the combination of the strength, speed and the agility of his four legged beasts, he had nothing to fear and he would leave the horsemen chasing shadows.

Swinging confidently into his saddle Jem tipped his Tricorne towards the beauty and boasted. "Until we meet again." He then heeled his horse into motion.

"Not in this world." She disappointed admitted to herself knowing the highwayman's destiny.

With the pursuers closing in fast the portly man suddenly found himself injected with another thrust of courage and he sprang up from his knees waving his fist at the villain.

"And may the devil take you down to hell. You coward!"

As soon as the words had left his mouth the fat man's face dropped to an expression of horror and disbelief as he saw the highwayman swiftly change his direction of travel and swerve back towards him.

There was no time for him to respond as within an instant the highwayman had returned to the carriage and smashed his passing foot against the side of the motionless man's jaw. Rendering him instantly unconscious, he spiralled once and dropped to the floor with an uncontrolled thud.

The attack was not done to impress anyone, it was merely the normal reaction from Jem's fiery and at times uncontrollable temper.

The time lapse had only been a matter of seconds, but it had cost him dear as it now seemed he could feel the pursuers breathing down the back of his neck. Arching down low into his saddle and spurring his barb into a bolt Jem glimpsed late the coach driver taking aim at him with his regulation musket. He could do little, but to duck lower and swerve the barb and brace every muscle.

Branches shattered high above from the discharged lead and seemingly unimpaired Jem had vanished into the shadows with the noise of galloping hooves fading rapidly from the ear range of the shaking victims of the robbery.

A gap of about 40 yards soon opened up between Jem and the chasing pack when suddenly and totally unexpected Jem's speed began to decrease and his horses head began to stoop lower and lower.

Something was drastically wrong and Jem glanced down for signs of blood from the horse. He saw nothing, he looked again and still he saw nothing. The horse began to lose all it's rhythm and coordination and Jem anxiously sensed the riders gaining upon him fast.

The Barbs pace slowly reduced to an unbalanced and unresponsive trot and Jem pulled the reins with all his might as he fought with all his might to keep the horse upright.

His mind and thoughts were frantic as he searched for the reasons to the horse's sudden demise and collapse.

He ignored the calls from behind which ordered him to stop and it was no surprise to him when a volley of pistol fire erupted. He ducked down low and shuddered as the orange flames bellowed out of the blackness behind him. For the first time in years fear began to claw it's way into his spine as he heard shots thud into the rump of his horse and splinter the surrounding bark.

The horse screams pierced his ears and in his heart he felt pain for his obedient servant, but he had no option, if he wanted to avoid lead or the gallows he had to urge the horse on and on. Within seconds the effort was lost and Jem knew it, for some strange reason his trusted horse had let him down and now shot had reduced his power to nothing more than a stumble. Jem spun from the waist and without aim tried to discharge his own retaliatory fire. He cursed his bad luck, the Lord and the Devil as unavoidably his over coat got caught between the flint and the steel Frizzen and the discharge failed.

The chasing pack now closed in fast to within a few feet of the slower horse and faced with a vastly improved target one of the pursuers decided to take no chances with an arrest and he released a second volley of pistol fire, this time assured of success.

The instant that the flame bellowed from their barrels and the explosion of noise erupted in Jem's ears, his horse had dropped, tossing him perilously from the saddle. Falling into a roll he tried to turn himself into the undergrowth, but he was rendered almost paralysed by an intense burning pain in his left shoulder.

"Got ya." Exited grinning faces of surrounded pack crowded to look down at the brigand.

"Don't look so fearful now does he Smithers?"

Jem's vision was blurred with water and the deafening echoes of the gun shots dulled the mob's ebullient exclamations.

"Which knuckleheads fired?" Shouted out an older toothless man as he tried to barge his way through the gathering. No one answered, they were too busy hustling to get the best view of the incapacitated prey.

"You useless faggots were given strict instructions not to open fire. We were told to bring him in alive!"

This time the raging man grabbed one of the mob and hurled him backwards so he could near the motionless man and improve his view to examine the outlaw.

"Is he dead?"

"Don't think it will make much difference except in the death register."

The statements failed to make raise any response from Jem, but the forceful nudging of an unfriendly boot into his body brought an immediate yell of pain.

All but one of the men was ecstatic with their success. They congested around the fallen man, laughing and boasting of their achievements. Without care or consideration they prodded, pulled and hauled Jem over onto his back so they could see and spit in the face of the notorious villain.

Gradually as his head cleared and his equilibrium began to return, he could feel hot blood seeping into his clothes and warming the painful area in his shoulder. He now began to understand that he had been shot in the back and his life was ebbing away.

He fought hard to stop the bile from rising in his throat as he writhed in agony. He never imagined in his darkest nightmares that such an end was his destiny. He struggled for breath and his level of response wavered. The voices became distant and the hovering figures surreal as they blended into reddening darkness becoming indistinguishable from the overhanging branches. He felt his eyes roll uncontrollably, his breathing faltered with rapid and shallow pants and his jaw and limbs dropped slack as he fell deeper into an awaiting blackness of nothing.

He did not feel the tugging at his clothes or the cutting of his hair and the stripping of valuables from his body by the wretched souvenir predators.

Chapter 2

Earlier that day in Carlisle.

Walking hurriedly in the direction of the Kings Arm's, Trevean the tenor was a man so preoccupied with his thoughts that he ignored all activity around him. His face stern, he was unrepentant to the people that he brushed aside with his rotund bulk. Forehead rutted he displayed all the characteristics of a man deeply absorbed by his problems.

He was just returning from the local constabulary where he had been interviewed concerning an incident which occurred at the last of his shows in Durham which led to the subsequent disappearance of one of his assistants. The fact that his statement was redeemed as satisfactory by the officials did little to relieve his state of nervous tension that had accumulated over the passing week since leaving Durham.

He spat in the charcoal coloured mud, nobody would have been able to relax when engaged in such a serious business as trying to raise aid and support for the Jacobite Stuarts with their attempt to cause open rebellion amongst the English people and against the British monarchy, which is what Trevean the tenor and the other members of the Society of Revolutionary Jacobites had been trying to do in Durham.

For years the Society of Revolutionaries had led campaigns of agitation against the British monarchy and it had failed on every occasion to create substantial support for a Jacobite uprising.

Prosperity had once more returned to the lands in the South of England, peace had settled and the people of England had no desire for a resurrection of the hardships and all the bitter consequences caused by a civil war, but now with news that Charles Edward Stewart had entered Scotland with an army for an invasion hopes amongst the Catholics were once more inspired and the message had spread, they must prepare to act now, there will never be a better time to oust the current regime.

The Welsh and Irish uprisings were gaining support and the war with France was not going well. The English was now beginning to show their condemnation for their ruler, the German born, King George.

1

All these factors once more aspired the Society of Revolutionary Jacobites into raising sufficient funds to equip a small army, this however was not enough to satisfy the leadership behind the conspiracy, there had to be no mistakes and there was to be no room for failure. The Society realised a long time ago that they would need massive support to overthrow the Hanoverian monarchy and they intended to aid Prince Charles's invasion by instigating a fiendish plot from within the community's own structures.

Choosing the northern towns, on this occasion Durham because of the notable hostility between the Catholics and the Anglicans, the guest of honour at their show was a strategically selected and well known, but widely respected for his moderate opinions and his support for peace, Lord Halivard, himself a Catholic.

It had been decided towards the end of the show that members of the Revolutionaries would invade the stage to make agitating political speeches implicating Lord Halivard to their movement. Then later that evening, Jeremiah Mortimer, who was second in command of the Revolutionary Jacobites, would disguise himself as a government official along with several other members of the movement and they would arrest and execute Lord Halivard on charges of treason thus creating the rapid communal uprising which they sought.

Unfortunately for the Revolutionaries one of Trevean's assistants Mary Dibbler had panicked and fled from the stage just before the Revolutionaries interrupted the act.

Fearing that she might warn the authorities of what was planned for Lord Halivard and reveal the organisations agents, Trevean suggested to Mortimer that the second part of their plot should be postponed. Infuriated by the girl's actions Mortimer, who was at the best of times an arrogant, ill-tempered and bad mannered leader volunteered himself to capture and return the girl.

When Mortimer had failed to return by the following morning Trevean ordered his cast to dismantle the stage set and pack up. He sent a message on to Luc De Winter, the Society of Revolutionary Jacobites leader, warning him the plan had gone wrong and that the theatre production was moving on to their next venue where he intended to continue with the prearranged plan of raising funds to support the cause.

It was when they reached Berwick that Trevean read in the Daily Courant that Jeremiah Mortimer and his accomplice Mary Dibbler had met their deaths for what the paper described as treasonable activities. Turning himself into the Commander of the barracks at Berwick, Trevean endeavoured to clear himself and his cast of any suspicion. He fabricated his story so that when his statement was compared with the recollections of the audience, it would prove him innocent to any part of the treachery.

He was allowed to leave and continue with his business under condition that he would inform them if there was to be any more developments.

Trevean had emerged free from suspicion, but still all was not well. He did not know how or why Mortimer and Dibbler had died and he could not understand why the authorities should have suspected Dibbler of being a traitor. When he raised what few questions he dare the constables and commander seemed to be evasive and answered only by saying that Dibbler had been working covertly for Mortimer.

Trevean knew this was not true. Dibbler being the latest addition to his entourage was the only one who was not a member of the Society of Revolutionary Jacobites. He suspected that she may have overheard some of the performers talking about the uprising and he concluded that this was the reason she had panicked and fled.

Finally, just before he left the barracks, he was informed by the Commander that they no longer concerned themselves with the capture of any more traitors as they were sure the group would disband now their leader Mortimer was dead.

Nearing the reek and the noise of the Kings Arms there were three other immediate problems that concerned Trevean. Firstly, he hadn't heard from the Society's leader Luc De Winter and he wondered if he had taken the correct decisions. Secondly, he was lacking a leading lady and finally and most importantly the Society was a leader short.

For the first time in over a week a smile briefly appeared on his face as his cunning mind contemplated the future possibilities. He aimed to fill the vacant leader position himself and become De Winters right hand man. He knew that there would be immense financial rewards for the leaders of the rebellion if a new monarchy could be crowned and to ascend the ranks, he needed to impress De Winter. To achieve this he concluded that he would firstly have to resolve the minor problem of recruiting an actress so that he could continue to produce the show. In doing this, the show could continue on the circuit allowing members of the Society to meet in secret without raising any suspicions concerning their presence in the area.

Licking his fingers and drying them on his side whiskers to leave them shining he raised the latch to enter the inn and meet up with the rest of the performers as arranged.

However, unexpectedly he was met with the amusing sight of his magician, Nat Futrell being tossed backwards to the floor by a woman. Tables, bottles, jugs, ale and bodies scattered in all directions as everyone found their attention being drawn to the amusing havoc.

Nat scrambled to his feet, his face livid with rage and embarrassment, his eyes veined and his reactions handicapped with excess alcohol.

"You thieving bitch! I'm going to beat you good." He slurred clenching and raising his fists.

"Don't come near me, you drunken swine or I'll scratch both your eyes out."

The women instantly spat back and judging by the mood she was in and by the inebriated state Futrell was in, Trevean believed every word she threatened and watching her stance with deep interest he believed that she could back up her threat with more than words as she too looked equally livid and she matched his stance with her small fist clenched tight.

"No you don't Futrell." Trevean ordered as he intervened by wrapping his meaty arms around the drunkard, catching and clasping down tightly by his side his threatening fists.

"Get your hand off me, you fat bastard and let me go." Futrell raged to no avail as ignoring him, so that his own volatile temper would not be raised Trevean began to pull the magician away. He wanted to defuse the situation quickly.

Although scuffles were rife in alehouses he did not want to attract any unwanted attention from the town Charlie's and constables.

"Refused to satisfy your pleasure has she?" Trevean taunted as he referred to Futrell's persistent and insatiable, but often failing womanising.

"No!" He yelled back as he struggled "The bitch tried to steal my purse."

The accusation more than interested the tenor and even now in the midst of this struggle he began to study the girl.

"I did no such thing. He touched me!" She screamed an accusing riposte whilst holding firm her stance with unwavering defiance, "and he tried to get me to lay with him."

That sounded just like Futrell, Trevean mused, but one thing was sure, he knew his magician was not a liar.

"You lying little bitch. I'm going to..."

"Do what?" Trevean cut in holding tight the man as their bodies stumbled across the room parting the crowd.

"I'm going to ..." Futrell struggled to break free from the vice like grip and they collided against the wall.

"You're going to put your hands down, calm down and get out. That's what you are going to do." Trevean ordered into Futrell's ear as he spun him around and tossed him in the direction of Goss and Turner, two of the production companies more reliable members.

"Take this maudlin to his room and make sure he doesn't come out until he has sobered up." Releasing Nat he knew that the pair would carry out his instructions to the full and that Nat would cause no further trouble tonight. Knowing the inn would return to normal it's custom very soon he dismissed Futrell to continue his assessment of the girl.

He knew that that she was lying and judging by her nerve, her arrogance, the signs of under nourishment and her tattered clothing, he knew she was desperate for money and his tempest thoughts concluded she might be a candidate for the newly vacated post.

He decided that he must get to know her better and he approached her with an artificial apology for the magician's behaviour, but just as he thought she saw straight through it.

"If you are after the same as your friend forget it because I'm not interested." She raged.

"If I feel the inclination, I will bear that in mind." He assured her with a placating smile and an accompanying nod.

"Well, if you're not interested what do you want?" She snapped to give to Trevean the impression that she was now annoyed because he found her unattractive.

"Allow me to introduce myself." He beamed loudly.

"Only if you make it quick. I'm on my way out of here."

"Somewhere to go?" He quizzed the stray.

"What's it to you?"

A conceited smile raised Trevean's cheeks to openly display how proud of himself he was. The girl's eyes rolled with disgust, she could avoid the self-esteem of the man whose face exposed half a century of debauch living was behind him.

"Oliver Trevean. I am the owner, manager, producer and the resident tenor for the Royal Oak theatrical company which is performing a production of Lancelot Blacks, The Wicked Cousin in this, your lovely town." He opened his arm wide to emphasis openly his egotistical boast.

She took the opportunity to increase his curiosity and quaffed.

"It's not my lovely town."

"It's not. Did I hear you say it's not? " He prompted for more falling into her trap.

"I'm only here because I have no place else to go for now."

Interesting Trevean muttered silently and keeping the conversation going he grumbled. "I'm afraid that's your problem. I just hope you haven't created another one for me."

"And just how might have I done that." She scowled.

"By causing injury to my entr'acte, the 'Great Magestico.'"

"The great what?" Her face twisted with puzzlement to convince the tenor she had no idea who any of the performers were.

"The Great Magestico. My magician." He repeated.

"Magician?" Her jaw dropped and eyes open wide to feign disbelief. Her performance was perfect and it was he, the tenor who was being duped and not the girl as he wrongly assumed.

"That's right magician. If he had been wearing his stage make up maybe you wouldn't have been so foolish to try and lift his leather." He decided probe and check if his assumptions were correct.

"How dare you!" She refrained from launching a vicious slap towards his rounded face.

"Oh, I dare alright. I didn't the pinnacle of my profession without being able to read into people's appearances and expressions correctly. You could call it an asset of mine, and a very valuable one at that." He said confidently holding his smile.

"Then tell me mister clairvoyant. What do you read into this?" To his surprise she slapped him across the face so hard that her palm left a burst of white and then a purplish imprint on his cheek.

"I read the embarrassment at being detected a would be thief." He calmly replied, ignoring the smarting burn from his cheek.

"Rubbish. You're trying to annoy me because you thought the same as your friend."

"And that....?" He asked.

"That I would comfort you."

"No, no my dear. You are far from the truth. You have it completely wrong." Trevean turned around to face the landlord of the inn.

"A jug of ale for me and... a gin perhaps?" He turned over his hand and raised his eyebrows to complete the offer "For the lady."

"Not for me, I must go." She dismissed. The landlord paused with his knuckles supporting him against the bar.

"Go where? Judging by your raggy appearance one could assume as though you've got no place to go." He noticed her eyes widen as he calculatingly pulled from within his coat his bulging leather purse.

"Well well. Just aren't you the clever one?"

"Not really or I wouldn't have upset you so, but it is, as I said. An asset of mine." He released a hand full of coins on the counter for the landlord to scoop and he nodded to settle the purchase. "One of many I might add."

"Well, I would have a place to go if those damn tax collectors hadn't taken all our stocks for the fat King." She lied with scowl to equal her tome of disgust. "A nice respectable place it was too." She appeared to momentarily reminisce.

"I don't doubt it for one minute, but please you must be careful with what you say about the King. You don't know who is listening." His eyebrows raised and his enlarged eyes flickered from side to side.

"I don't care. I don't care about anything anymore."

"You shouldn't talk that way. Now please have a drink with me before you go on your way. Maybe some food as well?"

"Why do you want to buy me a drink when you know I have no money to repay and I've already told you that I will not lay with you." She knew he was desperate to keep her engaged.

"And so my dear girl, you keep reminding me, but maybe I will be able to offer you a little comfort and something for you to care about."

The clatter of two tankards being slammed on the counter top broke the conversation briefly.

"If it's money you are offering for my body, then I'm not interested in that either."

"I'm sure you're not. I wouldn't even offend you with such a thought."

He forced the tankard of gin into her hand.

"I'd rather starve than lay with a stranger." This was her first statement of truth.

"I assure you my dear girl I do not need coin to revel with the ladies." He tested with a sip his warm ale.

His effrontery made her bilious and her stomach tightened.

"However I admit. I like a girl with principles."

She knew that she had impressed him and that she was controlling the situation just as planned. Her face twisted as the gin ruined her tongue and burned her throat.

"And that's why I would like to offer you a job with my theatrical company."

"A job doing what?" She acted surprised, hiding cleverly her satisfaction.

"Entertaining the public of course. From what I've just seen of you I'm certain you'll fit in perfectly." He gulped two swallows for the tasteless ale then wiping his mouth with the back of his hand he added, "If you can put a performance across on stage showing the same anger and enthusiasm that you showed a just few moments ago," he enthuse, "you'll be perfect for the part I'm offering you. Come, let's sit down and discuss remuneration over a hot meal and a few drinks."

Seating themselves down around a barrel which served as a table, Trevean asked. "Now my dear, let us begin with your name."

"My name is Dorathea Nibley."

Chapter 3

York Castle, Fishergate cells

Jem Rose had allowed his mind to become possessed by the alchemy caused by shock and pain and as one image would gradually lose it's perfection and began to disappear then another one would arise from it's fusion until once more his fevered mind was occupied with happy reminiscences.

The thunder of hoofs throwing up divots of mud in their wake was perfectly synchronised to the heartbeat of young Jem as he galloped away from Ferrybridge.

Bolting down the North Road on Jack Cartwright's treasured gelding without even so much as glancing back, this was the second time that day he had stolen Jack Cartwright belongings from right under his nose.

Jem's face beamed the huge delight that the thrill had given him. He was being pursued on foot by several members of the village which included his parents, the local constable, Mister and Mrs Cartwright, Toby Smyth the innkeeper, Matthew Dalmer, a trader William Gaunt the school master and a local farmer Neville Moore.

They had all just moments earlier been engaged in a heated discussion concerning the swindling antics of young Jem.

Jack Cartwright started the dispute by stating that Jem had wandered into his orchard earlier that morning and stole from him a basket of apples whilst he was still up the tree and scaling back towards the ladder. He said he called after the boy and ordered him to return which he duly did. But instead of returning the apples the youngster disobeyed the order and kicked away the ladders laughing and shouting abuse as he sped from view.

William Gaunt confirmed that the young Rose did not attend his lessons that morning and farmer Moore added that he and the boy swapped the basket of apples for a rabbit after the boy claimed Mr Cartwright had allowed him to enter his orchard to collect the windfalls.

Trading the rabbit with Dalmer for a sack of flour, Toby Smyth claimed that Jem had been sent by his father to exchange the flour for a keg of ale.

Considering this to be a good deal and taking the boy's word for the truth he eagerly obliged.

An astonished Mrs Cartwright then made it known that young Jem had the audacity to call upon her at her cottage and convince her to buy the ale as a surprise for her hardworking husband. She acknowledged Jem asked for a very reasonable 1d for the keg and she had mistakenly jumped at the opportunity knowing that her husband's throat would be parched when he eventually returned home from the orchard.

The bickering had congressed upon the village green where unbeknown to the group the young vagabond had listened with a mixture of trepidation and amusement at the tales from the safe seclusion of a large obstructive old chestnut tree.

It was just as Jack Cartwright demanded the return of his apples and farmer Moore answered by telling him that they had already been stewed and most of them used in a pie filling that Jem saw the means of escaping the wrath of his father's anger.

Using the advantage of surprise and his youthful speed he darted out from behind the cover and leapt into the saddle of Jack Cartwright's old Bessie who was grazing on the long summer grass

And so it was from this trivial escalation that young Jem Rose embarked upon his quest for adventure. He did not know or care what this journey had install for him. All he knew was that he wanted out, out of the dull and dreary poverty stricken existence which everyone else seemed to accept from birth.

He rode all day and most of the night ignorant of all direction, until saddle sore and bone weary he could ride no more.

Wandering aimlessly in both mind and body, he found himself contemplating his future on the banks of Hull's thriving dock yard and watching the comings and goings of the export ships his naive thoughts were soon influenced and by the end of the following night he was a stowaway entering a Belgium port.

The distinct clanking of heavy keys and the turning of locks roused Jem from his memoirs and into semi consciousness for the first time, in what was unbeknown to Jem, was almost a month.

He slowly became aware at the presence of onlookers and he suspected that their voices, which were almost lost in an indistinguishable hum, were directed at him. He tried to respond by opening his mouth, but paralysing bouts of pain held him both mute and motionless.

He could smell the freshness of a gentleman as someone neared him and he could feel the warmth of their breath as a face lowered down nearer to him for a closer inspection. He fought against the pain to crack open an inquisitive eyelid, but spiralling spasms of excruciation flashed up from his back to his head and around temples which held tight his eyelids.

Once more inaudible comments and questions failed to register his ears and he was unresponsive until all of a sudden he felt a prodding in his chest that spread into an all-consuming raging fire of misery that ravaged throughout his every nerve and fibre until he readily allowed the first vestiges of oblivion to relieve the impelling affliction.

Having to steal to survive young Jem could only evade the law enforcers for so long and before the month expired the inexperienced thief was to experience life in the gaol for the first time.

His desperation for food increased his risk taking and all his thoughts of reasoning waned leading him to make irrational decisions until he was finally apprehended.

It was amid this filth, suffering and unimaginable wretchedness that the young Jem Rose began to develop and nature the instincts that were to be essential if he was to survive the ordeal in the hellhole of a pit. During this period Jem experienced an instinctive transformation as he fell under the guidance and friendship of another English prisoner, Elisha Tropp.

A man of considerable size, Tropp was in his younger days a man of whom to fear, but now in the autumn years of his life with his brawn and vigour declining fast he relied upon his strength of cunning wisdom to see him through these dark days of punishment and torture.

It was due to Tropp's vital assets that the pair broke away from the bounds of confinement and made a break to freedom. Fluent in the Flemish language Tropp overheard a group of prisoners planning a protest and so waiting with patience they timed their break to perfection and the pair was able to take advantage of the manic chaos leaping onto the roofs of some adjoining buildings and from there they scampered to freedom across the hazy morning skyline of Zeebrugge.

Reliving these the dreams over and over in his mind they seemed just as vivid as the reality which they had once been not so long ago for the ailing highwayman, however the sudden removal of a tattered rag from the window allowed shafts of blinding sunlight to beam down through the cell bars and directly into Jem's ghostly face forcing him to fight against the probing brilliance as he began to stir to the edge of consciousness.

"Welcome back to the land of the living Mister Rose."

Jem heard the voice clearly, but he was still too frail to respond.

"You're just a mite sore I take it."

Squinting in the brightness he pried open an eyelid just enough to distinguish the elderly gent from the mould covered walls. He tried to raise his head, but his mind seemed to explode under the barrage of pain as a result of the light and so with all his might he just managed to tilt his head into the shadow by his side.

Crippling palpitations clasped his entire body as the sustained effort had been too great for him and his level of consciousness began to waiver once more. Evil marathons of agony caused his eyes slowly rolling over white and their lids closing down over them, he tried to study the man seated opposite. Who was he? He certainly wasn't the jailer or a constable Jem wearily concluded. He was dressed with a style of quality that Jem had become accustomed. Possibly he was someone whom he had robbed or swindled he reflected, but gradually that thought became dim as uncontrollably the man's stern face became a distant blur as he verged death and lapsed back into unconsciousness.

In his short, but eventful existence, Jem's past had become intangible but, here trapped in the state of senselessness within the confinement of cold stone walls he had just enough power and imagination to evoke the reek of the alehouses and to taste the wine which was dredged from every sacred bottle. He could hear the moans and groans of the suffering who had endured the many enforced long marches and he still winced from the ear piercing screams of anguish, pain and death which was inflicted indiscriminately on the battlefields.

Since their escape, the young Rose and the aging Tropp had robbed and pilfered their way across Belgium and Holland and were just contemplating on a return to their homeland when they inadvertently stumbled across a company of English infantry volunteers who were on active service in Europe. Wanting to avoid and suspicion they reluctantly enlisted for military service.

These torrid days were certainly full of adventure, but they did not supply the type of thrills young Rose had been in pursuit of, instead of a careless youth he had been forced endure his growing years with a wild bunch of cutthroats, thieves, tricksters and cold-blooded killers.

Twelve months had elapsed with active combat before Jem's association with the volunteers came to an abrupt and untimely end. After an evening session of drinking in the small Dutch town of Eindhoven the young Englishman insulted a Dutch officer by making advances towards and caressing with his chosen woman. In the ensuing argument which followed Jem was challenged to a duel at dawn.

Pistols, swords or sabres he knew that he was no match for the highly trained officer and rather than face a certain death, he decided to retire the officer for the night by striking him with a blow of perfection which rendered the Dutch man unconscious. Immediately Jem fled the tavern and made his escape upon the officer's horse.

He fled Eindhoven with his honour in shambles, but his life intact, which in his mind was a far more dignified way of living than what had happened to many of his companions including Elisha Tropp. Blinded and crippled from a Frenchman's musket ball Tropp was reduced to an insane half-wit who was sent home to rot away and die in some festering gully. Such a pathetic end was not to be in store for Jem, he was going to make sure of that.

Returning to the English camp on the stolen horse, Jem sparked bitter jealousy which eventually escalated into raging arguments concerning his horsemanship. At the heart of the arguments was a cocky and arrogant Captain named Alun Peats. He had insulted Jem by boasting that the Dutch horse, which he branded a pit pony, was well suited to it's new owner and this provoked Jem into issuing a challenge of chivalry which everyone else considered as foolish retaliation by claiming that he and his pit pony could safely jump and clear the wide dyke at the camps boundary.

It seemed impossible, but bolstered by the pressures enforced by his colleagues Peats was forced to try and equal the feat. With the officer's horse being of a superior breed and size, gilders exchange hands with speed and confidence and enhanced by the prospect of making a certain profit the soldiers assumed only the Captain stood any chance of making the clearance.

Having drawn straws to see who would go first Peats charged with his head down in a gallop towards water only to find himself moments later crashing down into the muddy banking with humiliation when his mount skidded to an immediate halt as it's nostrils scented the first smell of water, thus tossing Peats high and clear from the saddle.

Watching Peats arise with only his pride hurt Jem knew he did not stand any chance whatsoever at making the crossing so he decided that he would double the wager of any bet if he was allowed to make the jump on the officer's horse.

With all the soldiers emotions fleeting from the extreme of relishing the expected yield rather than suffering from the torment of being out of pocket with Peats failure, they were again elated at the new proposal and they urged their superior officer to accept the new challenge.

Peats, after an influencing heated bout of convincing from the soldiers began to see the rewards and accepting the new rules he rubbed his hands together with a new belief and boasted that if he couldn't do it on his horse then no man could.

Jem never had any intention of honouring the bets and once he was seated in the saddle and travelling at full speed he veered off the run up and before anyone had the chance to react and respond, he reached out for and grabbed a hold of the bag containing the stakes out of the numb standing red coats hand.

Impelling the animal on with driving confidence Jem cleared a small hedge at the boundary of the camp and left the stunned onlookers running for their muskets wide eyed and gasping with awe and desperation.

Here as in every reminiscence the weather seemed warmer, the sky bluer, the clouds more sparse and the days longer, and now and with his fee for transportation back to England clutched tightly in his hand Jem began with the journey home.

A loud involuntary rumble from his stomach niggled Jem once more back into reality. Riveting pain still dictated his every breath and so carefully and very slowly he tried to gather spittle in his parched mouth to ease the burning, dryness that seemed to rise from the pit of the stomach to the top of his throat.

"Glad to see that you are still with us Mister Rose."

He recognised the voice spoken in the calming tone and he saw through a hazy blur it was the stern countenanced gentleman who had spoken to him before.

Jem's reply caught in his throat and a mouth full of vomit was spat out instead of the words that he intended. His insides felt as though they had been sliced with a sabre and they burned like something from hell.

It was then that the vile stench of his own detriment pierced his nostrils and the shock of seeing himself lying in this incapacitated body forced his mind back to that baneful night. He let out a yell of anguish as the sustained efforts had been too great for him. His head and limbs sagged as his over worked lungs panted for breath.

He now understood why his mind was occupied with the past events of his life and that his memories were all that he was surviving on. He had acknowledged that he was now in the final chapter of his life and all he found appealing was the thought of endless sleep so he once more readily submitted to the state of unconscious remises as he awaited the shroud of death to enclose it's vices upon him.

Fleeing with elation pulsating through his veins, yet another hold up had gone perfectly to plan for the master of the highways, The Yorkshire Raider, Jem Rose.

Since returning to England a little over 2 years ago the adolescent Rose had found employment as a highwayman. Applying the skills attributed to him by his former tutor, Elisha Tropp, Jem had returned to the ways of the outlaw without effort and without flaw.

Adding to the interest and adventure he travelled throughout the country posing as a gentleman in pursuit of ending his bachelor days and he found on a couple of occasions fathers who were so desperate to marry off their daughters they were prepared to put up the dowry instead of the customary bridegroom to be.

Socialising within the circles of the wealthy with money in abundance to support his portrayal of a Koopman trader and enhanced by his robustness and affability he found success came without peril.

His plan was simple but cunning and only required nerve, confidence and plenty of spare time which he had in abundance.

Choosing his victims carefully the priority lay with a soul heiress, but more importantly wealth. Appealing looks were not essential because Jem knew if a proud man's daughter was unattractive then he would only be too pleased to seize the opportunity to marry her off whilst he had the chance.

The game would end for Jem when he had conquered the father's confidence and secured a dowry of cash and a future inheritance for the exchange of marriage vows. He would then set up a bogus marriage in some far away and remote village.

With no intention of going through with the wedding Jem would then take to the road as a highwayman and steal the dowry from the family in transit. Fleeing into the night and never to be seen in those parts again or by the rueful family, he had broken the hearts of two brides and the pride and resources of their fathers.

Although the profits were rewarding Jem began to grow weary of all the travelling. It was all too easy for him, the element of risk involved was of little challenge and the conquests failed to provide the thrills for which he searched.

The pursuit of wealth had become a habitual all time consuming effort and so whilst soliciting a young woman from Nottingham he gave considerable thought this time to marrying the girl.

Violet Boulding had all the qualities Jem admired in a woman and she adored him much more than he could expect any woman to do. With her attractive lure, loyalty and considerable dowry the matrimonial union took place in her hometown of Nottingham and after a lengthy honeymoon in Devon the newlywed's set up home in Badsworth which was just a safe distance away from his birthplace in Ferrybridge, but an area he remembered well.

Living under the pretension that he was still a Koopman, Jem had given himself the freedom to travel away from Badsworth whenever he desired. He had established for himself the perfect lifestyle. A comfortable home, a devoted wife with children soon to follow and the excitement of being a highwayman. To the townspeople of Badsworth, the Roses looked like a high class and dignified family who respected the law, themselves and others alike.

Unfortunately the wedding bliss and perfect family life all came to a premature and tragic end when Violet died after giving birth to their second son. For months Jem's soul was lost in a world full of grief and true guilt in which he concluded God had administered his own redemption upon him for the violations and sins he had committed.

Although he continued to live in Badsworth he reluctantly permitted Violet's sister to take the two boys to live with her on the outskirts of Nottingham until he stabilised, found another suitable companion and remarried.

However, as the months passed Jem's thoughts did not include finding a legitimate suitor and in an attempt to numb his heartbreak he willingly returned to the secret life of the lothario and outlaw.

He found it easy to prey upon the maidens and widows from far away towns and he would put to use his womanising skills of captivation. He would grow in their confidence as they hopelessly succumb to his charms and readily accepted him in their hearts.

Acting as a bachelor, he would court them until he could either move in and live with them as he had done on previous occasions or continue with the false promise of marriage, all the time using their homes as safe havens and new locations for raining terror upon the roadways.

He wasted no time on the suspicious, unresponsive or the reserved. He directed all concentration on the lonely and gullible. He was a natural charmer, who could decide upon a victim only moments after being introduced to them. He kept himself one step ahead of the law and he would tease and fool it whenever he struck.

He was as evasive as the human shadow, which taunted the touch, but always escaped from the detaining grasp as enclosed around it.

Reaping rewards of both the dual life and easy existence, he would simply leave everything behind him and return home to his awaiting life as a bereaved businessman whenever he sensed peril.

Settling back into the familiar routine and splitting his time between home in Badsworth and regular visits to Nottingham he could only wait a short while until the impelling urge for insatiable exploits once again dictated his feelings and tested his nerve.

The sound of muffled voices and the intense penetration of sunlight through his eyelids roused Jem into another semi consciousness bewilderment.

"Good morning, Mister Rose." Jem's mind could just acknowledge the words of the old gent, but still pain dictated his every breath.

"How do you feel?"

"I hope he feels like he has begun his journey to hell because that's the only place he is going!"

"Not now, Cornell. There's no need for comments like that at this stage."

Without moving his head Jem managed to roll his eyes towards the other side of the cell where he saw the obese man who had just expressed his opinion raise and swing back a pail but before he could fully comprehend what was happening freezing water had splashed over his rigid body. His instincts jolted him and he let out a scream of anguish as a huge unmerciful contraction seized his stomach and chest.

The scream echoed around the hollow cells and corridors, but before they had diminished into the vaults the fat man's rancorous bellows rumbled loudly over them.

Jem tried to control his dizziness, but black swirling dots distorted his focus then slowly the repeating bellowing of the man's amusement softened as did his spectre shape until it began to fade into the distance and it had totally been banished from the subconscious world of Jem's mind.

Jem and his father were seated on an empty barrel in the smoky corner of the Three Bells tavern in the small market town of South Cave. A four hour journey from Ferrybridge, but chosen because although idyllic, many traders rested here on their way to Beverly market and conducted illicit business without raising suspicion from the retailers or authorities in the main town. The Rose's were finally joined, as arranged by a man named Palmer.

Lankly reaching into his teenage years young Jem Rose was developing an interest for adulthood and rising in his father's esteem and confidence he was privileged to be asked to accompany him on this latest trading engagement.

Dressed in a red doublet and brown overcoat Palmer seated himself and immediately, with a lowered tone began to talk terms with a regional accent never heard by Jem before. Always looking for extra ways to make ends meet James Rose had been buying sheep from Palmer at Beverley Market for the past 2 years and now taking him into his confidence Palmer offered him a far more lucrative deal which seemed too good to refuse.

The Roses had travelled down from Ferrybridge the previous day and spent the night at the tavern in South Cave. It was the first time that young Jem had ventured beyond the borders of his village and he absorbed the scene, every face and every conversation on this exhilarating journey.

The deal was negotiated and completed within a matter of minutes. The exchange of two shillings for 5 fouls and a further two more deals which took place outside the inn away from prying eyes ended their trading and the Rose's association with the strange sounding trader. They parted ways planning to meet again at the next market day in Beverly a few weeks later.

Undoubtedly, while Jem's father more than suspected Palmer of being a cattle and horse thief due constant low valuations of his stock he certainly had no idea that the man who he was trading with was in fact the notorious highwayman Dick Turpin.

Suddenly Jem and his father were no longer stood outside the Three Bells on that warm August afternoon, Jem found himself propelled into a bitterly cold April morning. Shivering in a hail of ice and wind, he had ridden to the Knavesmire in York and along with the eager crowd he now waited for the execution of the robber, murderer and philanderer known as Dick Turpin.

Still in shackles Turpin had been in conversation with the tops man on the gallows for almost half an hour and the congregation were beginning to grow impatient with the hated man's obvious evasion of the noose.

Jem's eyes flickered between the highwayman and his father's daunting face, wandering what thoughts flurried in his mind. If only he had suspected, if only he had an inkling of whom the man Palmer really was then they would have been claiming the two hundred pounds reward money, but how was he to have known. There was no way he could have ever suspected Palmer of being anything other than a cowardly cattle thief. He was short, so short in fact, that even the young Jem equalled him in height. He had a dower and unpleasant personality and he was totally alienated of any humour or jovial spirit, he was morose and sullen. He seemed a dull little figure who was wallowing in self-pity, a man void of all the initiatives needed for a long survival.

Discontentment lay in his sullen eyes and his fiery ginger hair had long lost it's sheen of health and it mangled his miserable pot scared face. He was in total contrast to the dashingly handsome figure which the Rose's and the rest of the public had been duped into believing he was.

Saying the customary prayers and singing a penitential hymn from the book of palms, Turpin had recaptured the huge congregations floundering attentions. He mounted the ladder and began to climb, but he was forced to pause momentarily as a weakness in him allowed a quivering to take control of his legs. Looking around and gazing into the expectant and eager eyes of the onlookers Turpin drew a deep breath and suppressed the trembling by stamping his feet down hard. Finishing off the short ascent he had the rope fixed around his neck and he began to make his final speech.

"Friends and enemies alike. You have come here to see me suffer my punishment and I guarantee you shall not be disappointed." His words were laconic due to the excessive alcohol used to promote his false courage.

"I freely confess all my sins to the Lord God Almighty and I wait for his judgement, but before I expire my final breath I truly hope my ignominious death will arouse a consciousness and strike fear into all those who are sinful, dishonest and mischievous throughout this beautiful land. It is written in the book of David that there is no peace for the wicked, for a robber is continuously restless, whether riding, walking or sleeping. Frightful dreams disturb him, daily crimes fill up the measure of his iniquities till at length he finds himself in despair."

With the end of his life approaching fast Turpin looked more serene and at peace than he did all those years ago in the Three Bells

"I tell you all who you all watch my death so that you can tell those who hear my fate that this is true. For all the wealth I have stolen I did not once ever get contentment of mind." He paused to nod at the hangman. "I take my leave of you now begging for your prayers so that my sorry full spirit may find mercy and proceed into the heavenly kingdom. Come Lord Jesus and receive my soul, for I trust in thee."

With those final words he pulled down the death cap over his face and the hangman tossed him from the ladder sending his writhing body into infinite eternity.

Although the name Jem Rose was mentioned in the same breath as Turpin, Nevison, and Bracey, Jem secretly epitomised everything that these outlaws represented. He may have been in the same profession, but he did not consider himself in the same despised category. He liked to think himself an avenging entrepreneur who stole only from the rich and privileged. However these were only his own biased assertions.

The conclusion of this latest memoir served as an untimely reminder of what awaited him and both the shock and fear jolted him from the depths of his sub-consciousness and back into grim reality.

With his numbed senses gradually waking, dread began to spread from his bowels and into his head bringing with it perspiration to his skin and desperation to his mind. He drew a long deep breath and held it for a moment as his mind allowed the acceptance of survival to gradually dissipate the remnants of the past.

"Starting to feel better are we Mister Rose?"

Jem had no need to open his eyes to see who was questioning him, as he was now familiar with the frail drone of the constant companion.

After a short moment the bearing pressure around his chest forced him to expel his breath, cough violently and then pant to regain his stability.

"Nice and easy does it, Mister Rose."

He sensed the aging gentleman near to him. No need to start and hurry things now. You're doing just fine as you are."

Jem's mind was confused by the comments and his thoughts in disarray, he could not understand the man's concern.

"Take a sip of water and it will soothe away the irritant in your throat."

At that moment Jem felt a metal ladle touch against his lips. He raised his head and accepted the hospitality. At first the water seemed to burn and agitate the soreness in his throat causing him to wince and momentarily pull away, but the second swallowing cooled the raw passage as it lubricated and he began to feel slight relief.

He raised his hands and using his fingers as a filter he allowed the daylight to pervade through to his eyes. Squinting against the brightness slowly, very slowly he looked around the dark enclosure. He squinted at the four stone walls, the small and securely barred window, at the solid looking door and the concrete bed. A pile of befoul straw stenched his nostrils and watered his eyes, but ignoring the irritation he rubbed his hands along the shackles and tugged the chain which secured him to a detaining ring on the wall.

He sat up and every bone seemed to snap into position discharging another spasm of pain.

"Just you sit there and rest a while Mister Rose whilst I go get the physician to take a look at you." Said the elderly attendant to Jem's surprise.

"I don't want you to exhaust yourself." He added rising to his feet, "not now that you're on the way to recovery." Then he gently tapped Jem on the shoulders with his hands to politely insist he remained still.

"He's the best in this district." The old man winced and pressed his hand in the arch of his back indicating he too had been sat too long, "I've secured him a room nearby." He turned towards the door.

"Why the interest?" Jem gritted his first words, "worried I won't be able to walk up to the gallows."

The gentleman halted and twisted to look back over his shoulder to reply with in his usual affable calmness.

"No, no, no. Not at all." He began, but then he suddenly silenced himself when he saw Jem pushing himself up from the concrete slab of the bed with the palms of the hands.

With almost disbelief he watched Jem, with great effort straighten up and stretch out his crumple body.

Pain braced itself upon Jem's face as he tensed his stiff and extremely sore muscles. Both his legs were shaking with numbness and he clutched onto the detaining ring on the wall to steady himself. His body began to shake violently and blinking through the tears and sweat, he raised his right leg, it jerked forward and uncontrollably slammed down. He then raised his left leg which seemed to step higher than it should causing his right leg to buckle under him.

He collapsed onto the edge of the bed with his back propping him up against the cold wall. His lungs wheezed and his entire body quivered, sweat dripped from his brow. He felt like he was trapped inside the body of another man, a crippled war veteran.

Such was his pain that he had failed to hear the turning of the lock and the entering into the cell of two more males.

"Edmund it seems the good Lord wants our villain to suffer his punishment after all."

"Or maybe he thinks I've suffered enough." Jem answered sharply recognising the voice to be that of the overweight man who doused him with the water.

"Oh no Mister Rose. I can guarantee you are going to suffer for your crimes like no criminal has suffered before." Came the instant retort.

"That's quite enough Cornell." Edmund demanded.

Jem struggled to associate the sharp rebuff with the politeness that he had come to expect from the old man.

"I think that you and I need to converse immediately."

"Yes, Edmund I believe we do!" Replied Cornell from the doorway as he held firm his glare at the prisoner.

Grabbing his cane and hat with haste the Edmund joined Cornell and together they vacated the cell and disappeared into the darkness beyond.

"Your future does not look bright, Mister Rose." Quipped the remaining jailer as he tossed in Jem's direction fustian garments and an old pair of leather boots.

"It doesn't matter if they don't fit. You won't be wearing them for long."

Turning his back to slam and lock the door the echo from his laughter could be heard from the corridor beyond.

A chill ran down Jem's spine as speculation clouded his mind.

Chapter 4

Carlisle, Cumbria

Named after her mother, who forfeit her own life in the birth of her daughter, Jacqueline Pymm was the only child of General Fraser Pymm of North Allerton.

She was raised to the only standards of which he knew in the male dominated military and manly world. And so it was that she learned at an early age how to ride, shoot, master the noble science of self-defence with the use of the small backsword and quarter staff, the sabre and her fists.

It was not until she had reached her teenage years, when her father was assigned to a post abroad that she began to learn under the guidance of her aunt, all the social and lady graces to an equal standard.

Having failed to return home from foreign service, General Pymm had forward instructions that his dying wish was that daughter should continue to live with her aunt in Ripley until she had reached her time of marriage.

It was here in Ripley that the flourishing young starlet fell in love and married Edward Beechey thus becoming daughter-in-law to the Baron of Ripon.

Always an ambitious and daring man, Edward Beechey's profession was that of an undercover agent for the English secret service.

With her upbringing and skills it was naturally accepted to Beechey and the English spy network that she should join her husband in his profession and starting with simple errands and working her way up in the associations confidence it wasn't too long before she had earned herself a leading role within the organisation thus enabling her to join in a partnership alongside her husband.

Working throughout various regions of Germany, France and Spain together they infiltrated and exploited many of the crowns arch enemies and they were soon regarded with the highest degree of respect from of the most senior ranking officers within the service.

Unfortunately, it was to be in a dark, isolated field in Flanders as they were making their homeward journey that the marriage and successful alliance was suddenly and prematurely ended.

Deceived and betrayed, they were led into a trap by the leading Dutch Jacobite, Luc De Winter and they were struck down in a hail of musket fire.

Left for dead in the dark of night Jacqueline Beechey, spawned on by the will for revenge survived by calling upon resilience and courage to craw her way to the safety of the remote farmhouse.

Cared and tendered to by an aging farmer's wife, her ball wounds made a slow, but full recovery however, the deep scare of hurt, loss and hatred remained eternal. Not even the mellowing lapse of time eased the pain and anguish which she had suffered daily since leaving her husband in that distant field.

It had taken her three years to get back on the trail of Luc De Winter and no matter what the stakes she was determined to grasp revenge.

From her remaining connections within the English espionage service she had learned of the affair with the Jacobite's at the Durham theatre and she was informed of the capture of one of their leading sympathisers, Jeremiah Mortimer. Travelling north with haste she witnessed his torture and interrogation.

He confessed to murdering the actress Mary Dibbler, but that was all and eventually his stubbornness and silent tongue claimed his life. There was no pain spared with his treatment because the actress, unbeknown to Mortimer was in fact an undercover agent working alongside Beechey for the Crown.

Men like Mortimer turned her stomach and she found secret enjoyment at the expense of his suffering.

Although the English intelligence agents did not know for sure, Mortimer had cut the actresses throat before his capture, they presumed that Nora Ludgate alias Mary Dibbler had suspected she had been exposed of being a spy and had fled in panic whilst she could.

Piecing fragments of information together from her colleagues in Durham, Beechey had learnt that one of the leaders of the plot was known as Luc De Winter.

Immediately, she left the authorities in Durham to debate on their own what action they would be taking next and she travelled as quickly as she could to Fenchurch and to the retirement home of her father-in-law the Baron of Ripon.

After updating him of the news she pleaded with him to use all his powers of influence to get her an assignment involved deep within the treachery. Noting her determined state of mind and fearing that she might try something of a more desperate nature which he would have absolutely no control over he swayed in her favour and against his better judgement and by the end of that week her orders had arrived and she was making the preparations for resuming her pursuit of the murderous Dutch Jacobite.

It was agreed with the authorities in Durham and Carlisle that under no circumstances must the discovery of the Jacobites within the Royal Oak theatrical company be made public knowledge and nor should any of the rebels be approached.

The English intelligence believed that their best way for them to discover who all the ringleaders behind the plot was for Jacqueline Beechey to simply fill in the role and carry on from where the unfortunate Nora Ludgate had left off.

She gathered all the information she could from the Northumberland authorities and set off for Carlisle where she had decided to intercept and get acquainted with Oliver Trevean before anyone else could.

Knowing that Trevean the tenor might be more suspicious and weary than usual of hiring an unreliable stranger Beechey had invented a false name and character which she believed would dupe the tenor and satisfy his requirements. She had calculated both the introduction and her newly adopted personality to perfection and returning a brief smile to Trevean and raising her jug of ale to toast her newly found employment within the theatrical company she mused at the thought of the Society of Revolutionary Jacobites hiring their most implacable and dangerous enemy.

A meal and a couple of drinks later and Trevean trusted and felt completely at ease with his new employee, Jacqueline Beechey.

Her story revolved around the loss of her father's crops failure due to adverse weather conditions and the tax collectors claiming all their seed to pay off the debts which they had incurred.

Falling further behind the payments her father and brother were arrested for protesting and her mother fell ill and died from the upset caused by this turmoil. Losing everything they had worked for, her father lost his own will to live and deteriorated in the squalor of a cell never seeing the light of freedom again whilst her brother was transported to the Tangiers. She was forced into marriage to escape the life of a pauper, but fate was to deal her another vicious blow. After less than twelve months of marriage her husband was killed in a barroom brawl.

She had left an impression upon him, which more than suggested she was tough, clever, but most essentially she had a deep hatred for the crown, the government and anybody involved within it.

She had displayed, as many of this nation's people did, the frustration of being restrained by this government's policies and like many of the population she had been scarred by the loss of her parents, her husband and her home.

Trevean the tenor had accepted her story of resentment, hatred and poverty and he did not feel the need to examine her past for any more for details. He was highly pleased and satisfied that he had found the ideal candidate to fill the vacancy in such a short period of time.

During the following week Jacqueline Beechey alias Dorathea Nibley had learnt her duties, rehearsed the performance and made her debut on the stage.

Although over the years she acted out of many different scenes and portrayed several different characters to aid her work as a spy, this was her first appearance in front of a large audience. It was not a pleasant experience, but smiling on through the embarrassment she forced herself to go through with the act knowing that she would soon become accustomed to the situation and so far all had gone relatively well.

The show consisted of a drama called The Wicked Cousin and an entree act with a mixture of demonstrations of magic and short operatic ballads.

Beechey's role was that of a landlord's daughter who was having an affair with a leading member of the aristocracy. The play revolved around her affair and the bribing in return for silence concerning the affair with the aristocrat by her jealous cousin. The nobility within the play was portrayed as being a greedy, non English speaking German who was draining the country of it's wealth whilst he was living a life a lavish frivolity.

The first week passed by without any incidents, but during every performance, she noticed what she suspected was an exchanging of signals between the tenor and several different members of the audience. Biding her time she did nothing, but play her roles and report back to the Baron of Ripon with coded messages via the local constabularies.

It was after the second week in Carlisle that she got her first chance to impress the tenor with her courage and astuteness.

The evening's performance was over and she has decided to stay backstage for a while to see if she could find anything new about the organisation. The rest of the performers had gone their separate ways for the remainder of the night, all except the tenor.

Out of her costume and re-dressed in her street clothes Beechey had left her dressing room quietly to investigate the muffled conversation which was echoing in the backstage corridors.

Reaching the tenors changing room and the source of the conversation, she peered undetected through the ajar door and into the half-light of candle lit room. The tenor was accompanied by the theatre owner. In front of them both and partially tipped from a purse was a collection of glimmering coins.

"I'm sorry it's not more." The tenor apologised.

"It's what we agreed on." The theatre owner confirmed with a smile and a nod as he picked up the leather purse of coins. "I just don't know how you can afford for the production to continue." He continued the nod now replaced with a subtle shake as balanced the purse on his palm as if he was weighing the haul.

"It's all I require Mister Tasker. Just enough to keep the show running. You see the rewards I seek cannot be found in profit alone." Trevean reached down to pull a wet rag from a pail of water. "No, I get my rewards from the pleasure of entertaining the real people of this world. Not just the rich and noble all who sit around decorating the high streets of London." He began to vigorously wipe away his face colouring. "Oh no, I like to perform for the people out there who work hard and strive for everything they've got in life." His smudged face resembled a distressed clown. "The pleasure of enlightening the lives of the discontented, the miserable and the plain old poor folk of this society, albeit, if it's only for an hour or so." He submerged the cloth back into water and rung it tight then closed his mouth to wipe off the rouge around his lips.

Tasker admitted. "I'll be sorry to see you go Mister Trevean. You give me a full house every night." Another slight shake indicated his regret.

"I'm sorry. I've got other commitments." The tenor cut in displaying sympathy as if to support his comments. "Unfortunately."

The opening and closing of a door at the far end of the corridor forced Beechey to quickly avert her attention. Stepping back into the darkness, she watched a huge and burly contour of a man approach the door.

Hearing the voices from beyond the door he showed caution and halted himself from entering. He hadn't seen the women stood in the darkness at his side and he stood in the same position, peering and listening to the conversation between next to the ajar door she had done only seconds earlier.

Beechey noticed he held firmly in his hand a pistol. Hurriedly her eyes traced along his arm and up to his face where a yellow beam of light spliced the gap and glowed on his red hair. She recognised him from the audience where she had noticed him several times passing hand signalled messages to the tenor.

Squinting in the blackness about her, she was hoping to find something of which to make a weapon. A plank of discarded scenery lay at her feet and she decided this would fulfil her needs. Silently and slowly, she lowered herself until both hands were tightly gripped around it's solid girth then stealth fully she crept up behind the motionless and preoccupied dark form and guided back the wood to swing it ferociously forwards in the direction of the man's head.

Connecting with a loud and echoing crack, the man was knocked downwards and forwards. He omitted a gasp of surprise and with no control over his movements he collapsed through the door to sprawl at the feet of the tenor.

Too dazed to raise or respond and too confused to speak, he lay motionless as both the tenor and Tasker jumped back and bolted upright.

"Tom! What the hell." Trevean yelled loudly his surprise, his mind confused and his face contort with the fear of detection that all conspirators secretly held within.

Towering above the innate figure and still wielding the wood Beechey entered the room and approached to dispel the look of fear, but not the scowl of confusion.

"This bastard was planning to rob you." She enlightened.

"What?" Trevean's forehead lined and his eyes narrowed.

"Yes, it's true. I followed him down the corridor and watched him pull out the pistol and ready himself."

She slid the fallen pistol across to the tenor's feet with her foot as she spoke. "He knows it's our last night and he's been watching you settling up. What shall we do with him? Call in the Charlie's or teach the bastard a good lesson." She finished raising high and to her rear the wood.

"No, no." The tenor yelled as he put up his hands in front of her to prevent more violence. "Stop!"

"But Mister Trevean it's so obvious." She furrowed her brow acting totally puzzled to the tenor's reaction.

"No, no my dear." Now both his hand spread out in front of her face as barrier. "You are mistaken. This man works for me."

"No, it cannot be." She shook her head with her mouth open to continue with her pretence of disbelief.

"Oh, but Dora …. I'm afraid it is true." Trevean slowly reached for and lifted the wood out of her grip, she willingly surrendered the piece.

"I will explain it all to you later." He then half turned to Tasker. "Could you please bring us a jug of water and something of which to bathe his head Mister Tasker?" With his chest rising and falling rapidly Tasker submitted a speechless nod and disappeared into the blackness of a corridor.

Trevean released the wood and dropped is face into his open hands mumbling to no one in particular. "Poor fellows going to have a thumping head when it comes to."

Then hiding the amusement he found from the girls mistake he lowered himself over the stunned man.

"Tom." He repeated his name again, but louder and he continuing to speak louder than he normally would he shook the injured man by his shoulders. "Are you alright Tom?"

Cursing something inaudible the big man began to slowly move. Trevean rested his palm upon Tom's chest urging him to take it steady.

"What the hell happened?" Tom finally blurted out in a distinct Scottish accent and he rubbed the back of his head. Stumbling up to his feet, Trevean had to hold him firm with both his hands until the Scottish man regained his balance. His face revealed pain and he winced as his palm found the sore point at the back of his head.

"Tom I want you to listen to me." Trevean spoke to the man as if he was talking to a child. "You've been the victim of a mistake.....an accident."

Tom didn't answer back. He just stared blankly at the floor as he gathered his senses about him.

"Do you hear me Tom?"

Trevean knew Tom had an extremely unpleasant and nasty temper and he was trying hard to abate the anger which he knew would erupt.

"I hear you, but .... but I don't understand."

He raised his head in the women's direction as he answered. He looked exasperated and mean. "Just what the hell's happening Oliver!" He demanded shaking his head to clear his vision.

"Keep calm Tom. There has been an innocent misunderstanding.

"I am calm." He sharply cut in pushing away the tenors aiding hand.

"What are you doing here so late?"

"I've come to deliver a message." He blinked several times still trying to regain his focus.

"She thought you were a robber." Trevean began, but he was immediately cut off by the angry man's raised tone.

"She what?" He tried to rise as he bellowed, but his sudden movement caused him to stumble back against the table, he had not yet regained his equilibrium.

"I'm sorry, truly I am. I thought you were a robber." Sounding convincingly apologetic, but deeply wanting the traitor to suffer Beechey thought that hearing the words from a woman might help to calm him down. She was wrong and immediately she knew it.

The Scotsman tentatively shook his head, firstly to try and remove the blurriness that clouded his vision and secondly at the disbelief of realising it had been a woman who struck him. Suddenly all traces of bewilderment vanished and his eyes glared resentment at the woman.

"You took me for a robber!" His tone cast hate as regaining his faculties he erected himself, drew breath and expanded his chest.

"Take it easy Tom. It was a mistake." Trevean professed holding out his arms straight as if to make a barrier.

"A mistake!" He moved slowly forwards his right fist clenching into t tight ball. "The bitch damn nearly took my head off." He declared rubbing his head where the swelling lump had already protruded through his ginger hair.

"She did what she thought was necessary."

"Necessary!" He raged turning over his left palm to show the bright red blood. "I'll show the bitch what's necessary."

He relaxed the fist and drew out a dirk then crouched to prepare his revenge. "Nobody, but nobody draws blood from Tom McCoy and gets away with it."

Beechey's response was not one of fear, but one of natural defence. She instantly stretched down to seize the piece of wood and raising it high behind her head she balanced herself and yelled without any trace of fear.

"Just you try it and I'll flatten your face!"

"Why you cocky bitch." Tom ferociously raged slowly encroaching, "I'm gonna make you bleed."

"Stop it, both of you." Trevean's demand fell upon deaf ears as the two stalkers encircled each other to secure a position of advantage.

Tom lunged forward, swinging his outstretched arm towards the woman's midriff, but in the blink of an eye and reading his intentions perfectly, Beechey easily side stepped him and countered his attack with her own powerful blow slapping the wood hard against his back as he embarrassingly stumbled past.

Turning his face etched with shock from the woman's invasive speed and confidence his instinct was to retaliate with harsher punishment. He inhaled another long breath and his lips tightened, his nostrils closed and his eyes grew wider as demanding more concentration from himself he attempted to strike again.

"Tom! Dora! Stop it now." Again Trevean shouted to no avail.

"You stay out of this Oliver." Tom ordered, his eyes flicking between his face of his pray, her feet and the wood. "This is between the bitch and me and she's just begging for all she's going to get."

Bluffing an attack Tom jolted the dirk forward. A smile creased his cheeks as Beechey jumped back out of range and then he added as he encroached with his arm extended. "And a whole lot more besides!"

Knowing Tom's anger well, Trevean realised that the words would not be enough to halt him and so in desperation he reached down and grabbed a hold of the Scotsman's abandoned pistol.

"Back off and drop the knife Tom!" Trevean's first call did not register in Tom's ears, but after the second call the Scotsman averted sideways his eyes just enough to see his own pistol levelled directly upon his head.

Cursing he stopped his advance and when he felt the metal of the barrel press against his forehead he lowered the blade.

"What the hell are you doing Oliver?" Moving very slowly he angled himself towards the tenor whilst still keeping his vigilance on Beechey. "Turning enemy to your own men." He insulted

"It's not my choice Tom, but I'll fire if I have to." Trevean's threat was calm and his words clear.

"Oliver Trevean turning sides. I would have never thought it true if I hadn't seen it with my own eyes." Tom spat.

"I'm as loyal as the day I joined, but I will shoot if you don't do exactly as I say."

Trevean's aim was still and his voice firm. Tom was not scared or intimidated, but he was no fool and he knew full well the damage his weapon could inflict at short range. He also did not doubt for one minute that Trevean would not hesitate to use the weapon against him.

"For the Society's sake Tom. Drop the knife and back off."

"Societies sake?" Tom questioned with a wryly smile. He knew Trevean harboured plans for his personal advancement and he considered himself a threat which Trevean would not hesitate to eliminate given the opportunity.

"You heard me. Drop it."

Trevean's eyes quickly flashed to the woman and back upon Tom. It was the first time he had hinted that he was involved with something more devious than just a theatrical production and realising his error he looked at her face for a response. He did not get one.

"You're a good man." He began to prattle, but Beechey interrupted, knowing that it would cause the Scotsman more annoyance.

"But, no one's irreplaceable."

"Dora shut up! Haven't you interfered enough?" Trevean rapped and she responded by locked her lips tight to conceal the pleasure she had found from aggravating the traitors within.

"Is she with us?" Tom wanted to know before deciding what action he would take.

"Not just yet, but I hope she soon will be."

"With you at what?" She understood Tom's reference, but she responded just how she thought a common girl would.

"Dora. I told you shut it and I won't tell you again. Now Tom for everyone's sake calm yourself and let the knife go so that we can clear this misunderstanding."

Just as Trevean's words finished Tasker re-entered the room with a pail of water hanging down by his right side and a towel folded across his left arm. His every fibre froze halting him in motion as to his shock and surprise, he found himself in the middle of a confrontation with weapons brandished by all 3 combatants. Water wavered across the top of the pail and spilled over to splash down onto the wooden floor and across his shoes as he became the fourth statutory person in the room. Beechey, Trevean and Tom's eyes all shifted rapidly across each other, but no one made a move.

"This is the last time I say it Tom. Drop the knife and meet me back at my room. We'll discuss this misunderstanding rationally." Trevean made the ultimatum and everyone waited.

Shaking his head, Tom threw the dirk down with such venom that the point of the blade struck the wooden surface and it landed perfectly upright just a few inches from Beechey's foot. He scowled his disapproval at the outcome and spat in the woman's direction then he turned away to leave the room in such a rage that his shoulder bumped against Tasker knocking him off balanced and causing him to completely drop the pail of water and drench the lower part of his body in the process.

"I knew good sense would prevail, Mister Tasker."

A false smile accompanied Trevean's lie as he quickly gathered together his few belongings. He wanted to get out before Tasker could compose himself enough to start asking questions or think about informing the constable of the disturbance.

"Come on Dorothea back to the Crown, it's payday."

"Now there's a word I haven't heard for a long time."

Trevean was relieved that his employee had not noticed and tried to correct him on his deliberate mistake. They were not going to the Crown, but to the Kings Arms which was 5 miles in the opposite direction. Trevean had cunningly wanted to throw the theatre owner off his trail just in case he should get some after thoughts or ideas with regards to submitting a report to the authorities of the incident.

Linking the actress by the arm the tenor almost swung her around to leave the room with haste whilst Tasker, who was still bewildered and rooted to the spot with his jaw hanging agape, said nothing and scratched his head with confusion.

Beechey had noticed Trevean's error, but intuitively she understood his reason for it and she also knew that to point it out would have made her seem too astute for the undercover role she was portraying and possibly cause some suspicion from the tenor.

When Trevean and his actress entered the lodging room it was empty, Thomas McCoy had not yet arrived and by the time he did Jacqueline Beechey alias Dorothy Nibley was a sworn member of the Society of Revolutionary Jacobites.

The tenor had keenly expressed that he wanted women like her to join the movement and he did his best to influence her tendency's to support the organisation by explaining in specific detail his own biased assessment of the Society's aims and aspirations and what the financial rewards would be for it's members.

These she already knew, but the information she sought regarding leaders names and locations, Trevean had cautiously omitted. She dare not at this early stage ask too many questions or press any issues in fear of arousing any mistrust and provoke suspicion concerning her loyalties.

Interrupting the initiation in it's final stage, Tom entered the room to finally pass on his message from the Society's commander, which he had intended to do at the theatre.

The conversation was blunt and sparse, but direct. Tom expressed his disapproval at the new recruit the tension and hostility ensure there was not a celebratory induction.

Tom's report from the Society's leader to Trevean informed the spy of little. He grudgingly told the tenor that their leader was pleased with the actions he had taken after the Durham incident and he believed the Society of Revolutionary Jacobites reputation had survived unblemished. He sent orders that the production company should continue with their performances on the circuit already arranged but instead of spreading the news of the Durham uprising, they were to simply carry on as before, gathering support and funds from all of the towns they played.

Chapter 5

Since the start of her employment with the Royal Oak Theatre Production company three weeks ago Jacqueline Beechey's time had not been wasted.

She had portrayed her role as Dorothea Nibley with such enthusiasm and perfection that she had been welcomed by her performing companions so much so that no one hesitated to speak freely in her presence.

She was not surprised to find out that the cast were still worried about being implicated with Jeremiah Mortimer. Although most of them cared very little for the man and were not concerned with what sort of an end he met they were still obviously nervous and apprehensive of what information he might have told the authorities.

The undercover agent could have given them the actual details of his fate and confession, but she enjoyed witnessing their anxiety and she felt disinclined to ease their worries. However, there was one thing that she did want to establish with her work colleagues and that was to avoid any unwanted amorous advances she made it clear that she was still a grieving widow and she wanted no intimacy. The tenor and the rest of the cast understood her position and they had accepted and would honour her decision, but she feared the resentful magician would not be so obliging.

His pride was still hurt and she sensed it would not be long before he came looking for his revenge. He alone was the only member of the cast that she did not feel completely at ease with, even though she did not fear him, she knew that she would have to take extra special care when she was in his presence.

Fortunately since the night of her first encounter with the fiery Scotsman her only interactions with him were conducted at a distance when she was on the stage. Several times she had noticed his aged battered face in the audience, but they never had cause to confront each other since that night in Carlisle. She presumed the tenor had timed his meetings with the envoy so that a repeat performance or continuation of hostilities could not ignite and reoccur.

The production had moved south from Carlisle stopping to perform in Kendal and Lancaster and it was now engaged in a week long-term in Preston.

Beechey had learnt plenty about the Society of Revolutionary Jacobites by cautiously picking up information from Trevean and his crew, but she had failed to make contact with someone whom she could trust with her information in both Kendal and Lancaster therefore she had not yet reported back to the Baron of Ripon for over a week.

Now in Preston she must once more try to find a constable of a reliable and trustworthy nature so that she could pass on her coded messages to the Baron.

This was now a priority as she gathered urgent and important information. She knew that the Society leaders were in England and somewhere within close proximity because word had been sent that a meeting was soon to be arranged between Trevean, Luc De Winter and some of the other conspirators.

Her blood had boiled with the thought of vengeance when the name Luc De Winter echoed into her ear drums, but she had to force her own personal incentives to the back of her mind for the time being at least. She had discovered that the Society had gathered about four hundred well armed soldiers and their numbers were increasing every day with outlaws, ex-soldiers and criminals from every walk of life. She also knew that these soldiers were in encampments scattered nearby and that eventually Trevean would receive orders to take his employees to this secret training camp.

Until that time arrived however, they were to carry on gaining as much support as possible and influencing the more prominent members of the public into funding the Society. These most prominent members of the public were chosen for either their wealth, social or political status or even their military knowledge and they were hand-picked by another member of Society whom the English spy had not yet met.

After this secret member of the Society had aroused the interest of their target they would invite either him or her to attend Trevean's production of The Wicked Cousin where they would then be encouraged to attend one of the secret meetings. The topic of conversation would be the living conditions and unjust hardships forced upon them by the Hanoverian monarchy.

Dorothea Nibley's role was to condescend upon these meetings with morose and spread her tale of grief and sorrow. She was to gain the sympathy and support of the mainly female listeners with her opinions of the Hanoverian oppression.

Oliver Trevean would converse with the guests on an individual basis promising positions of power for those who were seen to be highly competent and offer rewards of wealth for those who would play a brave and active part in the approaching uprising by giving their support to Prince Charles Stewart with his ambition to crown his father James as the true King of England, Scotland and Wales.

Titles and positions of influence were offered to those who were prepared to give loyalty and sacrifice their income to raise sufficient funds for the cause.

Everything Trevean echoed was calculated to boost the guest's morals and appeal to their beliefs that a new monarchy and government would conform to their own avarice. Oaths of allegiance and secrecy were sworn and arrangements for the donation of funds were implemented, passwords were exchanged and messengers employed. A treasurer was elected by the gathering to hold secure the funds until convincing proof had arrived to indicate that the day of the revolution was near. This was Trevean's clever idea, he wanted to establish local interest by impressing the audience with his own trust and he also wanted to stop the inevitable moans and grumbles of the unsympathetic who would imply that the Society was nothing but a fake organisation that was only interested in pilfering the hard earned money of the working people.

Parting company with his new recruits Trevean gave his honourable promise that the days of cruel hardship and embitterment were soon to be at an end for the day when the countries true leader James Stewart would be crowned King was drawing ever nearer. And all this was falling upon the eyes and ears of the English secret service's most distinguished female spy.

For the next two days they continued to perform and promote but nothing out of the ordinary happened except that Trevean's magician, Nat Futrell's dislike for the shows latest recruit began to increase and an impending confrontation began to look certain. The 'Great Majestico' was a brawny thirteen stone colossus that had the good looks to match his self esteem. Sharp with his tongue, fashionable with his dress and a personality as false as his stage act, he was everything Jacqueline Beechey detested in a man.

He was a compulsive womaniser who was intent on having as much fun and as many sexual conquests in every town they visited as he could. Mixing his addiction to women with his pleasure for drink he never attended any of the after show meetings and was rarely seen outside the bounds of an alehouse or his bedroom.

Whilst this arrangement suited everyone the fact that he worked in the same production as the one woman who had publicly humiliated him made him irritable and hostile towards his fellow performers and her presence served as a continual reminder of the embarrassment.

The friction finally became overbearing when his assistant for his magical routine fell ill and Trevean ordered, because there was no one else suitable, that Dorothea should take on the role for that evening.

Herself feeling embarrassed by having to clad the revealing costume and stand in for the assistant, Beechey forced herself to go through with the performance, firstly for the sake of revenge and secondly for the sake of her country.

Everything flowed as normal until the finale when she accidentally knocked over a piece of Nat's equipment which fell with a loud, distracting clatter, much to the audience's amusement and to the annoyance of the magician. Scowling his thoughts of hatred to the woman he awaited until after the show to accuse her of deliberately trying to ruin his act and only the tenors care to avoid the clash, which may have resulted in one or both of his employees leaving the show, halted the argument before it went any further.

Later that same evening when the secret meeting with the local and potential supporters was over and only Trevean and Beechey had remained to tidy up more trouble followed.

Trevean had just informed the spy how satisfied he was with the progress she had made and with the direction things were generally heading when suddenly the door burst open and in staggered Nat with a female escort hanging to his arm.

"My, my... look at our little Dorothea."

Nat began to remark with his veined eyes running up and down the spy's threadbare dress which she specifically wore to accompany her story of tragedy and ruin.

"Doesn't she look the poor unfortunate?"

"She looks like the harlot you described Nat honey." Nat's escort hissed.

The women's appearance and style of clothes suggested that she was not from the gentry class or an aspirant to the Society.

"Whores are all he knows how to describe. They're the only women that will accompany him." Beechey snapped at the courtesan.

Both the whore and the magician were worse for drink and their abusive and hostile attitude showed that their sole intention of this visit was to cause trouble for Beechey.

Trevean was wise to their play and he levelled out his arm across Beechey's front indicating he did not want her to get involved.

"Lower your cursed voices down. We don't want the constabulary around here." Trevean ordered trying to control the situation before it got out of hand. "Nat you're drunk again!"

"I've had a few, but not enough to make me forget that this is the bitch." He raised and pointed an accusing finger. "That not only humiliated me in front of my friends, but now she also does it in front of my audience."

"That's enough Nat." Trevean interrupted. "Get out! Go and retire to your bed. You've obviously drunk too much to realise you're overstepping the bounds of decency and more importantly loyalty."

Suddenly Nat's face braced a stern expression as if Trevean had touched upon something the he held significant.

"Loyalty! I'm loyal to what I know and what I believe in and I know that I don't trust this little tart you're protecting."

Trevean's face drained of all colour as he immediately understood and disliked what his magician was implying.

"I earnestly advise you to say no more. Get out of here and never appear in front of me in this despicable state again."

Before Trevean's words had finished, Beechey who had a detestation for all members of the Society of Revolutionaries decided to provoke Nat and his woman hoping that it would lead the traitors into a squabble.

"I don't need protection. Especially from the likes of you and your whore."

"Whore! You little bitch." The woman screamed back lunging for and grasping at Beechey with her long fingernails. "I'll whore you!"

The spy did not respond as the cool and calculated Jacqueline Beechey, but as the aggrieved and seething Dorothea Nibley and instead of stepping back to avoid the wild assault she barged past Trevean's barrier to clash with the whore.

Arms rotating, fingernails clawing and hair flying in all directions the pair began to tear each other apart. Clothes ripped, blood splattered and furious screams pierced the air as eventually they fell to the floor with legs and arms interlocked.

Managing to grab a handful of the whores long ginger hair Beechey forced her over onto her back and trapped down her opponent's arms tightly with her legs then she raised and slammed down the back of the whore's head against the floor until all resistance wavered.

Trevean, motionless and stunned allowed the wicked beating to continue as he found himself concerned only with the whore's breasts which were partly exposed through her torn garments.

However, realising his fun time girl was taking a serve beating Futrell stepped in and having already received and suffered from the new girls surprising combat talents he wasn't fool enough to succumb to them again so from a measured distance he pulled his right leg back then catapulted it forward so that the impact of his boot against Beechey connected with maximum force.

Slamming against her, the blow was powerful enough to knock Beechey clear off the whore, force out her breath and render her prostrate alongside her stranded opponent.

Futrell's unexpected action ignited Trevean's volatile temper.

"You're finished Nat Futrell. The Society is done with you."

"Then it will be done with you too!" Futrell slurred as he fumbled to grab a wine bottle from the nearest table.

Smashing it's base against the table corner, he menacingly waived the weapon towards Trevean. "You're not worthy of your position so I'm taking over the leadership of the Royal Oak."

"I'm the headman and it will always be that way." Trevean retaliated.

"You're no headman you're a fool and that's what you always will be."

"Oh no Nat. You're the one that's the fool. You're the fool of want! You want gin and you want women and your gluttonous habits flounder to them both as only a fool could allow." Trevean insulted.

"You amused me Oliver, but I always knew it would end like this." Nat's confidence was enhanced by the consumption of excessive alcohol

"The ending is yours Nat." Trevean finished as he whipped out from beneath his waist coat Tom McCoy's razor sharp dirk.

Futrell delayed his advance as soon as his eyes caught sight of the blade, but Trevean's mind was now controlled by an infernal obsession that was intent on satisfaction and devoid from all reasoning.

He lunged forward, stabbing the knife in the magician's direction, but moving his huge bulk with the swiftness and the accuracy he needed to gain success, even against a drunk was impossible.

The tenor was slow and cumbersome and Nat easily sidestepped leaving Trevean to wildly miss his target and unable to halt his stumbling momentum Futrell was able to drag the jagged edge of the broken bottle against Trevean's unprotected face.

Evidence of horror and disbelief appeared on Trevean's face as blood spilled out from his flesh. He lost all vision and control of what he was doing as incensed, and acting out of anger he charged recklessly forward again.

Trevean was an easy target for Nat and this time the bottle ripped open the tenor's knuckles forcing him to release the knife. Stunned and hurt and he collided into the table, but he was in no mood to yield and stumbling back upright and raising both his fists in an act of defiance he took up the stance of a knuckle fighter to the encroaching Futrell.

"You really are a fool Oliver." Preparing himself to finish off the tenor, Futrell saw too late that the woman whom he hated so much was closing near to him fast and he could not avoid the right fist that lashed forwards in the direction of his chin.

Beechey had pivoted forward from her waist so that her full body weight lay behind the blow. It was not a risky gamble, but a perfectly timed execution that connected hard enough to snap his head backwards and send him staggering to an involuntary retreat.

Following up the attack with a hard kick to the groin, she made certain that Futrell could only respond in the way she had intended, on his knees screaming in agony with his hands free of any weapons and shielding the painful area.

Momentarily inspecting for damage and rubbing away the stinging from her knuckles Beechey failed to notice the frenzied tenor re-arm himself with the dirk and attack the stranded magician. With blow after merciless blow he continued to thrust the dirk into the magicians back.

Blood spurted high and burst out from the many perforations on the dying body as it squirmed it's last moment, but savagely and relentlessly Trevean hacked into the flesh only stopping when the blood of his victim squirted into his own eyes and he could see no more than a red blur.

In her short but eventful life time Beechey had witnessed many acts of cruelty and many brutal crimes, but this barbaric act of inhumanity equalled all that she had seen before. Her stomach turned and her legs almost buckled, she felt unusually weak as watching in horror, she realised that he had not yet finished. With a cold and calculating callousness that would normally be associated with only the most ardent backstreet cut throats and not a theatre performer, Trevean calmly straddled the unconscious and limp whore, pulled back her head with her hair exposing her bare neck and sliced his blade deep into and across her throat.

The slash opened wide as Trevean continued to hold back her head as if he were savouring in her death and for a brief moment the whores gaping windpipe sucked for air until it became engulfed in a flood of blood.

Turning away from the macabre scene Trevean moved towards the static spy. His face soaked with dripping blood expressed a manic glee.

"Sacrifices have to be made for the cause." He said nonchalantly as he dropped the knife into the dead woman's pooling blood and wiped splattering's hot liquid from his face with his sleeve.

Concerned her life was in danger, Beechey stepped back in an attempt to avoid the tenor's approach. She had witnessed a psychotic trait within him that she could not imagine he possessed. Now she knew he did not rise to become one of the Society's leaders by just relaying on his affable influences.

"Do not worry yourself with the loss of these lives Dora." Suddenly he was calm and apart from the smudged blood the signs of savagery and mania had totally disappeared from his face.

"This unfortunate day was inevitable. The society will not accept or tolerate those of a weak constitution."

Beechey frowned and the tenor obliged to reveal his thoughts. "He had a weakness for the ale and the lust for easy women and these my dear are the invitations to ruin."

"And his friend?" Beechey thought it was only natural to ask.

"I'm afraid her death was necessary. She could have prescribed irreversible complications and believe me we are well rid of them both."

"I couldn't agree more."

Replying, she could not avoid his deep probing eyes that were in searched to find some kind of weakness.

She felt the need to beguile him. "Nat always resented you because you have a strong disposition for leadership and success."

Turning away satisfied that the girl was still loyal to him and the society Trevean moved over to the sagging lifeless body of the magician.

"You useless womanising bastard. I always knew that you're sinning ways would drag you down to hell." Trevean used his foot to lever the body so that Nat's greying eyes were not fixed directly upon him. "Dear God, what a mess." He added flickering glances across the bloodshed. "Dora, are you alright?" He unexpectedly asked partly turning his head to address his visibly distressed college.

"Yes." She replied adjusting her bedraggled clothing, "I will be fine in a few minutes." She flawlessly continued to control her deceit, "a little bruised and shaken but nothing serious enough to warrant any attentions." She lied.

"Good because we must act quickly. I want you to go and find Goss and Turner. Tell them what's happened and that they need to be here at once. Be sure that they bring with them a cart, my spare coat, waistcoat and breaches .... Oh and a spade."

She responded instantly by heading straight for the door.

"And Dora." She stopped to listen, but holding her breath she did not looking back, "You did good, real good tonight."

"I did what I had to do for the society's sake. Not my own."

"Yes and I will personally make sure that your bravery and courage is repaid in full come the day of our triumphant resurrection."

Early the following morning Trevean sent word that he wanted all his fellow collaborators to attend a meeting at the town hall where they were performing. The location of backstage had been chosen carefully to ensure that they did not arouse any suspicion from within the local community and so the gathering could easily be explained as a rehearsal if it should become necessary.

The tenor addressed the sombre audience with the news of Nat's death and even more importantly death of one of the local whores. He explained the execution had been unavoidable and had resulted from a sudden change of attitude concerning his loyalties.

Although Nat was well liked by the cast no one questioned Trevean and he continued without any interruptions. He stressed the importance that everyone's explanation of Nat and the whore's disappearance should be coherent and not contradicting under any circumstances. If questioned, the tenor instructed to the few who had been in the alehouse with Nat to say he left the late promising to show the accompanying whore all the hidden treasures of this beautiful country and a better way of life and that they have not seen or heard from him since.

The rest of the cast who had not been in the Inn were to simply say they hadn't seen him since finishing the night performance, but they were to add on many occasions he had shown signs of discontentment with the show and he had spoken several times that he had more than enough of the dull routine. Finally, Trevean enthused the assembly with the news they had been waiting to hear for a long time.

The coming Friday night's performance was to be their last and early Saturday morning they were going to move the production company into a small village near Manchester where the Society of Revolutionary Jacobites had based their headquarters.

Here they were to make their acquaintance with the organisations leaders and wait along with the military presence until the nearing day insurrection. Until then, he announced that he would have to re-write the script to include his facial wound into the story and lengthen several of the acts to consume the time gap left by the magician's routine. Therefore that afternoon there would have to be rehearsals for everyone. Beechey wondered if the lack of questioning, accepting silences and knowing glances amongst the gathering were a confirmation they had encountered Trevean's antithesis capabilities before.

This was the information the English spymaster had been waiting for. She now knew that she could not delay in sending forward her knowledge any longer.

No matter how great the risk involved she must act before the entourage left Preston. Once in the boundaries of the traitor's headquarters it would be impossible to trust anyone and there was even a distinct possibility that she may be recognised. If this proved to be the case, then at least she would have succeeded in informing the English secret service of the society's headquarters location, the leaders and of their trained armed force.

Quickly heading for the sanctuary of her room Beechey produced from a hidden sleeve in her bible the secret services coded alphabet. Sealing the secret correspondence firmly within a letter she descended into the morning bustle that congested the main street of Preston.

The bright midday sun caused her to squint along the haphazardly congested array of buildings. She stepped into the shadows of the high and overhanging tudor terracing which led the way to the fusion of architecture that had been hastily erected for merely functional and not attractive purposes.

Starting her quest for a reliable and trustworthy emissary, she had nothing to rely on except for her instincts and a small purse of coins.

After a couple of hours of carefully scouring the streets in search of a messenger there seemed only one available option, the parish constable.

Calling upon Symon Cutch in the privacy and discretion of his home, she told him only as much as he needed to know. She did not introduce herself or reveal the contents of the sealed and coded letter. She merely besieged him to deliver the dispatch with the utmost urgency to Edmund Beechey, the Baron of Ripon. An obvious pauper, she trusted the coins would ensure his loyalty and she left the sealed message in his agreeing hands.

The rehearsals in the afternoon soon past by as did the first evening's performance without the magician. There were no blunders and the evening pass by without any concerning events.

In the solace of her boarding room with only the crackle of rising ambers from the fire disturbing the silence, unable to relax Beechey was combing thoroughly the long shiny locks of hair. It was her own ritual habit which she performed every night before she retired to bed. Her mind was still very active with the conjecture of events and she intended to comb until her eventual tiredness would dispel any doubts and fears so that she could relax and get some much needed sleep.

The temperature of the evening had dropped dramatically as the darkness closed in and Beechey was glad she had taken up the landlords offer to light her fire.

As only the orange flicker of flames from the chimney piece illuminated and shadowed her room Beechey began to consider burning the secret code. She held out the translation instructions in the flat of her open palm and subconsciously allowed her eyes to re-examine the letters and their subsequent codes.

Arising from the stool she decided it must be burned. Taking it with her into the lair of the traitors would be a risk far too dangerous to take. Should she be recognised or captured, allowing the code to fall into the enemies hands would jeopardise the entire English spy communications links. She had in any case passed on all the information to her employers and so to dispose of the codifier now would be no great loss to her.

Stretching her hand containing the paperwork out to the flames a sudden explosion of noise and activity behind her door shattered the silence and alarmed her.

After was a couple of thunderous rhythmic bangs against the door it collapsed inwards and two men she had never seen before followed in after it and stumbled forwards both falling into her and onto the floor . Behind them followed a stone faced Tom McCoy, Oliver Trevean and the parish constable, Symon Cutch.

"Is this the woman of which you spoke?" McCoy demanded from Cutch as he pointed an accusing finger at the rigid female.

"Aye, this is the one." He nodded avoiding her distressed glare.

At that moment the revolutionary's eyes locked onto the paper that she was still holding. It was obvious they knew what it was.

"You traitorous bitch! Your time has come to an end." McCoy warned moving forwards.

"You have a care for what you say." Beechey quickly answered back.

"Oh, that sounds royal coming from you.... You slimy bitch." McCoy was the only one doing the talking.

The two heavies stumbled back to their feet and Trevean stood silent, looking both disappointed and crestfallen. His face openly etched disappointed failure from the treachery that she had humiliated upon him.

Beechey knew that she was caught and that her information had not got through to her father in-law, but with McCoy stood only four feet away from her, she was determined not to let him get the code.

"A man's loyalty cannot be bought by small coin." He teased her about the small offering to the constable with a grin stretching satisfaction from cheek to cheek.

Beechey turned his confidence into a startled grimace of shock as she tossed the paper into the flames.

McCoy rushed forward, pushing her aside and reaching into the flames to retrieve the piece, but quickly Beechey rebalanced herself and propelled forward and used the flat of her foot to knock McCoy, head first into the fire. His screams of pain screeched loud above Trevean's order.

"Get her!"

Before either of the men could react Beechey had twisted herself down, took hold of the stool by it's legs and spun it back around in a half circle. It's wooden seat collided perfectly with the temple of one of the onrushing giants splattering blood across the adjacent wall and sending him crashing unconsciously to the floor.

McCoy pulled himself out of the flames, dazed and hurt his charred fingers were cindered onto the remains of the codifier. He stumbled against the chimney piece unable to balance himself. His right arm was blackened, the side of his face blistered purple and his hair singed to a wizened black crisp. One eye gaped the anguish and pain he and the other was closed tight by a layer of molten skin.

Beechey called upon all her combat knowledge and resources and ignoring the burnt man and his pungent odour of scorched flesh, she swung the stool towards the other assailant. This time she was too slow and the agile man blocked her aim before it could gain momentum and he forced the fist of his free hand and into the woman's stomach. The savagery of the blow folded her completely breathless over his arm, but still having her wits about her and being trained for blood feuds she was able to draw away as she fell.

The big man, thinking that his job was complete mistakenly turned to attend to his senseless friend, but Beechey was up aiming a kick into his midriff as quick as a flash.

Trevean saw her arise, but he was too late to warn his colleague and her foot cracked against his unprotected ribs, forcing him to lose his balance and trip forward over is unconscious associate.

Trevean ignored the pleas of help from McCoy and injected himself into the fray. Throwing a left and right combination he was able to land the blows upon Beechey before she could readjust her stance to fend off the new angle of attack.

With everything spinning in front of her, she threw out a wild right hook, but it was only partially successful landing on Trevean's face without gaining it's full force and power. Blood trickled from Trevean's old wound, but uninjured he aimed and landed a right hand to Beechey's defenceless jaw.

She stooped defeated in front of him, swaying on her unbalanced and weak legs, but through watery eyes she could just make out that the paper codifier was burnt beyond salvation. She closed her eyes and gasped a shameless sighed of relief as blood poured from her mouth and down onto her night dress.

She was dazed and too frail to move, but Trevean had not yet finished. She had conned him into trusting her, he had killed one of his friends for her and now he must to answer to the leaders of the society for her.

His dreams were on the verge of collapse and all because he was capacitated by her deception. One woman had virtually demolished within a few weeks everything he had lived for over the past eight years.

He looked at her in an all compulsive hate. He shook his head and groaned as still he struggled to believe what he had witnessed with his own eyes. This smaller than average woman had crippled Nat Futrell in the Kings Arms, knocked Tom McCoy unconscious in the theatre in Carlisle, then only last night defeated both Futrell and the whore and now she had incapacitate the brutish McCoy yet again and rendered his two heavies useless.

He shot a cursory glance to the trembling constable who still occupied the doorway then clamping his teeth hard he summoned all his hate into one mighty punch which snapped her head sidewards and tossed her limp body to the ground. She did not feel the second impact.

Chapter 6

The iron lock clunking causing Jem to cut off from his thoughts and look up from his shackles to see the door thrust inwards with alarming speed. He was confronted by four prison guards and judging by their intimidating approach and their stern countenances he knew they had come for him.

No instructions were hailed and he was given no time to think, react or question their intentions as within an instant they were upon him. He was gagged and his head covered with a muslin bag then with the shackles still fastened to both wrists and ankles the four guards who were barely concerned with his weak struggling resistance hauled him from the floor and out of the cell. He felt himself bundled into some sort of cart and he felt it's swaying motion as it began to take him on this journey into the unknown.

Shuffling into a corner and wedging himself into a seated position, explanations began to overpower his thoughts. His muscles tightened until rigid and his stomach milled queasy as he considered the possibilities. They had conducted the trial without him, he thought and he was being taken to Tyburn for his execution. Maybe he had been lucky enough to be sentenced by a generous judge and he was on his way to be transported to the Americas. No, he shook his head to dispel the thought as he would rather hang than spend the rest of his life without seeing his children ever again.

Fearing he had reached a sudden end to his life's journey he felt bile obstruct and burn his throat. Again he considered the possibilities and, though he feared the worst he hoped and prayed that he had reached the wrong conclusions. Beads of cold sweat damped his forehead, palms and the centre of his back as he could do nothing but await his fate.

Despite Jem being an excellent judge of time and distance he was totally unable to predict either how long he had been travelling or in which direction he was heading. He had no way of knowing where he was travelling from, he assumed it could have been either Doncaster, York or Beverley, but considering how he had never been inside any of the gaols he just did know from where he had left nor to where he was heading.

Some considerable time after the journey began, the carriage steadied and slowed. Jem noticed the distinctive sound and textured feel as the wheels rolled from the usual mud road surface to strange hardened cobbles.

He prepared himself as the changed suggested to him that he was now on the approach to the destination and the journey was about to come to an end.

Moments later his assumption was correct and immediately after the carriage pulled to a halt he was handled from the vessel and forcefully led up some steps into another building.

Jem knew it was a large impressive structured because of the echoing from the shackles and footsteps. In the distance the banging of distant doors from long and stretching corridors was heard, but no one spoke. He concluded he was well away from any town or coastline because he hadn't smelt either a town's pollution or the sea air so he assumed he was not going to be deported. Nothing but the pure freshness of open wild fields and forests had scented his nostrils since shortly after leaving the cell.

Now, polish wood, melting candles pierced the layer of muslin confirmed to him that he certainly wasn't at another jail or at a dockyard. He was brought to a halt and he could hear for the first time muffled voices. After a short moment he heard a door open close by and as detaining hands forcefully gripped to hold him firm he was pushed forward a room.

Suddenly his eyes were exposed to light as the cover was tugged from his head. He instinctively tried to pull up his hands to shield his eyes, but they were restrained by the shackles, all he could do was lower his head and squint against the brightness until his eyes slowly adjusted themselves to the shock.

"Lift up the vagabonds head and let me see the face belonging to the infamous master of the highway, The Yorkshire Raider!"

The gag was violent pulled to below his chin and his hair pulled at the back to raise his face. Jem did not need to see the face of whom the words belonged, he instantly knew it was the obese man who had ridiculed him when he was fighting against the pain and misery of torment in the gaol.

Seated behind a highly polished writing desk he sneered a look of contempt at the prisoner and then he sucked heavily on his pipe until his fat cheeks reddened.

Blowing out a cloud of blue smoke, he twisted his fat neck and raised his eyebrows towards the elder man seated in a huge green reading chair in the corner of the room and at an angle from him.

"And you think this pathetic coward is of some use to us?" He exhaled the remainder of the smoke.

Jem glanced around the room grandiose surroundings his eyes adjusting to the light, he recognised the older man as the man who seemed to be constantly watching over him whilst he suffered for his overconfidence.

"Remove the irons, please Jenks." The elder man instructed deciding to ignore the comment directed at him.

"Leave them be! This man is a dangerous rogue and his code is violence and villainy." The fat man's overruling bellow forced Jenks to hold still his position with the key to the shackles still some distance away from the lock. He looked to the older gentleman for a contradicting order or some indication of what to do.

"As you please. Sir Clifford." The calmer older man ceded and Jenks lowered the key and took a step backwards. "You may leave us now Jenks." He then added with a smile and subtle, but assuring nod. "We will take care of things from here."

At first Jenks hesitated, cowering he expected Sir Clifford to oppose the instruction.

"You have done your duty and delivered the prisoner into our custody. We are grateful for your service." The aged man prompted waving his right hand in a fleeing motion.

"Very well sir." Jenks nodded and backed towards the door without turning as he still expected there was more to come.

"Be sure to stand close by the door and with an alert ear." It came with a concerning tone from Sir Clifford Cornell and he signalled with his finger where exactly he wanted Jenks to position himself.

"Very well sir." Jenks tapped his fingers on his pistol which was secured at his waist by a wide shiny leather belt. "I understand sir." He winked disappearing behind the door.

It was the older gentleman who began to speak first with his usual genteel manner. "Mister Rose it's good to see you looking so much stronger than the last time I saw you."

"Is it?" Jem wondered his eye narrowing and questioning the frail looking man's examination he flashed confused, repeated glances between the ostentatiously attired men.

"It is indeed. Very much so." Jem's mutter was heard by the sharp eared gentlemen.

"Stop the bantering Edmund and let's see if this gamble of yours is up to it." The fat man urged displaying impatience.

"Very well Sir Clifford. Who is to begin? You or I?"

"You do it. It's your damn foolish idea." He roared replacing his pipe and clamping his mouth.

The older man arose to near Jem bringing with him a padded chair. "Please be seated. You must be fatigued after such a journey."

"Thank you." Jem's reply was lost in another of Sir Clifford's impromptu outbursts.

"Good God, Edmund. Offer him any more comforts and the scoundrel will think he's died and gone to heaven." Again a cloud of grey smoke hung thick in the centre of the room.

Turning his back on both men the old man paced the room as he began to enlighten Jem, if not confuse him.

"Jem Rose. I am the Baron of Ripon, Edmund Beechey and this is my lifelong friend and business associate Sir Clifford Cornell."

To Cornell's annoyance, Jem did not acknowledge the smile cast in his direction after the introduction, instead he unnervingly returned a withholding glare.

"Sir Clifford is the member of Parliament for Harrogate. He is a leading member in the cabinet and he is a principal representative of the English Secret Service who reports direct to the Lord Chief Justice himself."

Jem's demeanour did not alter, his face remained stoic indicating disrespect and Cornell's cheeks flushed purple with displeasure.

"Now then........"

The Baron paused and scratched his head as if wondering where to begin.

"Our Prime Minister Henry Pelham has long been concerned with the idea that Jacobites are lurking around every corner just waiting for the right moment to strike and return this country to the chaos of the Roman Catholicism."

Impatient at the drawn out introduction and failing to comprehend it's reason Jem arose from the chair. "I have no doubt to what you say is true but."

"Be seated!" Cornell bellowed using his lungs to their full as he simultaneously smashed his tightened hand down on the table top so hard that it shook the decanter and accompanying glasses. "And be quiet or I'll have you hung, drawn and quartered before you have time to wet your breeches!"

Unresponsive to the member of parliaments raging outburst Jem stood firm.

"Please Mister Rose be seated and allow me to finish." The older man's attitude agreed more to Jem's liking, but still fronting a scowl of impertinence he re-seated himself.

"Oh this is a waste of time and effort. How can we trust an insolent vagabond who is devoid of all respect?" Cornell thrust back his chair and leant on the table using his huge knuckles for support. "I'm sorry, Edmund but I don't think this is one of your most favourable ideas. We'll have to think of something else."

"No Sir Clifford. We've come this far. Let us at least try." The Baron's words were almost said as a plea.

Shaking his head as he contemplated nothing but failure Cornell said. "Arr go ahead for pity's sake." Then he turned his attention upon pouring himself a measure of claret.

"Please try to be patient and understanding Mister Rose. I want to give you a full appreciation for the duty I hope you will undertake. Now where was I?"

He paused to think with his bony hand feeling the point of his chin as he searched for the words to come back to him.

"Return the country to Roman Catholicism." Jem prompted.

Nodding with a smile that suggested the outlaw's attention pleased him, he began once more.

"Yes, yes and while this is so often proven as true and many plots of rebellion have existed so far only a few have ever been considered as serious, but now Mister Rose it appears there seems to be genuine reason for concern." He paused only to refill his lungs. "The exiled Stuarts are once again plotting to overthrow our regime which, I think we can all admit is weak and unpopular at this moment in time, but nevertheless it has to survive for the salvation of our country."

He paced the room with short deliberate steps his eyes expressionlessly fixed on the walls as he explained.

"No one can afford the sacrifices and savages that can only result from our failure to defend against and destroy the Jacobites once and for all. The government is preparing for this eventuality, but there is a lot of work yet to be done. Our main problem and concern lies in the two forms that this rebelling consists. We have both an escalating internal rebellion and an impending Jacobite invasion led by Charles Edward Stuart himself."

The Baron noticed Jem's stolid countenance manifest quickly into a display of confusion.

"Just bear with me Mister Rose. You will have all of the details when necessary."

The Baron seemed to be looking at Jem for some kind of response, but other than a frown of bewilderment he did not find one.

"The internal rebellion is being fuelled and funded by a body of traitors calling themselves the Society of Revolutionary Jacobites. Yes, it's quite a mouthful." The Baron remarked as he reacted to the slight crease in Jem's cheek.

"And quite a fancy name for a bunch of traitors." Cornell added with an admonishing tone of disgust.

"Their aim is to gather support, cause widespread disorder and agitation then reinforce the Jacobite army when it enters England."

"When it enters England?" Jem repeated his eyes widening. "You seriously believe they will invade?" Jem asked in disbelief.

"We hope not." The Baron flicked an optimistic glint towards the uninterested looking Cornell. Jem noticed he seemed buoyed by the interest.

"We hope not. Our agents are keeping us well informed, but at the moment we are powerless to intervene."

Now graveness quickly descended slowing the Baron's delivery and instilling an expression which revealed fear and concern.

"We know Charles Stuart is already in Scotland and momentum is gaining rapidly."

"You seem to know everything concerning the matter of events." Jem interrupted hoping his confusion would be relieved.

"It may interest you to know Mister Rose that," it was beyond Cornell's own restraint to remain a silent bystander any longer, "we have Hanoverian agents posted as far afield as Scotland to Russia and they operate in such varied positions under the command of the principle clerk in the Holy Vatican and the high commission in Parliament."

The Baron walked between the desk and prisoner blocking Cornell's view then he cut in and continued. "We know of the French and Scottish contacts and we know who the conspirators on the French, Scottish and English sides are."

"Yes." Cornell stretched his neck to intervene. "Antonio Walsh, his brother in law Richard Walsh are accompanied by a business counterpart named Walter Rutledge. They are the ones responsible for providing funding and the transportation."

"King Louis XV has provided the backing for the raising of the army and Charles Edward Stuart will lead the invasion onto English soil." The Baron interrupted. "It is a hereditary Jacobite, the wealthy Dutch master spy called Luc De Winter who has pledged to provide support from within England when the time comes and now to add to our troubles we are receiving further information that certain influences in the Welsh regions are offering their own support and loyalty to the traitors."

"Their aim is to divide the nation and draw as many factions into the battle against each other as possible." Said Cornell adjusting his position so his view was unobstructed.

"You're well informed of everything there is to know." Jem still wondered to his presence.

"Everything there is to know and more Mister Rose." Cornell corrected.

"Then I fail to see what this treachery has to do with me, an insolent vagabond." Jem quoted Cornell to annoy him more.

"It would have nothing to do with you if I had my way." Cornell remarked with a sneer of contempt.

"Please Sir Clifford allow me." The Baron gesticulation gave the impression that cooperation and agreement were vitally important to him. "I'm afraid Mister Rose all this talk of treachery and treason is linked only to you by the unfortunate or should I say fortunate in your case fact that you happen to bear a remarkable resemblance to one of the English Jacobites most celebrated protagonists."

"What?" Jem frowned with an accompanying shake of his head.

"Your likeness to the goddamn traitor Lazar Benedict, son of the Earl of Penrith is incredible." Cornell stated.

"Now .... I begin to see." Jem snarled disapprovingly as his mind worked on the men's motives.

"Let me explain." The Baron proposed. "Would you like a drink?" He asked, raising the lid of the decanter.

"No, I don't think my stomach could stand such delicacies just yet." He declined gulping salvia.

"Water perhaps?" To Jem the Baron seemed to be excessively belaboured on politeness.

"Nothing." He answered sharply to indicate his concern as to where this intelligence was leading.

"Very well." The Baron took the bait, "we want you, Mister Rose."

Deliberate enhanced coughing by Cornell indicated his condemnation and shaking his head the Baron moved nearer to the table permitting the two men to begin a private discussion with lowered voices.

"My dear Edmund, may I remind you that this is your idea and I am only in agreement with it's action because of our long-standing friendship. You are solely responsible for it's failure and the consequences shall rest solely upon your shoulders."

The ball wound and the time spent in the prison cell had not eroded Jem's hearing and he listened to Cornell's warning.

"And the gratification for it's success as well, I hope."

There was an exchange of menacing leers before the Baron broke away to once more pace the room and after a considerable pause where he seemed to deliberate by rubbing his chin he continued.

"I want you, Mister Rose to work undercover for the English secret Service. I want you to take Lazar Benedict's identity and work your way into the confidence of the Jacobite traitors that are associated with this plot." He tilted his head back slightly and fixed his glare at Cornell as he continued. "In return for your cooperation and I must stress your success, you will receive a full pardon for your crimes and reward of £100 to set you up a new life with your children."

"If you so wish to be reunited of course." Cornell added with a wryly smile.

"This is my punishment. To serve you?" Jem scowled disbelief.

"No this is your trial. Your trial is a test of freedom." The Baron said.

"Not to serve us, but your country you laggard." Cornell raged.

"Freedom?" Jem ignored Cornell again and quoted the Baron to clarify his meaning of the word.

"Yes, if you succeed you will be a free man and we will be free of the death and misery caused by civil warfare."

"This is all very tempting," Jem shook his head. He could not comprehend the message and dispel his confusion, "what if I choose to refuse?"

"Refuse!" Cornell blurted rising to his feet with exasperation, the word echoing throughout the building.

"Refusal will not even be considered. You have no option but to cooperate and agree to all of Edmunds requests." Cornell's face released at perceptive smile that impliedly, he knew Jem would be forced to oblige the Barons satisfaction. "Because you see Mister Rose, you no longer exist. Jem Rose scourge of the Ridings, the Yorkshire Raider was shot dead on Tuesday 10th of May whilst he was attempting to hold up the six o'clock Lincoln to York."

Jem suddenly felt numb and he looked to the Baron's face for confirmation. The Baron remained silent allowing his fat associate to thrive in the outlaw's demise.

"As far as everyone is concerned, you are dead. You're no longer England's most feared and wanted criminal, no longer a loving father and no longer the gentleman impostor and lover. England is well rid of you and she didn't waste any time in mourning your death." Cornell finished by gulping down in one mouthful the Claret.

Jem's face and reply concealed the bitterness he felt and containing both his anger and shock to the facts he questioned the Baron.

"I still don't understand why you need me or this Benedict. You could use bribery or one of your own men."

It was the now the haughty Cornell who led the conversation by bellowing another answer before the Baron had time to respond. "Results from bribery return rarely more than marginal value and besides, there are complications." He then reached for and drew on his pipe allowing the Baron to clarify.

"Yes." Leather treading on the highly polished wooden floor sounded as the Baron moved closer to the highwayman. "You see Mister Rose one of our most valued and a courageous spy has been captured or maybe," he clasped his hands together and looked up to the ceiling as he finished, "heaven forbid even worse." The Baron's voice trembled with a fearing nervousness and Jem wondered as to the obvious personal concern.

"Many of your men must be in danger." Jem prompted.

"That is true, very true. But this agent is not just a spy. Jac."

"No names my dear Edmund." Cornell hastily interrupted waving his hands to increase the emphasis.

"This agent is the last remaining member of my family." He admitted now bowing his head, "Lord forgive me." He sighed. "Our aim was to contain and keep a constant check on the scheming Jacobites, but somehow it has all gone wrong. Terribly wrong and it's my entire fault. I am solely responsible for this catastrophe."

Jem listened without questioning and Cornell for once remained quiet as unconcerningly he took to restocking his glass with claret from the decanter.

"A few years ago Mister Rose I lost my son. He was a spy and he died doing his duty for the country he loved, and now I fear I may have sacrificed the life of another loved one and jeopardised the entire structure responsible for the failure and the banishment of the Society of Revolutionary Jacobites." He paced the room, eyes cast downwards. "No one can ever get over the loss of a son Mister Rose and that's why you are so important to me. My last and only hope for something to be salvaged from this disaster lies with you."

"You must have capable men who are more qualified than I to undertake such a task."

"I'm afraid not. You see Mister Rose to get deep within the lair of the traitors we need a special type of beast." He now raised his head to stare blankly into grey dullness beyond the window pane. "We decided upon you a long time ago."

"What, but how? You did not know me and you would have never caught me if it had not been for General Preeceton tipping you off." Jem recalled with a cussed regret.

"And my great and long time friend the Baroness Waldon for drugging your horse." Cornell informed curling his mouth.

Jem clenched his fists tight and braced his muscles as a woman's deception struck him hard. He breathed in deeply to control and restrain his anger and not wanting Cornell to see the hurt he had just inflicted, he tried to disperse the memory of recent times and concentrate on the unveiling opportunity.

"How do you know I won't take my chance to run out on you and disappear?" Jem's words faded as the sudden stimulation left him short of breath.

"Because Mister Rose." Cornell could not resist inflicting more distressed upon his prisoner, "ever since we found out about you we had our men keep you under surveillance. They tailed your movements from Cridling Stubbs to Pontefract, from Doncaster to Blyton, from Badsworth to Nottingham."

Cornell noted the hardening of Jem glare. "Oh yes," he nodded with derision detectable in his tones, "we must not forget about your activities in Nottingham must we Jem."

Jem knew what he was implying and it sickened him. To the fat man's obvious delight he felt himself tremble nervously and once again cold globules of sweat trickle down his forehead.

"If there's one thing we did ascertain about the Master of Deceit, it is that he loves his children and he would rather die than let any harm come to them."

"Damn you bast …." He hated the man seated opposite so much that his words and normal affability failed him.

"Are we not correct?" Cornell's eyebrows raised.

"Is all this necessary." The Baron asked sympathetically.

"It would seem so." Again Cornell answered holding his deliberate smile to the shackled man.

"So you're holding me to ransom?" Jem understood.

"Don't think of it that way." The Baron tried to calm the situation with his intervention, "we chose you because the Baroness informed us of your striking resemblance to Lazar Benedict and because we know what you're made of, how you think, and how you survive. We know from your army records that you were to be decorated for your bravery so we tracked down your old Sergeant who remembered you for your strength and courage. He confirmed our beliefs that you are built of Grenadier material." The Baron approached the prisoner and standing directly in front of him he rested both his hands on his shoulders calmingly.

"You also have the ability to transpose yourself into a phantom. You can make yourself undetectable and uncatchable. Even when someone thinks they've got their fingers around you, you seem to find your way out like elusive smoke. You have the ability to detect danger and escape traps. You're as wise as an owl and as cunning as a fox.

"Which is exactly what the societies leader, Luc De Winter is." Interrupted Cornell.

"You will understand we have no option in choosing you, Mister Rose because only a fox can outsmart another fox."

"I am weak, my finances are exhausted and I know absolutely nothing about either spying or Lazar Benedict. You might just as well send me to the grave right now and be done with it."

"That's just the sort of negative answer I'd expect to hear from the man who steals a living from the vulnerable." Cornell chided tilting his head towards the Baron to confirm he had anticipated this kind of response.

"Although urgency is of the essence, you will be given an expert education regarding everything you need to know, especially Benedict's exploits." The Baron assured with the pat of his palm between Jem's shoulder blades. "Your strength will return as your confidence grows and I can assure you, you will have absolutely no need to worry yourself with the expenditure."

"You will be funded with sufficient resources for the position and a little more to comfort your needs." Cornell shouted.

"If I agree and succeed?" He needed to hear their terms again.

"You will be given a full pardon and a reward of £100 pounds as I said before." The Baron nodded.

"And if I fail?"

"Makes very little difference to you as far as I can see." Cornell anticipated reaching again for the Claret decanter.

"If you fail then I fail." The Baron continued with his persuasion undeterred by his friend's lack of faith, "and all hope is lost. Not just for me, but for the whole country. That is why I besieged you Mister Rose not to allow your conscience to be smeared with the blood of the thousands who will perish in the struggle to rebuke an open rebellion."

Jem's mind was already made up. He decided to accept the challenge and agree to the terms even as soon as a proposal registered in his ears and long before the Baron began his soul-searching plea, even if it did seem impossible.

He was prepared to do exactly what they wanted and place himself in whatever danger was necessary in a bid to regain his freedom and rebuild his life.

"You can stop this slaughter before it escalates." The Baron finished with his eyes searching Jem's for a sense of integrity.

"Where do we begin?"

Contrasting expressions emerged and being held mute Cornell's flustering consternation and confoundment distracted him to overfill his glass. The Baron, suddenly energised, invited Jenks back into the room with instructions to once more remove the shackles.

Knowing any objection would only result in death Jem would not let the thought of failure cloud his slim opportunity. Even now with the shackle marks still embedded in his skin his mind was occupied with only the thought of success and the slim prospect of a once banished vision, returning home to his adoring children. He did not contemplate failure nor any kind of deception and buoyancy sped through his veins and enthusiasm oozed throughout his body.

Up before dawn and retiring only when totally exhausted Jem's remaining time spent with the Baron of Ripon was not allowed to elapse with idleness.

Experts in their own subjects of, health, Flemish, fencing, self-defence, secret agent savoir-faire and etiquette were ready and available to provide and perfect all the attributes that Jem would need for the role and the mission to succeed. The expert's directive was to make sure his education became a natural possession that would be impossible for anyone to infiltrate. Their methods repetitive and difficult, but taught in a language that Jem understood and oozing with his own enthusiasm the Baron and other instructors found their pupil to be agreeable and capable to fulfil almost all of the training objectives.

The information and instructions he readily digested, but exercise and fitness he found extremely difficult. He was still weak, extremely sore and stiff. Hearty meals were provided to build him up and copious amounts of salted stout and calamine tea were used to flush out and purify his system, but he found he had no appetite for the delicacies which he longed and dreamed of only a few days ago.

Many of the days were tedious and he found all eagerness for the mission was mitigated against with discipline, rudimentary tonics and curatives. Often each day seemed like every other with the exception of the gradual increase within his strength and the mastery of new abilities. Goose grease was liberally massaged into his joints A nauseous brew of berries and bark was administered to sharpen his mind and dull the headaches and a mixture of cinchona and hyssop was taken to purify his cleanse his body from within.

He found a relentlessness borne from new convictions and his recovery to the next stage soon progressed to fresh air activities and exertion.

He studied hard the life, travels and adventures of Lazar Benedict and he soon found himself understanding and respecting the man's addiction for the daring and he acknowledged the similarities both Jem and Lazar shared in their life of risk.

Even though they were both from very different social classes Jem Rose and Lazar Benedict lived for and searched for the thrills gained only from the excitement of high risk danger and adventure.

He memorised every detail given to him by the informants and by doing so he was enlightened and educated to all there was to know about the once nobleman.

Lazar Benedict was the only son to the Earl of Penrith. Born in May 1715 the same year as Jem Rose they were to age with the same colouring, build and height.

Educated to the Earl of Penrith's Jacobite ethics and principles young Benedict was highly expected to follow in his father's footsteps and take up a prominent position in Parliament, but defying his father from an early age he had made his mind up to seek the life of an adventurer.

As the years passed and the Jacobites uprisings continually failed to make any political impact the Earl of Penrith along with many of the other hereditary Jacobite protagonists found that old age and pressurised submissiveness eventually led them into silent obliteration.

It was it was from this decline that the young Benedict launched himself into the heart of the perfidiousness. With his aged father now just a fading memory to all concerned Lazar Benedict took up the position of a Lieutenant under the command of General Wade and serving as a spy for the local Jacobites in Scotland where he used his position to relay information concerning Wade's orders and moments. He revelled in disrupting operations which Wade was responsible for enforcing including the Disarming Act, the Malt Tax act and several which involved crushing minor rebellions and suppressing all smuggling activities.

For two years he successfully caused chaos and havoc within the ranks of the English army and in particular the much hated General Wade.

His penetration into the armour of the enemy came to an abrupt end when his serving Captain intercepted, through the means of bribery one of Benedict secret messages. Foolishly the inexperienced Captain took it upon himself to see that justice was done and whilst he sent his knowledge to General Wade he failed to wait for an escort of men to assist with the capture of the traitor. The rash Captain was no match for the Lieutenants swordplay and it cost him his life, leaving Benedict to escape to France.

News of his successes, the death of the Captain and his subsequent escape sped fast within the structure of the Jacobites and he was hailed a hero by his father and those he had served. In his native Cumbria he was famous, but he was never to have the opportunity to return home and revel in is acclaim.

The Baron of Ripon guaranteed Jem that there will be no chance whatsoever of an encounter with Lazar Benedict because whilst he was still working under cover for the Jacobites in Europe, he was unfortunate enough to fall into the grasp of the English secret service and he had been rotting at the bottom of the River Meuse for the last four years and had not been seen by anyone in this country for more than six years.

The Baron was confident with his intelligence reports, stating that although they have respected him as a hero, no member of the current Jacobite uprising from within England had ever seen Benedict.

It was at this point that the Baron informed Jem that he would not be told of his contact's name. The reason for this was simple, should he choose to run out on the secret service, betray them or even be captured he would have no information of worth for the Jacobites.

When questioning how he would recognise the undercover agent, he was told that they would approach him because this particular agent was involved with and responsible for the termination of Benedict's life. By engaging with an imposter the English spy would recognise the counterintelligence.

With his time with the Baron almost at an end he was enlightened with the movements and people concerned within the Royal Oak theatrical production company and he was informed of where the Baron wanted him to fit in.

Jem's skin was cleansed with lavender milk, his chin shaved with a flamed finish to add radiance and he was clad with expensive cambric shirts, accompanying taffeta bows, silk stockings, embroidered waistcoat, warm overcoat, the highest quality Tricorne made from beaver skin and a powdered wig. At his disposal, to accompany his image was a purse full of coins and a leather case stocked additional clothing and accessories. He was transformed from convict to gentleman spy. He was strong and ready, he was now Lazar Benedict.

Chapter 7

Darwen was shrouded in both darkness and dense fog. The night air was damp and the thick mud roadway muffled Jem Rose's, alias Lazar Benedict's becalm approach.

The village lay silent and the streets deserted. There was nothing much for Jem to see except for the inviting glow of lanterns which lit up the occasional window indicating that hospitable warmth lay beyond the misted panes of glass, however he knew his mind was conjuring up thoughts of comfort just as it always did when he had been sitting in the saddle for too long and travelled too far without having a proper rest or meal.

He entered Darwen's main straggle of buildings and followed the long, narrow and winding track until he reached the distinctive noise of collective merriment.

His eyes rested with relief, but also great anxiety upon a motionless sign which hung high above the main doorway.

'The Black Horse' He had reached his point of destination as instructed. Now he must make himself known to the locals and prepare for the consequences, whilst remaining hopeful that a contact could be made soon before his restless loitering aroused any suspicions as it inevitably would if the charade was to a last for more than a couple of days.

He dismounted evicting all the preconceived notions and trepidation from his mind. The Baron of Ripon had assured him that this vicinity was rife with the rebellious Jacobites and that the mere mention of the name Lazar Benedict would have them tripping over themselves to make such an important acquaintance.

He stretched out his stiffened aching limbs and he shook his head to dispel sluggishness then he rubbed the tiredness from his eyes with his knuckles. Stretching out his arms as far as they would extend and straightening his back tall he then filled his lungs with massive breaths of the crisp night air. He wanted to look as strong and fresh as possible and not weak and tired like he felt within. He led his horse to the rear courtyard and unstrapping his case he hauled his way up to the rear entrance of the tavern.

Raising the latch he released an explosion of noise and a spray of jaundice yellow across the previously dark and undisturbed courtyard.

No one seemed to pay particular attention to the distinct well dressed gentleman who worked his way through the crowd to the approach the bar except for the landlord who jerked his gaze up from the rearranging of bottles at his feet just enough the see the face of a new customer.

"What do you want?" Shouted the huge man with the cannonball smooth head and battered faced.

Jem did not hear the question, he had turned his head to survey the crowded room of convivial and garrulous prattle. Nothing concerned him, amongst the revellers he saw four loose mouthed labourers playing dice, a round faced coach driver perched on a stool swaying to non existent music and a few glum looking men and women sat together in sullen silence their minds void of all liveliness.

Noticing the customer's eminent attire as he arose from behind the bar the tightness in the inn keeper's face eased. "Ah .... Good evening Sir," his deep tone softened signalling reawakened hospitality. "What can I get you on this miserable night? A large brandy, Claret or gin to cheer your spirits, perhaps." He greeted with a now friendly if not a curious smile.

"Not at the moment thank you. A bed or a room to rest a while will suffice my needs adequately for the time being." Jem returned the smile. "Oh and keep for my horse?"

"A room." He frowned as the prospect of additional money raised his mood. Although many coaches stopped to change horse and rest, very few passengers requested lodgings.

"How long for?"

"Just a couple of nights to give myself a rest."

"Travelled far?"

"Far enough." Jem swivelled at the waist to scan across the crowded room.

"Just so happens you're in luck." The landlord confirmed not listening or showing any interest to Jem's reply. "What name will it be?" He slapped down a room key on the damp bar top.

"Benedict."

"Benedict?" He repeated raising a curious eyebrow.

"I did. Lazar Benedict" Jem confirmed bluntly.

"Is the special clean?" The Landlord unexpectedly turned his bulk to shout over his shoulder and towards a dark room behind the bar.

"Cleaned only this morning. Why?" Came a screeched reply.

"We have a guest, a special guest." The landlord answered with a broad smile. Suddenly his attitude had changed to one of immense interest.

He was proud that a man with such an honoured and respected name in these parts should choose to rest and refuel himself at his lodgings when there are so many in the local vicinity to choose from. He would be the envy of everyone in the region once the news that Lazar Benedict had graced his establishment had spread amongst the gossipers, and spread it soon would.

He could not prevent himself from looking at the traveller with open admiration, he had listened regularly to many barroom tales of Benedict's legendary exploits during his tenure as landlord.

The man stood opposite looked just like he had imagined him. Tall, large shoulders tapering to a lean waist, handsome with tough facial features and clothed in the highest quality of garments to suit his gentlemanly status.

"This time of night." The woman in the back noted. "Must have good reason to be travelling so late." Her voice grew louder as she neared the doorway to the landlord's rear. "Especially with it being so ruddy damp and foggy."

"Be quiet woman and stop your wittering."

The landlords raised tone displayed his annoyance at his wife as she emerged with a crate pressed tight against his bosom.

"What have I told you about your nosing?" He waved a finger in front of her face as he reminded her of her obligations.

"Your place here is to cook, serve and clean and not to interfere." Dropping the crate with a huge clatter she angled her neck to stare straight past his condoning finger and focus her attention on the handsome customer in front of her.

The landlord was within moments of exploding into a jealous rage when the source of the jealousy asked.

"How much do I owe you for the room?"

Hissing at his wife, but managing only to repel his anger because the man who had attracted her attention was Lazar Benedict, the landlord waved both hands.

"No, no, no. You go rest yourself and we will deal with the insignificants over breakfast."

"Thank you very much. That is very kind of you." Jem tilted his head and smiling, tipped his hat with his forefinger.

"Not at all. Anything to be of service." He proffered as he slid the room key nearer to his guest. Jem acknowledged the man's generosity with another appreciable nod and he curled his fingers around the oversized key.

"Would there be anything else you might require this evening?" The landlord asked leaning over the bar top and lowering his voice to below the range of his wife's ears.

"I can highly recommend a couple of the local girls for their expertise in relaxing the mind and let's say help the body to forget about all the aches and pains."

"Tomorrow night, maybe." Jem politely declined. "But there is one thing you could do for me if it isn't too much trouble." He confidently added expecting his requested would be fulfilled.

"Please, just name it and if it is at all possible, I will oblige."

"I haven't had a good meal since yesterday and I wondered if you have any scraps left?"

Jem didn't get to finish his request as the admiring landlords wife could not prevent herself from impressing by imposing herself.

"I have some beef ribs, pottage and bread." She beamed wiping away sweat from her brow with her soiled apron

"A meal you want, a meal you shall have." The landlord boasted with a smile of genuine pleasure that was generated from his wife's ability to be of service. "Is there anything else we can do for you Mister Benedict?"

"You have done more than enough already and I'm obliged to you both." Jem again raised his Tricorne to support his gratitude.

"Well, if there's anything else at all, please don't hesitate to ask."

"Again sir, I thank you. It's so good to know that I am getting near to home." Jem lied as he reached down for his case.

"Don't just stand there woman! Come and get the gentleman's luggage." Snapped the bald, pug faced landlord to his diminutive wife.

"No. No." Jem declined as the woman moved fast to obey her husband's command. "I can manage."

"Then let me show you to your room." She had continued her forward motion and she surprised both of the men by removing her bib and discarding it on the bar whilst grabbing hold of the room key from out of Jem's grasp. "This way Mister Benedict." With a teeth revealing pleasing smile she led the way upstairs leaving behind her husband aghast to reflect upon her unusual zeal for her duties.

Shaking his head, he grunted disapproval under his breath and turned to serve other now impatient customers. He resented her enthusiasm, but concluded that it was only natural for a woman to react in such a way.

Emerging from the combustive chatter and smoke of the bar room the woman gladly strolled the way to Jem's room. She swayed her hips enticingly in front of Jem keeping herself at the absolute minimum of distance from him all the way.

The long creaking corridor was dark and narrow and it reeked of sour ale and tobacco smoke which hung thick and swirled in the damp cold air around the solitary wall lantern.

"And what brings you back to these parts. The love of a sweetheart?" It was beyond the woman's restraint for her to resist a prying quip.

"No. Nothing as pleasurable as that I'm afraid. I'm here on duty only and to pay my respects to my father."

"Business then?"

"No. I've had news that he has taken severely ill and that it won't be long before his time of passing." He lied.

"Oh, I'm so sorry." Her sympathy was as genuine as her honesty and her directness.

"Time has passed so quickly. I'd like to see him once again before his time has beckoned."

The Earl must be very proud of you Mister Benedict."

Almost at that precise moment a door to which they were passing creaked open and a stranger's face appeared. The woman cut off her opinions in mid sentence, but judging by the visible twisted expression of concern on the ghost like face both the woman and Jem knew that the name Benedict had reached the ears of the concerned man.

Dressed in the attire of fine quality, Jem's eye were attracted to a large linen cloth which was secured around the man's head concealing half of his face. Hiding his interest the man merely smiled and nodded to offer polite acknowledgement to the pair before closing the door and returning to his affairs.

"For what? Running away from my country and deserting my kin." Jem finally answered.

"No. That's not the way I heard it. You never ran from anyone and certainly didn't abandon your country."

They stopped at a door with the number seven scratched deep into the grubby wooden surface.

"Is that so?" Jem said nonchalantly hoping that his comment would stimulate her into explaining more of what she and her friends understood and believed regarding Lazar Benedict's adventures. Turning the key and starting to enter the room she began to oblige without hesitation.

"The way I heard it is, that you had no option but to leave."

Before he followed her into the room, he glanced quickly over his shoulder in the direction from where he had just walked. It was just as he suspected, he glimpsed the stranger, only for a brief moment before he disappeared, but he definitely saw the bandaged wearing man peering around the corner to see which room the famous Lazar Benedict had been allocated. He suspected that things were going to start happening rather sooner than he had anticipated

"You had to stand up for what you believed in and you were let down by cowards that failed to stand by you when things got difficult. Isn't that correct?"

He had missed the middle part of her explanation when she had vanished into the room and he paused to peer back at the stranger, but somehow he knew that he hadn't missed out on anything of importance.

"Yes, it was something like that." He affirmed.

"I have heard every tale that's ever been told about you, Mister Benedict."

"Oh. Often memories are glorified and unimportant acts get exaggerated. Whispered falsehoods spread like disease."

"But there's so many tales of daring that some of them just have to be true. Hero, adventurer, leader, duellist and gentleman lover." Her giddy voice rushed.

Jem hadn't been listening to the women's prattle he was preoccupied with thoughts of the man in the corridor and discarding his case and coat he turned to quickly scan across the surprising comforts of the room.

"Do you like what you see?"

"Yes, very much so."

Turning to face the woman he realised he had spoken with haste. He pulled back his head with surprise as the woman had moved up close to him and was standing with one leg raised on the bed with the top of her dress unfastened. She was not referring to his opinion about the quality of the furnishings. Leaning against him she squashed herself against his trunk she removed his hat.

"Take your fancy do they?"

He could not avoid noticing and savouring the tempting huge mounds of flesh and the separating gorge of a cleavage that she shook in front of his eyes.

"Be something wrong with me if they didn't." He admitted.

He found it hard to ignore her advances even though he was wise enough to know her awaiting husband downstairs looked every part the rough and tumble ex-pugilist type that usually took up the role of the inn keeper during their semi retirement.

Although the woman was at least ten years his senior, she was neither unattractive nor overweight and the mellow light of the lantern softened her features and diminished the telling signs of age.

Jem was tempted to respond positively and ignore the vision of the jealous ridden husband and his actively distrusting mind.

"Well then." She giggled almost childishly as she cupped her hands firmly on his buttocks, pulling him even harder up against her.

Jem knew that any normal man would consider it foolish and dangerous take such a risk for just a few minutes of passion and pleasure, but taking into account everything he had learnt about Lazar Benedict, and not being comforted by a woman in months he decided that he could only respond in one way.

Folding one arm around her shoulders, he began to lower his face down to meet her awaiting mouth, but she surprised him by impatiently lunging forward to lock their mouths together in an almost frantic embrace. Both their hearts began to pump rapidly, hers with passion and Jem's with excitement, but also trepidation.

The women steered herself onto the bed and Jem followed, lying himself along her side. Their mouths met again as simultaneously their free hands traced and felt their way along each other's writhing bodies.

Without breaking away from their kiss Jem began to unfasten the lacing to the woman's dress and she responded by starting to remove his waist coat. She continued the disrobing by pulling out his shirt from within his breeches and sliding her hand between his vest and skin. She moved her palm enticingly across Jem's naval and chest before lowering it and rest it upon his groin where she teased, taunted and provoked with her experience fingers.

Jem became distracted by a creaking noise from beyond the door in the corridor and he turned to pull his head away, but the women's cupped hands swooped his attention back in her direction and he felt twitching and tingling in his loins.

He tried to break away again to momentarily pause, but lasted less than a second before it was lost because the women had exposed her enormous breasts and she began to guide his head down into her bosom.

He dragged his tongue across to her nipple and flicked it rapidly across the erect core then he took it fully in his mouth all the time slanting an eye towards the door. She released a gasp of pleasure as she felt the warmth of his mouth enclose around her and the caressing of his fingers flurry through her hair and along the back of her neck.

Jem was well experienced with women and he knew how to control the drama to suit his needs, but the inn keeper's wife had lost herself in such a pleasure she had long since forgotten and a lust she had never before known. Fervently she began to kiss and bite the side of Jem's face and neck.

Suddenly the moment of lecherously was shattered as the room door was kicked inwards and the huge bulk of the woman's seething husband occupied the space between the wooden frame.

He scowled hatred upon the semi naked aspiring lovers before he marched forward to deliver his wrath of anger.

Jem did not have time to pull his hand clear of the woman before the husbands giant fist was thrust in his direction. The blow smashed powerfully into Jem's mouth splitting open his lips and forcing out a gush of blood. He was hurt and dazed, but the interference of the struggling woman gave him just the amount of time he needed to avoid the following blow. Screaming, the woman reacted by launching herself forward to scratch at her husband's face, but impulsively he swung his fist to deliver a right hook to knock her clean off the bed.

Jem was just regaining his senses when he saw the second blow being launched in his direction and he was just roused and skilful enough to jolt his head to the side leaving the powerful force to sink it's impact deep into the softness of the bed. This created just the opening which Jem needed and he was able to take advantage by grabbing a hold of the stiffened arm as it powered into the mattress and turn the landlord with force and throw him over the bed and on top of his stunned wife.

There was a mass scramble of arms and legs as everyone clumsily struggled to their feet in a bid to arise and gain supremacy. Neither of the men succeeded as they straightened simultaneously, both suffering from hurt of different strains which etched deeply on their incensed faces.

Jem's pain showed where the blow had been delivered and left it's bloody mark whilst the landlord's humiliated suffering was of a mental kind and his eyes bore the glare of a man whose pride had been shattered with his trust and beliefs destroyed.

Spurned on by having his perceptions of a man he once worship transformed into the hatred of the worst possible kind the landlord charged forward ramming his head into the body of his target. The force of the attack doubled Jem over and raised him off his feet, but he still managed to grab under the arms of the landlord and, holding him tight pull him backwards with the momentum. They collided heavily against a solid dressing table and the inn keeper head forced it's way deep into the Jem's midriff forcing out the last of his breath. Rendered winded he was unable to rise and once more he found himself at the mercy of the colossal brute.

He squinted to clear his vision and panted bitterly to regain his breath, but all he could do was watch with increasing alarm as the raging man towered over him to grab and raised above his head a solid looking wooden stool.

Jem feared for the worst and he tried to protect himself by sheltering his head under his arms whilst he waiting for the killing blow to strike.

He peered out between his crossed arms and watched the big man draw breath and steady himself then suddenly just as he expected the stool to come crashing down on his skull the big man's body locked to a monolithic hardness and his eyes gaped open wide. His expression changed from one of rage to immense shock, his mouth dropped loose and he omitted a gasp of breath as a small pointed tip began to protrude through the middle of his chest. His feet became unstable and he wobbled momentarily as he battled to retain his poise and stability, but as confusion blanched his skin he released the stool to aimlessly crash down to his side. He stumbled back a step and as he did the silver point in the centre of his chest protruded further tearing out from his shirt with a spurt of blood. Continuing to stagger uncontrollably the emerging blade continued until it could be forced no more.

The big man's vital signs ebbed in lingering agony, but slowly he stumbled forwards and slid free from the blooded blade to reveal the murderer.

Jem was still too winded to show any signs of relief as the bandaged stranger from the corridor now stood before him and not the inn keeper wife as he expected.

With an uttering of disbelief and a death bearing grimace furrowing itself upon the landlords pallid face he twisted to his knees, briefly glancing at his assassin as toppled sideways and crashed to the floor with his eyes and mouth still gaping open.

"Mister Benedict. I advise that you come with me at once."

"What?" Jem spat shaking the blurriness from his vision. He had heard and understood the man's words, but he was disorientated and unable to comprehend the sudden change of events.

"It's too dangerous here for you. You must come with me for your own safety."

"I don't," he gulped a mouthful of blood from his torn lip, "understand."

"Quick! Mister Benedict. We must go. I have no time to explain right now, but I give you my word, you will be informed of everything there is to know in due course."

The man had only one able hand, the other was dressed in a sling and so after wiping clean and putting away his sword, the man outstretched his arm down in Jem's direction to signal urgency by repeatedly curling up his fingers.

Jem responded to the offer by grabbing the palm and clasping it tightly to hauled himself upright.

"Who are you? Why are you here? And why did you do this?" Jem asked as he steadied himself and shook the dizziness from his head.

"I had no option or should I say you left me no other option. The poor man was obviously beyond any consolation and to use my pistol would have created too much attention from down below." Came the reply.

"You haven't answered my question." Jem pointed out wiping away blood from his beneath his nose and the side of mouth.

"Just trust me, Mister Benedict. It's in your best interest that you believe me and we both get out of here without delay."

Jem was unsure what action to take. The stranger had just saved his life for no apparent reason yet he did not trust the man. His accent made it obvious that he was of Scotch origin and his actions made it clear he had some sinister motive for being far away from his homeland.

Shaking his head to clearing the daze and finally restore his vision Jem began to fit the pieces together. He delayed agreement by looking about the room for his luggage his thoughts concluding that this man was a representative from the Society of Revolutionary Jacobites.

The case was where he had left it, but it had been knocked onto it's side in the scuffle. So lost in his confusion Jem failed to notice the Scotsman nearing the unconscious woman until it was too late. With disbelief he saw the Scotsman kick the women then almost as an afterthought he withdrew the sword and plunged it unmercifully through her left breast taking away from her what little remained of her life.

Jem heaved a sigh and the pit of his stomach wrenched as he saw involuntary twitches sped through her limbs and her venous eyes.

Turning without any signs of remorse or repent the man wiped clean his sword on the bed linen and calmly said to the sickened onlooker.

"Do not cast your judgement upon me just yet Mister Benedict or jump to any false conclusions. We are brothers you and I, united together with the same aims and beliefs."

"I know my father had plenty of amorous adventures in his younger days, but I know his adventures were firmly rooted on the English side of the border." Jem spat disgustedly his eyes locked on the twitching limbs of the dying woman.

"Please don't jest with me, Mister Benedict. We have neither the time nor the knowledge of safety." The Scotsman warned. "Now please I besiege you to hurry."

"I'm not moving out this room until you tell me exactly who you are." Adjusting his clothing he spun from the waist to face the murderer. "And why in hell did you kill these people?" Jem remained firm.

"Very well. Have it your way. But may I remind you that every second you spent here you are putting your life at risk."

Displeasure braced the visible side of his face as he again wiped the steel blade across the body then straightened himself to ensure he had slid his sword back firmly into it's scabbard.

"Then be quick with your reply and I will oblige your request."

"I more than suspect you already know who I am and why I'm here through your connections in Europe, but if you need it confirming to ease your mind, then I am Thomas Boyd McCoy and I am a member of the Society of Revolutionary Jacobites. If my judgement serves me correct Mister Benedict, you have not returned home to visit your sick father as you would have people believe, but you have returned because you fear you will be missing out on the glories and the beneficial rewards which the success our revolution will deliver." He paused to step over the women and added with a presumptuous smile. "Am I not correct?"

"If you are as wise as you are astute and your wits as sharp as your timing Mister McCoy then this Society you speak of has at least one member with the calibre that it is going to need to stand any chance of success." Jem praised in the hope of creating a false impression of admiration and compliance.

"Coming from a man with the distinction of yourself Mister Benedict I regard your comments with the highest esteem and I thank you very much." He half bowed. "Although I admit my timing and intervention was down purely to my prior knowledge of the allegiance between the landlord and the government."

"You mean." Jem scowled quizzically towards the dead man even though he suspected the Scotsman was lying to give credence to his actions and bias the conjecture of Lazar Benedict.

"Yes. Even this poor soul was bought and owned by the current government." He cursed. "He was after the reward for your capture. Like so many around here that have had the bail of a purse dangled in front of them."

"I'm afraid it's not just around here my friend. I've travelled far enough to know that the hardships being suffered all over England are making it hard if not impossible for even the most ardent of rebels to resist, never mind the ordinary folk."

"I couldn't agree with you more Mister Benedict. Bribery and corruption are never far away from the coin of the realm. Now can we please make haste before we too are slayed for our convictions?"

"That depends." Jem still pressed for more.

"On what?"

"On where you intend to escort me."

"To friends and safety." He smiled, but Jem remained still unimpressed.

Astonishment and frustration drained all colour from the Scotsman's ruddy complexion and his lips narrowed as he began to grind his teeth. His impatience with the Englishman was obvious, but the thought of receiving the praise from the highest ranking members in the society for enlisting to their services the talents of Lazar Benedict was a stake too high for him to lose and he was forced to repel his anger and any thoughts other than friendly obedience and compliance.

"Questions, questions and more questions. I suppose it would only be unnatural for you not to ask." He finally granted. "We are going to the society's headquarters where I want to introduce you to our leaders." A proud smile shifted the sternness as he added, "it will be a great honour for me."

"And the society's leaders will view you with the greatest esteem and repay you with their gratitude." Jem baited.

"Of course." McCoy answered firming up the linen cloth so it did not reveal his charred flesh. "Reward and respect naturally follow risk and danger."

Jem nodded agreement, but he once more ousted McCoy's smile.

"So what if I don't oblige you?" He did not intend on giving the opinion that he was weak and easily misled. "What if I don't want to be a part of your plans or the society's plans?"

"Mister Benedict." McCoy's rasped. "I have already stated that whilst I never take anything for granted, I believe your presence here is no coincidence with our movements. Now please let us stop wasting precious time and avoid any further delay."

The thought had crossed Jem's mind that McCoy knew exactly who he really was and exactly what interests really concerned him.

Explanations rapidly flashed through Jem's thoughts. The Society had already captured one spy so they would fully anticipate the arrival and infiltration of another. Even worse, they had already tortured their prisoner into confession and so they knew what kind of riposte to expect.

However, Jem's thoughts did not make any sense to him. If his way of thinking was anyway near correct, then surely it would have been in McCoy's and the Society's best interest just to let the landlord finish him off, unless of course they knew he was a spy and they intended to supply him with incorrect and misleading information.

He swallowed a large mouthful of blood and saliva that seemed to suddenly swell in the back of his mouth. Maybe they intended to apply torture to him for more incriminating information.

He had no way of really knowing what was swirling around in McCoy's head, but he knew one thing, the murderer had kept him alive for a good reason and so he decided he had no option, but to agree to the man's request and accompany him out of the inn. He grabbed hold of his case and walked nearer to McCoy.

"I have travelled far and I am now hungry. How long will we be travelling?"

He knew he had pressed the Scotsman's patience to the limit and there was no more room for any unnecessary duress. He was not surprised at McCoy's unresponsiveness. It was time to cut the dialect and follow his 'saviour'.

Chapter 8

Holding their horses at a calm and unhurried trot Jem and Tom McCoy had left the inn without arising any suspicion or concern.

The Scot had impressed Jem when he demonstrated his strength by hauling himself into the saddle with just the use on his uninjured hand.

The fog had not lifted and so they travelled without the illumination of the moon and stars through a contrasting array of winding tracks and paths all of which all seemed to be leading to nothing more than endless sloping trails through darkened trees and foliage.

Jem was apprehensive and suspiciously alert. Around every cleft and crevice he expected to find an awaiting ambush party. Out here far away from any dwellings and seemingly in the middle of nowhere it would be easy for the Jacobites to apply whatever inflictions they needed to eliminate the infiltrator and satisfy their requirements.

Conversation between the two men had been brief and frank. There was plenty of information Jem wanted and needed to know, but he did not feel either the inclination to press him for further information nor to talk to him.

Having already stated that he expected the Cumbrian luminary to know most there is to know about the Society of Revolutionary Jacobites from his own sources in Europe and he did not want to ignite any underlying doubts or suspicions that might be just lurking deep inside the Scotsman's thoughts.

It was McCoy who did what little talking there was. He was in an obvious buoyant mood, evidently pleased with his discovery and his handling of it so far.

"You will be most surprised and dare I say highly pleased with our organisations remarkable achievement thus far." He boasted with pride.

"I've heard many of the same words on my travels, but so far I failed to see any of them live up to their expectations."

"Yet it grieves me that you show doubt Mister Benedict."

"Then I fear I will continue to cause you more grief until I am convinced of yours and the society's sincerity."

"I assure you my friend. England and Scotland will have riches they have never known before and power so strong that we will be a nation feared by everyone. There will be no other country in the world with so much power. We will be the envy of all who desire respect and notability." His dialect was unwavering with supreme assurance.

Jem detected that there was an air of superiority and condescending arrogance about McCoy as if he was addressing a man of inferior abilities or position, but Jem did not fear McCoy and his dignity would not allow him to be passive under McCoy's dominance.

"It's a beautiful dream you speak of McCoy, but many dreams just fade away to nothing more than gallows lure as the labour less hours slowly ebb away with the passing of time."

"Ah, my friend." He arched over his horse to lean nearer to Jem. " This is more than a dream that we hold close to our hearts and you will see with your own eyes that it shall soon be a reality with all the consequences engaged so subject on where your loyalties fall depends on whether you are gallows bait or not."

"You predict mighty things."

"My friend, I speak only of what I know."

Jem hated every aspect of McCoy, his supercilious manner, his treacherous boasts, but most of all he hated him for the fact that he could exterminate the innocent without it even stirring or staining his conscience for the aid of the society and his own personal benefits. He did not appreciate being addressed as the Scotsman's friend and he objected to the term.

"McCoy, I admit I've a great curiosity for what you speak, but I advise you I choose my friends very carefully."

"And so a man of your position should, but I do not need to remind you that you did not choose for your friends wisely in Darwen did you?" McCoy's reference was implied with distain.

"True.... but you sir will not object if I ask you to restrain from using the term friend until my curiosity has been satisfied."

McCoy drew up his horse and swivelled his base to face Jem and with an offending scowl just detectable in the darkness he scoffed.

"You do not like the reference or is there more you want to tell."

"I merely state that I do not take things for granted. I find words of friendship come easy, but in reality, I find friendship can only be gained with loyalty, trust and respect. It isn't something which can be bought by cheap tricks, bribes or pure lucky timing."

McCoy rose a few inches in the saddle and he straightened upright to discharge his response.

"I care not for what you say and I beg you sir, do not distress me more." His Scotch accent emphasised a hidden threat.

Jem wanted to goad him a little more, but he knew full well that at the present time it would not serve to be in his best interests. He was tempted to ask about the face cover and the banded hand, but he decided to leave it and see if the Scotsman enlightened him further into the journey.

"I just want to make things clear McCoy. As you may well imagine, I have had to cross swords with many a foe whom I once trusted as a friend. I've had to learn the hard way not to trust anyone."

"You have expressed your opinion very clearly Mister Benedict, but rest assured you need not concern yourself with those fears now. When we reach Temple House you will be once again working amongst friends and you will once and for all lay your suspicions to rest." McCoy thought he now understood Benedict's indifference.

"Working? I don't recall offering my services."

Jem knew what McCoy's intentions were all along and he knew that he was desperate enough to kill to fulfil them, but then killing probably came as easy as eating and sleeping to McCoy.

Jem's motives for being obstructive were to create the perfect portrayal of Benedict. He had to display confidence, a strong determination and an unfearing will of anyone and their beliefs.

"It would be a great honour for all concerned to have you alongside us."

"You seem to be taking a lot for granted McCoy."

"Mister Benedict this sort of opportunity only comes around once in a lifetime and that's if you're lucky. I'm certain that you will realise the possibilities and most importantly the probabilities that will arise once the society makes it move."

"That may well be. But before I commit myself to any kind of involvement I intend to establish my own unbiased opinions."

"You will be able to convey all of your views and concerns with the society's leaders direct. Nevertheless, may I be so bold as to say I would have expected a man with a reputation such as Lazar Benedict to have shown his gratitude in a much more favourable and positive manner."

Jem knew what McCoy was getting at and not only did he resent him for it, but he hated him for it. McCoy considered the Cumbrian hero should be indebted to him and Jem suspected that McCoy had duped the inn keeper to ensure he had an easy kill. He knew that McCoy had been listening at the bedroom door in the Black Horse in Darwen and he suspected that he had relayed what he had heard through the door down to the landlord knowing full well how a proud ex pugilist would react. Pulling the landlord to one side as not to cause a scene at the bar, he had only to follow the enraged man upstairs and wait outside the a few seconds bedroom until he could time his intervention to perfection and guarantee success. The whole incident flashed through Jem's until McCoy jolted him from his thoughts.

"The Lazar Benedict I have heard so much about is famed for being eager to repay his debts."

A feeling of nausea overwhelmed Jem. He considered a coward and he wanted to kill him for what he had done, but he was forced, yet again to restrain himself. He knew that any lack of self control could result in the failure of his mission.

"You may well, for now hold me in your debt McCoy for I cannot and will not commit myself to something of which I know very little."

McCoy pulled tight on the reins to bring his horse to a sudden stop.

"Please do not insult my intelligence Mister Benedict. I have already expressed that I believe your arrival back on English soil and the potential risk of your capture and execution has not been undertaken merely to visit your sick father. You are renown for your contacts throughout Europe and therefore you will know all there is to know about the Society of Revolutionary Jacobites. So either I introduce you personally as my own recruit or we stop right here and sort out our differences."

Jem's blood pulsated as his heart beat strong and fast. There was nothing he wanted to do more than kill McCoy and nothing would give him greater satisfaction.

"Are you challenging me to defend my integrity?" Jem dared to equal McCoy's direct glare.

"It's more of an ultimatum. You can join the Society and once again recapture your past glories and thrive in the subsequent benefits or you can end your days here and now."

Before McCoy had finished his words he had drawn and levelled in Jem's direction his flintlock reinforce his threat.

Only the rustlings of overhanging trees and the breathing of the horses could be heard as McCloy held firm the pistol. The tension continued until McCoy demanded.

"Not only do you owe it to me, but you owe it to yourself Mister Benedict."

Jem knew that McCoy was cold blooded and barbaric enough to pull the hammer, but he guessed that on this occasion he was bluffing and he taunted.

"A grave is a grave and in the end we all are all just maggot fodder."

"Rotting away in an unmarked pauper's grave does not have the same appeal as the challenge that lies ahead." McCoy's desperation for compliance was clearly visible. "Does it not Mister Benedict?"

Jem decided to end McCoy's speculation, but not before he had scorned at his intellect one last time.

"I understand what your intentions are now McCoy. You want the honour of introducing me to your leaders to increase your influence amongst the Society." A sardonic smile creased McCoy's eyes as he said.

"I see the time away has not jaded the sharpness of your mind." He did not intend the comment to be a compliment and his smile fell away as he quickly referred back to the previous subject. "Commanding an army is a small reward for saving a life as valuable as yours. Is it not?"

Jem indicated a nod of agreement as he mused the admission then after a long pause he answered the Scotsman's question.

"You may replace your pistol and claim your reward McCoy. I intend only to fight against the true enemy."

"You have spoken like a true Jacobean and I honour you Mister Benedict. Let us quarrel no more."

With his pistol replaced out of view McCoy spurned his horse back into motion.

"If we make haste, I'm sure we will just make supper."

Much later in the journey McCoy pulled up his horse and stopped. Turning around his head from one direction to another he scowled and strained to see in the darkness as his eyes searched amongst the shadows. He waited, holding his horse motionless, but there was nothing to see except blackness and nothing to hear except the sway of the trees from the night breeze. Jem sensed he was not satisfied, he seemed agitated and he reined his horse around again to be sure he hadn't missed whatever it was he expected to find and he strained once more into the darkness to confirm his doubt. He said nothing to indicate his concern, but annoyance and agitation was demonstrated by his displacement.

Jem wondered what irked him, but he did not ask to what concerned the Scotsman with nothing around except the dark of night.

Maybe he summarised the Scotsman had pre-arranged a meeting to safeguard the arrival of his intended new member. Whatever it was and whoever it was had failed to appear and this had enraged him.

It was to be his innocent horse who first received the wrath of his anger. Digging his heels into the horse's side and rattling the reins he journeyed on with added pace. Only occasionally did he ease up from the determination to glance behind at his fellow traveller.

They continued on at this pace just a little further until out of the darkness a large stone wall began to form in front of them. Obstructive with it's height Jem could not see behind the stronghold, but he sensed they had reached Temple House, headquarters of the Society of Revolutionary Jacobites.

Slowing to a halt, McCoy dismounted and walked up close to a solid unostentatious wooden door. With no handles or latches on the outside Jem watched McCoy signal their arrival by banging on the door slowly four times, then again in rapid succession.

"Do not be deterred by this humble entrance Mister Benedict we rarely use the main entrance at the front as we don't want to create any unwanted attention."

"As I would expect Mister McCoy."

"State your name and business." A voice bellowed from beyond the solid mass.

"It is I. Thomas McCoy and I bring with me a very important new member."

"One moment sir." The caller returned and the sound of three bolts grating and a restraining board being removed could be heard. Finally a key turned in the lock and the door swung inwards.

A stooping man figure holding up a lantern moved forward and greeted them.

"Come on in sir and I'll get Finlay to attend to your horses. McCoy nodded his approval.

"Andrew who's on watch tonight?" He demanded

"Ah, that will be young Ainley sir."

"Ainley?" McCoy frowned to reaffirm.

"Yes sir" Andrew replied again unconcerned with the question, his eyes anxiously peering at the visitor beyond McCoy. "The Ostler's nephew. Didn't you see him sir?"

McCoy ignored Andrews question and brush past him. Jem followed nodding to acknowledge the small man as he passed him by.

"Don't suppose anything could have happened to him. Do you, sir?" Andrew enquired without receiving a reply.

Now McCoy's agitation and scowling search in the darkness made sense to Jem. He feared for the young Ainley, for if nothing had happened to him out there in the darkness he knew it would when McCoy locates him.

Crossing a large, dimly lit courtyard they reached the door of the main building, which resembled more of a fortress than a house. McCoy followed the same procedure, four deliberate slow knocks, then a quick volley of the same and the door opened to him. He crudely ignored the elderly gent who occupied the entrance and barging passed him the force of his shoulder unbalanced the doorman forcing him to grip tight on the door handle for stability. Unconcerned by the collision McCoy led the way into the building at an assuming pace. Jem followed on only a step behind through the narrow corridors of the ground floor which led the way by the kitchens, food store, wine cellar and laundry room of this mammoth building.

Finally arriving at a well illuminated reception hall McCoy began to tread a sweeping stairway which led them up to and passed an impressive landing, library, music room and finally deducing from the appetising smell of roast meat, the dining room.

"Good evening sir."

Again McCoy ignored the male servant's polite gesture and arrogantly he headed straight for the door handle which the male servant opened for his convenience just before he made the reach.

The conversations around the huge dining room table fell silent with the abrupt entrance of the Scotsman and his companion.

"Mister De Winter, M'lady. I hope you'll forgive the intrusion." Bowing he raised and extended his arm in Jem direction. "For I have great news!" He spat out with great enthusiasm addressing the male at the head of the table and the female sat beside him.

"The King is dead." One of the other male diners quipped through a mouthful of food and laughter.

"No, no. Tom here has got himself a bargain of a whore who's promised to make his dreams come true." Mocked another man opposite, but his drunken comments failed to raise any amusement.

"Don't mock me." McCoy's face reddend and he paced forward to smash down his clenched fist on the table directly in front of the first nuisance so hard that it spilled the man's wine and caused him to gag and cough out food.

There was no retaliation and after a moment's pause which entailed a challenging glare McCoy twisted his frame towards the head of the table.

"Mister De Winter, I have great news which will please the society."

"Well then speak man of what you consider so important that it makes you disturb our meal." The unruffled man with the foreign tone ordered directing his eyes from his plate to the stranger behind McCoy.

"Gentlemen, Countess Van Buren." McCoy angled himself side wards and bowed his head. "I have the privilege of introducing to you all." He extended his arm in the direction of Jem. "The honourable Lazar Benedict."

Trying to be polite and gentlemanly was alien to McCoy and he bluntly stumbled his way through the privileged introduction.

Jem stepped forward one pace, smiled and respectfully half bowed in the direction of the seated party with his eyes inappropriately detained upon the solitary female.

"Gentleman, my lady." He simply said.

"Mister Benedict?" The head of the table repeated the name, his attention distracted from the contents of his plate.

"The one and only." McCoy quickly confirmed with an ear to ear grin.

"Please join and honour us with your presence." The foreigner turned over his palm to accompany the invite then he clicked his fingers and two servants rushed to the table with two additional chairs.

Jem had already absorbed the scene facing him. Seated around the large oval table were four other men all clothed in equal quality garments, feeding their gluttonous faces. The woman of exceptional beauty had obviously spent much of her time preparing and pampering herself for the evening event. Feeling the need to dwell on her for a second or two longer than he should, initially the single female interested him more than the five males collectively. The top half of her body was restrained with a jewel encrusted stomacher which emphasised the small of the waist and the fullness of her breasts. He raised his eyes slowly and they levelled and set on hers.

Her immaculate structured face was white leaded to perfection and it contrasted with her hair which looked as though it had been tortured and stiffened into position with pins, lard and powder. It's unnaturalness agitated Jem and he felt a wanting urge to release it and undo the hours of work and patience to let it hang down freely. The women looked as though she had spent all afternoon preparing herself for these few hours and Jem wondered if her efforts had made any kind of improvement or not. Little did he know or care that Countess Van Buren's exceptional tastes originated from the expense of the latest European fashions.

Now upright in front of Jem and blocking his view of the woman was the fifth and most important man in the room. Luc De Winter had his hand extended offering a formal welcome.

He stood out from the others with his superior quality and ostentatious clothing, immaculate wig and tainted olive skin which was not in existence in the pallor of an English gentleman. From his strange and unfamiliar accent, Jem knew this man matched the description given to him by the Baron of Ripon.

"The honour will be entirely mine." Jem acknowledged nearing the table.

"Tebb! More food for our guests." The foreigner requested.

"Yes sir. Coming at once." The male servant answered and lowering his submissively he promptly moved to obey the command.

"Not for me, Mister De Winter." McCoy declined. "My business here is done for the time being and I have other urgent matters of importance." McCoy gestured with a flick of his head. He was highly pleased with himself, but he felt uncomfortable in the presence of aristocracy and he could not wait to leave.

Jem notice a hint of delight ripen on the faces of the diners as McCoy declined the invitation.

"Ah the whore is promoted to a matter of importance." The drunken man's comments which were only intended for his friend's ear carried throughout the room and McCoy halted his withdrawal and turned immediately.

He moved to the table and lent over the red eyed loquacious man who had just displeased him again.

"Captain Basil sir, would you care to step outside to see if your courage is as great as your mouth."

Coughing out his embarrassment and disinclination in an unrecognisable splutter the humiliated drunkard waved his arms in front of his face to support his message but still angered McCoy, turned his frustration upon the man seated next to him.

"What about you Oliver. Think that I am a fool? For I cannot remember on one occasion on which you have also acted with the slightest of wisdom."

"How dare you insult me! You highland half breed." Oliver Trevean's face mottled with rage and without hesitation and arose to his feet to defend his honour.

"Stop this foolery the both of you immediately." De Winter intervened. "Oliver be seated!"

The tenor paused, holding firm his alcohol tired gaze in the direction of the Scotsman until De Winter added.

"That is an order not a request!" His authoritative bellow resonated around the vast room.

Curling his top lip to indicate his disgust at the Scotsman, Trevean returned to his chair and De Winter moved around the table to place himself between McCoy and the diners.

"And you sir. Whilst I congratulate you for your service tonight I pray that you will not cause any more unrest around this table for, God help me, it will be I who will take up your request to step outside."

The red flush of McCoy's cheeks dulled pale. He knew that he was no match against De Winter, with sword, pistol or fists and deprived of an opportunity to demand satisfaction from Trevean he was forced to back down.

Although highly satisfied with his achievements McCoy knew the foolish incident had tarnished his deliverance and he yet again had failed to gain De Winters respect. He muttered something inaudible in a deep Scottish tone, turned and without offering any of the usual pleasantries left the room slamming the door noisily behind him.

He was convinced that his repeated efforts deserved a position of authority and high seniority within the Society and he was more determined than ever to make sure that he got one.

Full of impatience he stormed out of Temple House and set about completing the next task, to teach the night watchman, young Ainley and the rest of the societies recruits a lesson they were not likely to forget.

"Please be seated and intrigue us with your tales of peril and adventure Mister Benedict." De Winter defused the tension and anxiety which lingered and silenced the recreation.

"I care not to boast of what I have done. It is what we will do tomorrow which is far more important." Jem replied seating himself comfortably in the chair.

"Indeed you are correct, but please do not tease us with your folly. I hear you are no stranger to the smell of gunpowder." The woman smiled sceptically.

"There are many things which I am ashamed."

"And many things you should be proud of." She raised her wine glass and smiled, "For you see Mister Benedict we have got you at a disadvantage." She said then paused to sip wine and to deliberately delay and tease Jem with her knowledge.

Jem's heart began to pump faster, he thought he had walked into a trap and the charade was over. He slowly lowered his hand until it lay firmly upon his pistol.

"You see, your reputation as the man we need has proceeded you." She swallowed her small sip and finished abating Jem's concern for the time being at least.

"Then I sincerely hope I am as favourable in the flesh as I am in the estimation of words."

"It has to be said you have a lot to live up to." Once again she teased. "But then again we shall soon see." Her expertise at manipulation and her inscrutable expression protected her from revealing her true thoughts.

"Enough of this." De Winter intervened. "Arrabella our guest has only just arrived. Is it beyond your capability to make him feel welcome?" He scorned wondering if her ambition was designed for vice or virtue.

Jem sensed that there was a rift between the two and he became convinced of it when she simply tilted her head slightly backwards and scowled a look of contempt at De Winter before reaching again for her wine glass.

"Good night gentleman." She said with more than a hint of bitterness as swilled down the wine and calmly replaced the empty glass to the table.

"But you haven't eaten." The drunkard observed, innocently oblivious to the conversation.

"I have no appetite all of a sudden." She answered nearing the door.

"Be at the barracks by dawn Arrabella and you shall see for yourself whether Mister Benedict can be compared with his glorified reputation or not." De Winter called out to the echo of footsteps.

Not responding in any way that the men could see Countess Van Buren made her exit in the same way as McCoy, slamming the door angrily behind her.

"Please do not let my associate cloud your judgement or your opinion of me. We have to start somewhere, but I don't want you to think I am exploiting liberties or taking anything for granted."

De Winter paused to sip on his wine as he waited for Jem's reply. When he realised one was not forthcoming, he decided try and make light of the incident with the Countess Van Buren.

"And please do not let Countess Van Buren offend you, Mister Benedict." Restocking his plate, he spoke without looking at Jem. "She is a no nonsense woman with more than a hint of a temper. She does not like strangers and it's almost against her constitution to trust anyone."

True traitor Jem mused before his attention was displaced by the empty plate that Tebb placed in front of him. Simply nodding as if unconcerned he smacked his lips with visual pleasure at the huge portions of glistening meats and steaming vegetables.

It was an elegant meal such as leaders and their associates would expect to preside over. Venison, pigeon, chine of beef, snipe, trout, veal and eggs were displayed on the table centre.

"Now that we have all once again settled, let me introduce everyone to you, Mister Benedict." De Winter announced finishing a mouthful of chicken and sage.

"This is Captain Redfus Tavish who has brought us today great news of which we have been waiting to receive for quite some time." De Winter's face displayed a pleasurable smirk as it turned between the glass of wine he was pouring for Jem and Tavish.

"Good evening." Jem gestured and a nod was returned.

De Winter extended his arm across the table to the next man in line.

"Evan Rinold. Our Welsh contact and principal." Jem barely heard the name. He was wondering to what great news Captain Tavish had enlightened them with.

De Winter's arm continued to arc around.

"Captain Basil, who you will.... I hope be working alongside with and Mister Oliver Trevean who is responsible for raising both support and funds for the society."

"Gentleman the honour is all mine." Jem acknowledged raising his wine glass and standing to bow.

"Please tell me, Mister Benedict. What brings you back onto English soil?" With alcohol induced lethargic words Trevean began the conversation.

"I've been away far too long. In fact, I often wondered if I would ever come back." Jem admitted.

"You will have noticed that things have changed in your absence." Basil raised his face from his plate.

"I've been hearing rumours for a long time and now back on English soil I've been able to see for myself the spreading signs of growing resentment and hatred for the monarchy and government." He tore apart with his hands a whole chicken.

"You feel it is not too dangerous for you in this country?" Evan Rinold continued the questioning. It was nothing less than Jem expected and he was well prepared.

"It is just as dangerous as anywhere else in Europe and Mister Rinold." He gnarled at the hot crispy skin and tore the tender meat with his teeth. "It is sometimes safer to be where you're not expected." He abandoned etiquette by talking as he chewed. "I can vow for that."

"Not expected." Trevean questioned as if he was looking for something.

"Was I?" Jem fired back.

"No, your intelligence has not let you down. I admit we certainly didn't expect you to be back in England," the tenor shook his head, "and it was a great surprise to us all when McCoy informed us of your movements in Darwen. It was a coincidence that we could not ignore."

De Winter sipped on his wine choosing to remain silent, his eyes leering over the rim of his glass as he studied his guest. He knew full well that Lazar Benedict's sudden appearance in the area was no mere coincidence with the Society of Revolution Jacobites moments.

"Your suspicions are correct." Jem sensed increasing apprehension and he felt the need to convince of his sincerity. "It is no coincidence that I should return home. I have been monitoring the situation for some time and I've waited until the time is right for me to come back home and serve where I belong."

"Your timing is impeccable." De Winter pointed out.

"That is as I was hoping." Jem confessed.

"Then you're not averse to risking your personal safety to help the society achieve it's aims?" Rinold inquired.

"That depends on what you gentlemen have in mind."

Jem didn't want to sound too eager. A man of Lazar Benedict's position and status would only accept a leading role and anything else he would consider an insult.

"We need a leader of men." De Winter admitted as he emptied his glass.

"A man of respect and courage." Trevean nodded.

"We no longer have the advantage of time on our side Mister Benedict." De Winter reflected. He then leant forward nearing up close to Jem's ear. "You understand that every word spoken here tonight is spoken in confidence and I fully expect a gentleman of your renown to respect this confidence."

De Winter had already made his mind up. If Benedict should surprise him and decline his offer to join the society then he would have no option, but to have him executed before he had the opportunity to leave Temple House, he knew Lazar Benedict's knowledge must be controlled.

"Of course. I would expect nothing less myself." Jem raised his glass and skimmed it against De Winters to formalise the agreement.

De Winter sat back looking satisfied and he began once more.

"You will have noted I said earlier that Captain Tavish has brought us great and long-awaited news." Jem nodded, helping himself to more food.

"The news is Mister Benedict that Charles Edward Stuart is encamped on the banks of the Tweed at the border and he is preparing to move his troops onto English soil".

"An invasion, so soon?" Jem faked a reaction of surprise.

"He is ready and the time is right." Captain Tavish confirmed.

"I must admit, it concerns me that he should try to move an army of such a force in what shall soon be winter conditions." Jem responded." Jem looked at De Winter for a reply.

"The Scottish warriors are accustomed to such conditions, unlike the soft bellied English." Tavish boasted as De Winter paused from his wine to add discontentedly

"The weather is yet mild and of no concern. With the reinforcements of arms, men and food all of which we shall supply from here the Prince will invade London before Christmas." He then sighed, "The only problem is Mister Benedict everything is ready with the exception of our new recruits."

"Tell me of your concern?" Jem urged.

"We have the numbers, but not the quality of fighters needed to assist the Prince." Basil slurred into his plate.

"They are a mixture of farmers, labourers, coal heavers and shepherds. They are all hired hands that are only too sick of having their belly's filled on nothing more than tax demands and false policies." Trevean enlightened until De Winter once intervened.

"They are Catholic's fuelled entirely on resentment, hatred and discontentment for the current regime. They've massed themselves here because they're prepared to stand up, be counted and fight for a change. A change that will bring about a new monarchy, the rightful King, a new government, new laws and new investment. It will be a change to end their suffering and bring about a new prosperity. One of which until now they have only imagined in their dreams."

And it will be a change that will fill the purses of all the traitors concerned. Jem thought, hiding beneath the look of enthusiasm his own disgust and anger.

"But Mister Benedict, they are everything except soldiers. They lack morale, discipline and training." Trevean scowled as Basil's embarrassment blazed across his face.

"It's fair to say that our men are, at best, not amenable to discipline." De Winter concerned, then he added. "This is where I would like you to come in and lead the men."

"Your army credentials will be a great asset to us." Trevean remarked with more than a hint of admiration.

"Not to mention the morale boost it will give to the men." De Winter continued.

"Just what exactly do you mean?" Jem demanded.

"I want you to take total charge of the men and unite them as a fighting unit that are second to none then lead them into London alongside the army of Charles Stuart."

"But what about McCoy? During the journey here he openly and enthusiastically boasted that he had aspirations of such a post. He seemed so much looking forward to taking over and I quote, whipping the men into shape."

"Exactly," Trevean shook his head, "whipping the men into shape is not what's needed.

"We want to encourage confidence, determination and loyal obedience." De Winter stated.

"He would make an excellent gaoler or a torturer, but not a leader of men." Basil remarked to no one in particular.

"My thoughts exactly. The man is unpredictable and a liability when inebriated. " Trevean quietly said aiming his words in the direction of De Winter.

Jem heard the quip and he wondered to what Trevean was referring and he wondered if the reference implicated the capture of the English spy.

His eyes traced across the four faces of the men seated around De Winter. There was nothing to be noted either visually or from any of their comments with the exception of Trevean who held a stared at De Winter which suggested his comments contained a hidden message.

"Don't get us wrong Mister Benedict" De Winter now seized Jem's attention. "We are not ignorant enough to realise that some of our men have their limitations. However we believe a man with your knowledge, respect and reputation to inspire every volunteers own self-determination so they can perform to their own ultimate capacity."

"Of course I would gratefully undertake the position myself, but I have to return to London to make preparations there." Captain Basil absolved himself of the responsibility.

"Naturally." De Winter sneered a glare towards the Captain and Jem suspected scepticism.

"If I agree. What of McCoy?" Jem asked, trying to ignore the obvious disparagement and rebuke.

"McCoy is expendable." The Dutchman dismissed the Scotsman as no importance and after a short pause to swallow more wine he added. "He has served his purpose and we shall find a task, shall we say, more suited to his taste." Implied glances were exchanged between De Winter and Trevean. "Is it agreed then Mister Benedict, or should I say Captain Benedict."

"The thought fills me with exultation." Jem announced with a forced smile.

"It would fill me with one of dread." Basil whispered into his glass as he lifted it to his lips, but not quiet enough to prevent Jem from hearing the comment.

"Then sir, I propose a toast." De Winter exclaimed, refilling his glass and arising. "To you sir and our future success."

Simultaneously the traitors held up their glasses and echoed loudly. "Captain Benedict!"

Reseating himself and adjusting his comfort De Winter continued. "Charles Edward Stuart is dependent on support from us therefore we are dependent on you Captain Benedict."

"Rest assured Mister De Winter. I will abide by my convictions."

"Your words bring us all great comfort, but I consider it my duty to offer you a word of warning." De Winter began to advise.

"Please, if there something I should know then I would only be too grateful to hear it."

"It shouldn't bother a man of your repute." Basil chided with a mouthful of his meal.

Ignoring the drunkard Jem concentrated on De Winter.

"Our recruits all follow a brute of a man by the name of Elziver Gunn."

"Yes." Jem prompted for more pulling his chair closer to the table.

"They won't do anything unless he authorises it. Every order, command or training exercise must be approved by him. He appointed himself as the leader because he fought in the Battle of Dettingen, for the King."

"The King?" Jem repeated.

"Yes, but he left on bad terms." Rinold interjected.

"What he says they do," Trevean supported. "They are intimidated, bullied and damn scared to death of him. They fear to do or say anything unless he is in total agreement."

"They are a stubborn bunch." Rinold frowned.

"Sheep! They are sheep." Basil slurred.

"Nether the less break Elziver Gunn and you will have broken the men. This is the reason why I chose to warn you. " Said De Winter scowling disdain at Basil.

"He is a beast of a man who knows no restraint, shows no mercy and he has not the least bit of gentlemanly conduct." Trevean added.

"You want me to thrash this man?" He eyes browsed across the surrounding faces which were all now engaged upon him.

"If you want to commend and gain the respect of the volunteers I'm afraid you will have to overcome Mister Gunn." Tavish answered on De Winters behalf.

"Tame the beast and you will gain their ultimate loyalty and respect." De Winter said.

"Do you want me to thrash this man?"

"It would be easier to have done away with him in the dark of the night, but that is an act of cowardice. It would disillusion the men and compromise their loyalty." De Winter continued. "It would be contrary to our principles and we would still need to find leader who they would respect."

"To gain the men's adulation then you will have to conquer Elziver Gunn in full view of everyone. Do you think you are up to such a daunting task Mister Benedict?" Basil snarled.

"Captain Benedict." Jem corrected.

"I apologise Captain." He drunkenly slurred with more than a hint of jealousy.

"If a man strangle hold is too tight eventually it will snap." Jem hypothesised mainly to needle Basil, but he knew full well he would have to back up is braggartism. "I will destroy Elziver Gunn before breakfast."

"Then let us waste no more words on the issue." De Winter ordered.

"To the dawn Captain Benedict when you will find your initiation into the Society of Revolution Jacobites more of a challenge than I fear you estimate." Shaking his head Basil raised his wine glass to propose a toast.

"To the dawn Captain Basil. Gentleman." Jem riposte with a confident smile. "And to the true foundation of the."

"Manchester volunteers." De Winter confirmed.

"Tebb! More wine, gin and brandy for my guests. We have plenty to celebrate tonight." De Winter ordered with a jovial resolution as he emptied the last remaining droplets from the imported wine bottle.

"Maybe Captain Benedict might want to moderate celebrating until after the morning schedule." Basil could not prevent himself from releasing another jealous quip, his thoughts and reactions influenced by the amount of excess alcohol in his bloodstream. He saw and feared the new Captain as another rival who was sure, from his fame alone to embrace the praise of Luc De Winter and find himself rewarded with a choice of the most honourable positions within the Society's leadership to the detriment of himself.

"Nonsense, Captain Benedict here is famed for his revelry and his ability to withhold his alcohol." Trevean barked to Jem's dismay.

"It may be wise." De Winter began "To divulge less than your usual amount Captain Benedict, but please tuck in and eat to your stomachs content."

Jem smiled, but it was more from relief than acknowledgment of the appreciation as De Winter continued.

"That is if you can bear to stomach this second rate English fare. I unfortunately have not yet acquired a taste for this bland and dull disappointment that you English so proudly call food."

Yes, he could stomach it. His eyes rolled over the mountains of steaming food, the small of the roasted chicken stuffed to the full with apples, sage and onions teased his every taste bud.

"Come on now Luc, don't be harsh. These delicacies are far superior to that greasy fodder you're so fond of. Don't you agree Captain?" Trevean asked Jem.

"I must admit, it more than surpasses anything I've come across in any country for a long time." Jem answered thinking only of his meals in the prison.

"Then I insist that one day you shall come with me to my native Holland so you can enjoy my servant's culinary skills."

"It's a pleasure I am already looking forward to." Jem replied to a disagreeable moan from Trevean as he grabbed hold of a chicken and pulled apart it's legs with vigour to show his appreciation for the English food. Then tearing off a large chunk of the white breast meat he filled his mouth.

The intensity of the conversations and the constant reference to the tasks ahead gradually dissipated mainly due to De Winters subtle indication that he had heard enough on the subject for the evening.

Although he didn't actually say anything everyone around the table sensed that he was protecting the newcomer from embarrassment and possible deterrence. It was obvious that the new member was very important to him and he wanted to secure his agreed participation and influential connection.

Occupying himself by divulging into the assortment of food Jem was deeply concerned. He did not know and had no way of knowing if his portrayal had been accepted. If it had, then so far he had achieved his intentions, if it had not and Luc De Winter and the rest of the congregation knew he was a secret agent then they were toying with him and were deliberately feeding him false information.

He wondered if they intended to use him to get Elziver Gunn out of the way and once done they were going to capture torture him for information.

One way or another he was sure to soon find out and until that time arrived he could only continue with the assignment and his endeavour to find the missing English spy.

As for Luc De Winter, he was hugely pleased to welcome and enlist such a man of honourable quality into his exclusive organisation. He did not have any knowledge or reason to suspect that the real Lazar Benedict was dead and that the man seated next to him was in fact an impostor and a vagabond by the name of Jem Rose. The confident thoughts of ever assured success occupied his mind along with his rise in esteem and Charles Edward Stuart gratitude amused and comforted him and so he suppressed any doubts or suspicions that were underlying in the back of his mind.

He was relaxed and highly pleased with the evening's outcome, everything had gone perfectly to plan and tomorrow's instauration of the Manchester recruits could not arrive fast enough for him.

Eventually the evening past into early morning all the men with the exception of Jem, finding themselves incogitant and incoherent due to the copious amount of wine and ale they had glutted down their throats.

Jem had wisely stuck to divulging with only the food always keeping his mouth well-stocked so that he could buy himself precious seconds of which to think up and remember his answers for the inquisition which was fired upon him from all angles.

Slowly the conversations deteriorated and as the night ebbed away the probing subsided switching irrationally and regularly from curmudgeonliness annoyances to haughty and lecherous prattle of less serious subjects and the inevitable boasts of female conquests.

It was at that point, with the late hour that Jem admitted that he would like to retire. Tebb's was called back in by De Winter and designated to show the honourable gentleman to his quarters. Leaving the noisy room together, De Winter and Jem bid farewell departing separately through east and west leading doors.

Chapter 9

Jem sat quietly on the edge of his bed. He was allowing his eyes to roam around the expensive furnishings in the bedroom with the aid of the dawning hue.

He had been out of bed for almost half an hour yet he sat fully dressed and alone. He wanted it this way, he needed a few moments of privacy to contemplate what he had achieved and to what he was going to do next.

He was neither tired nor groggy. He had been awake most of the night and Tebb's morning call only prompted him to fully arise from the comfortable bed, wash and dress.

His mind had been too active to allow him to settle in comfort and sleep. It was not the prospect of facing Elziver Gunn which troubled him. He wasn't scared and he did not fear any man. The time he served in the Dutch jail and the English army accustomed him to that. He merely and easily dismissed the inevitable challenge of Elziver Gunn as an ordeal he was going to have to face and overcome regardless of the pain inflicted or suffered. He believed in his own strengths, skills and knowledge and he was not in the least bit concerned for his safety. After all, apart from Luc De Winter the society's leaders poised very little if indeed any threat to his life.

It had been the English spy that had occupied his thoughts. There had been no mention of a capture or execution and so he still had no idea who or where the English spy was being held.

"Captain Benedict." Tebb again politely called in a hushed voice from the other side of the door. "You're expected in the dining room."

"I'm on my way Tubbs." Jem answered, stretching out the stiffness from his limbs. Grabbing a hold of the door handle he paused and half turned towards the small window. Glaring into the murky grey he wondered if the spy was in any danger at all. The thought crossed his mind, that maybe, because the society's headquarters were so isolated and impregnable the spy had just been unable to get out any messages. Possibly it was just too greater risk take and even if the spy did suspect Jem of being a government contact he might consider him a weakness and a threat of exposure. He dismissed everyone he had met already knowing none of them were worthy of representing the King.

All he could do was reaffirmed that if he did make an eventual contact he would, along with the spy, judge the situation and carefully review their next proceedings.

Following Tebb's through the splendidly decorated maze of corridors Jem was finally announced at the dining room entrance.

This time as he passed by the rooms and corridors, he found himself attracted to the colour coordinated walls, drapes and Chinese carpets. He found it strange that this fortress type of building with it's high and small windows should be decorated to such a highly expensive standard. There was every latest comfort imaginable and it was in the highest of immaculate order.

Huge mirrors shone and the furniture was free of dust. Without doubt he considered the building had been furnished in exemplary detail by a woman. She had obviously gone to some considerable trouble and some extraordinary lengths to make sure everything was impeccable. He considered that maybe the Countess was responsible for the internal affairs and that she was here to scrutinise proceedings and report back to the leaders of the society in Europe or judging by the opulence possibly even Charles Stuart was planning to rest here on his journey south.

Seated around the table and having already eaten were Luc De Winter, Trevean, Evan Rinold and Captain Tavish. There was no sign of Countess Van Buren or Captain Basil and there was nothing which suggested they had already eaten.

Both Captain Tavish and Evan Rinold were ghostly white in colour, red puffy eyed and deliberately slow in speech and fragile in moment. They both seemed to be suffering for last night's extravagance.

Judging by everyone's reaction Jem thought he had at interrupted at an inconvenient time, but then after he was warmly greeted by Luc De Winter he discovered that the men's disgust and anger was directed Tom McCoy. Sitting to face a breakfast of bread, cheese, eggs, pottage, ale and milk Jem was told by Trevean that after McCoy left the dining room last night he had took out his frustrations on the Southside look out.

"Apparently," Said Rinold in a tentative and slow voice, "last night when you drew in close the lookout wasn't anywhere to be seen."

"Ah yes. There was no one on duty. " Jem confirmed braking open with his fingers a small loaf.

"Well, after he'd finished here McCoy went back to look the sentinel and unfortunately for the young lad he caught him sleeping behind a tree."

"From what we can gather he never even had the chance to open his eyes." Tavish spoke without raising his bowed head. "Cut the poor bastards throat whilst he was sleeping."

"Cut off his head and brought it back to the camp to show what happens if orders are not followed." Trevean enlightened with more detail.

Jem noted De Winters silence, he refrained from speaking whilst he deliberated.

"And he may feel the inclination to try out the same treatment on you when he finds out that you've taken his position." Rinold warned.

"Then I fear that McCoy's adventures with the Society are near to an end." Jem announced confidently.

"No!" Now De Winter arose out of his chair to reinforce his opinion. "I forbid any of you to go near or approach him. Although I do not condone his behaviour I have one more use for him yet, then I and I alone will personally deal with McCoy. Do you hear and understand me. I don't want any harm to come to him just yet."

"If that is what you want." Jem said.

"Absolutely it is." He nodded.

"Then it is confirmed." Jem agreed. "I will not incite nor antagonise the man."

"And we shall endeavour to keep our distance." Trevean added not wanting to be left out.

"But what if he should seek vengeance or retribution for my actions this morning?" Jem inquired. He wanted to make sure that there could be no mistakes or misunderstandings.

"Then I will not hold you accountable for your actions." De Winter answered without delay to Jem. "Now that is understood, let us deal with the priorities of the day. Captain Tavish I have here a reply for our leader." He swivelled towards the ill looking Scotsman and pulled from inside his coat a sealed document. "I want you to start back for Peebles and deliver this in person, immediately."

Although De Winter had no intention of revealing what information the document held everyone around the table assumed it was confirmation informing Charles Edward Stuart that the militia was ready and waiting.

"Gentlemen, it is time." He announced arising.

"Are we not waiting for the others?" Trevean concerned.

"I have already sent brave Captain Basil ahead to muster the men and my sister in law can suit herself.

Sister in law, Jem pondered. The connection interested him, he had assumed wrongly she was De Winters lover.

"I have waited for this day to arrive for too long."

Trevean and Rinold scowled at each other, they seemed concerned to how Countess Van Buren would react when she discovered that she had missed out on such an important event.

De Winter caught, interpreted and understood their expressions. "If she does not choose to attend then it is her own misfortune. After all, for once she is not the most important person of the day." He then turned to smile at Jem. "Are you ready Captain Benedict?"

"I was ready the day I left France." Jem announced discarding a piece of bread and straightening upright.

Following on the heels of De Winter who set an eager pace the other men excitedly followed Jem out of the building, across the courtyard, past the stables and through an archway which led the way into a massive secure compound.

Cramped upon the muddy surface was an unhealthy array of hastily erected shelters, weather covers and tents which perilously represented the living quarters the Jacobite reinforcements. Jem's eyebrows raised when he saw the squalor. He tasted the foul air that soured the morning breeze watching drowsy men urinate into splattering mud.

Captain Basil could be seen and heard in the fluky half-light shouting orders and trying with all his might, without success, to make the troops assemble.

"Now you see for yourself Captain Benedict exactly why we need you." De Winter said as they observed the calamity.

"Basil has no guts and the men know it." Trevean informed.

It was obvious to everyone that Basil was ruffled and could not control the situation. Most of the men were unresponsive, ambling at their own pace in front of him whilst others still slouched half asleep in groups. To the centre of camp a couple were mocking him and being urged on by a huge man one of them dropped his pants and directed his bare backside to the inept Captain.

"They will never respond to a man who hasn't even the courage to defend his honour." Trevean spoke once more referring to the insults spat at Basil last night by McCoy.

"Basil is a coward and McCoy a savage." De Winter opinionated himself. "Now let's see what our men think of you Captain Benedict."

De Winter walked forward with a brace of conviction and determination. Only Jem followed, Trevean, Rinold and Tavish all chose to watch the proceedings from a distance.

"Thank you Captain Basil. We will take over the proceedings from here."

With relief overwhelming him, the red-faced and panting Captain turned and with his head held low retreated back to the others.

At the mere sight of Luc De Winter all of the men straightened to attention, all with the exception of one. The giant amongst the men who had been the main cause of Captain Basil's grief slovenly barged his way to the front of the assembly. There was no need for any introduction, Jem had no doubts, this man had to be Elzivir Gunn.

Standing well above the tallest of the gathered and outweighing the heaviest amongst them Elziver Gunn's face was a symbol of suffering and punishment. Flattened nose, scarred flesh, puffed eyes and ears. It was obvious to all the bedraggled malcontents that over the years this man had suffered great wounds and sacrificed his natural features for the price of victory. The subsequent respect he demanded he now always received.

De Winter's eyes traced along the faces of the gathered and he drew breath.

"This is Captain Benedict and."

"And he is going to be our saviour." The big man bellowed out mockingly above De Winters voice.

"Less of your insolence or I will have your tongue cut out of your mouth!" De Winter uncompromisingly raged.

"Oh yes! Then tell me sir. Who out of your men would be so bold enough to carry out the deed?" Gunn fired back with his eyes fixed, challengingly on the stranger stood at De Winters side.

There is no doubting for one instant in Jem's mind and in the mind of all who were watching with great expectation that De Winter could and would himself kill the big man without even so much as a flicker of emotion, but everyone including Jem knew it was his own courage that was being tested by both Gunn and De Winter.

"Get back in line and respect your superiors." Jem shouted, stepping forward to meet the big man's glare of disrespect.

"I see no one here superior to me." Gunn confidently taunted back.

"Then I will oblige to enlighten you." Jem announced removing his jacket and striding to within striking distance. The late autumn breeze chilled his back.

"And you think yourself my superior because of your fancy words and cloth." Gunn spat back standing his ground and tilting his head back with a sneer of defiance.

"I congratulate you. For you are not as demented as your appearance suggests." Jem chided as the volunteers, their eyes transfixed with great anticipation backed away to form a large semicircle. "And now I see plainly enough none of you understand the meaning of superiority."

"And so it seems neither are you." Gunn began to roll up his sleeves. "But I will gladly oblige you with a lesson in manners." He bellowed walking forward with his fists tightened.

"We shall see, shall we not?" Jem gritted as quickly he discarded his coat to De Winter's awaiting arm, firmed his feet in the mud and raised his clenched fists to defend himself.

Grinning as though he was expecting to enjoy administering a beating upon a Captain, Gunn lunged forward swinging his ball of a fist in the direction of Jem's jaw, but anticipating the attack Jem pulled back his head, dropped his right shoulder and smashed his own right counter into Gunn's solid midriff as he let the big man's would-be blow breeze passed his ear and make contact with nothing, but the cold morning air.

Releasing mass gasps in unison the audience displayed their surprise and disbelief as the big man stumbled foolishly sideways and arch his body as he panted to regain breath.

"You turn away like a bitch of a woman," he wheezed.

"But I hit like a man." Jem boasted as he followed up by smashing a straight left into Gunn's undefended face with rapid speed and hurtful accuracy to the further dismay of the onlookers.

Raging, with humiliation rather than the sting of the blow Gunn snorted out a stream of hot blood which began to pour from his nose and erecting himself he charged forward again swinging left and right blows in the rough direction of the target in front of him.

Jem parried the punches easily with his forearms and sprung back on his left leg at the same time grabbing a hold of the collar on Gunn's shirt. Then with lightning speed and using Gunn's own momentum to an advantage he pulled the giant forward and tipped him over his right leg to toss him down into the mud with a thud. Whilst Gunn was once again void of all breath Jem glanced quickly about him to ensure that he was not about to receive a helping hand from a cowardly backer, but all he saw was motionless expressions change from one of surprise to one of amusement as the bully struggled in the mud to comprehend what had happening to him.

"You see, Mister Gunn. I do have a notion of the meaning of the word superior." Jem teased the dazed man.

Incensed beyond all control and reasoning Gunn hauled himself upright using his knuckles as a leaver. He wiped the blinding mask of mud from his face with his forearms and then rubbed the palms of his hands dry against his buttocks.

Much to Jem's confoundment and irritation he had not swiped the look of supremacy from the face of the soldier and disheartened him, rather he had incensed him further.

"By God! I'm going to make you suffer like I've never made any man suffer before." He threatened and once more he launched himself Jem's direction.

This time he feigned his punch and he tried to surprise his adversary by grabbing at his shoulder. A quick left and right pounding into his face from the retreating Jem did not deter him from his intentions and when Jem's right foot slipped in the mud Gunn seized his chance by wrapping his massive arms around Jem's back and chest whilst locking tight his arms by his side.

The instant that the arms latched secure Jem knew he was in desperate trouble. He was no match in size or strength against Gunn and he fully expected the big man to render him breathless with a slow vice like squeeze.

Gunn grinned insanely as he gave a little squeeze to give an indication of his strength and then he pulled back his head and snapped it forward with bolting ferocity. Bone cracked against bone as his forehead smashed into Jem's face to administer it's damage and he laughed loudly through blooded teeth as he felt Jem's legs weaken and buckle under him.

"You know it's the good Lord who says it is far more blessed to give than receive. Wouldn't you agree Captain?" Again he laughed as he held Jem upright in the hold.

The boasting was a fatal mistake as the delay in finishing Jem off gave him just enough time to clear his head and think of what to do next. Although his vision was blurred and his footing unsteady Jem summoned just enough strength to raise his knee and ram it painfully in Gunn's groin.

Screaming in an intense agony, Gunn immediately released his grip and in a spasm of weakness dropped to his knees with his hands covering the injured parts.

"Bastard." He whined.

Jem was still dazed and he staggered back a couple of steps to re-compose himself. Pinching his nose between his fingers he found the bone to his astonishment was not broken just extremely sore and throbbing. He calmly wiped away the trickle of blood from his brow, blew clear his nostrils and wiped the water from his eyes. Regaining his composure he waited to see what Gunn intended to do next.

Battling with all his might against the crippling pain Gunn gritted his teeth and began to slowly arch upwards. Once again, he spat out hatred.

"Bastard!"

Jem saw he was in no mood to yield and he understood the big man had one intention on his mind.

Ending any chance of a revived attack Jem coldly took two strides forwards and violently kicked out his right foot with lethal power and accuracy. The blow caught Gunn cleanly under the chin as he was rising and it's force stretched his neck and trust over into the mud.

The audience gasped watching in awe and disbelief as the big man lay on his back with only his chest rising and falling. No one moved to help him and no one spoke, disbelief held them mute and locked in their stiff bodies.

It was Jem who broke the silence after a moment's pause to satisfy himself the fight was over.

"Now you listen to me, you unruly a lot and listen good for I will say this only once." Realigning his clothing he turned to address the men. "You are all from this moment in time under my commanded and I expect you all to do exactly as I demand without question at all times." He raged spraying spittle and blood from his mouth. "Is that understood?" There were a few nods and some muted grunts of compliance, but shocked faces and clamped mouth looked down to avoid Jem's gaze.

He continued to pace along the front of the men glaring deep into the unfortunate countenances who found themselves opposite to him.

"That is unless any of you share the same views as Mister Gunn here?" There was no movement, no sound and to Jem's relief no more challenges.

"For if any of you have any questions step out here now and we will sort them out our differences before we go any further." Still there was no reaction.

"Good then I will endeavour to give you men the best training possible and in return you will give me your cooperation and loyalty at all times. Is that understood?" Only muted grumbles were uttered and it was not acceptable.

"Is that understood?" He barked venomously to force a more positive response.

"When I have finished with you. You will be the most feared fighting unit in this land."

Suddenly the expressions opposite him changed signalling concern and he became aware of movement to his rear. Arching low and spinning to face the danger he caught sight of Gunn lunging towards one of the inanimated soldiers.

Bundling him to the ground with ease, Gunn twisted his feet in the mud to face Jem he brandished a large knife which he had pulled free from the soldier's belt.

"Face thy doom bastard! And taste thy own blood for I am going to quarter you." He edged slowly forward and waved the blade out in front of him in an attempt to impel dread and fear with his weapon of destruction. He grinned insanely, his enlarged eyes breaching a mask of sludge and blood. Determinedly he slowly neared and jabbed out the blade towards Jem, but quickly slanting sideways Jem avoided the stab and prepared for the next attack by digging his heels deep into the slippery surface.

He circled Jem and twice more and lashed out with the knife to no avail. Jem was not intimidated, his confidence increased as Gunn began to look more and more clumsy and foolish in full view of everyone. He arched down low and swept the blade to no avail across Jem's chest. Finally growing more erratic in movement and void of all patience Gunn desperately rushed into a full lung forward with one last futile bid to conquer his enemy. Being both quick of thought and sure of movement, Jem easily evaded the fast moving blade and at in the same motion he sank a punch into Gunn's stomach allowing him to fling him once more over his tripping foot.

Gunn's legs spread and disobeyed him on the slippery mud and losing all control of direction and balance he fell on top of a blazing campfire, demolishing as he crashed a cooking stove and rack. Boiling water hissed and a cloud of steam arose as writhing and screaming in agony the flames instantly melted his flesh and ignited his waxy waist coat. He rolled frantically and blindly trying to douse the flames in the cool mud, but as he squirmed Jem marched forward, grabbed hold of the discarded knife and closed in on the writhing body. For a long moment he held his poise staring at the charred horrors of disfigurement. Singed hair and scorched skin wretched the air and turned the stomachs of all nearby. Gunn rolled skywards and pleaded frantically for Gods mercy. He tried to cover his melted eye lids with his hands charred bony fingers, but the pain rendered him senseless and he screamed again through his lipless blackened gorge. Jem had no option, but to end his misery and plunge the knife with all his might deep into Gunn's chest and to prematurely end his suffering. He felt Gunn's hot blood squirt onto his hands as the blade slid in deeper and deeper and he weighted his shoulder behind the press until finally the piercing screams eased to a whimper and the struggling ceased as his last breath expired.

Leaving the knife protruding from Gunn's smouldering chest Jem straightened. He flicked mud with his foot to cool the glowing ambers on the dead man then he turned to lecture the rictus of terror which mantled the faces of those around him.

"Now listen to me you men and be sure you listen to me good!" Jem shouted into the silence, "for I have never seen in my life before such a bedraggled and unworthy rabble of men such as you which stand before me this morning. You are a disgrace, not only to this moment, but to yourselves." He took one step forward and reached towards the man nearest to him. Unopposed he lifted the man's tatty shirt with his fingers. "Look at you. Look at you all!" Beneath the shirt and hanging from the frail skeletal frame was the skin stain of filth and neglect, open sores pussed freely on his chest and red blotches and scratches marked flea infestation. Disgusted at the sight Jem quickly released the shirt and wipe his fingers of his thigh.

"Call yourselves fighting men. It doesn't look like you could fight a good whore."

"I have purchased uniforms." De Winter disclosed to Jem as he inspected with the aid of his foot Elziver Gunn's dead body. Blood poured to the floor from the flooding around the knife as De Winter disturbed the body.

"Then where are they?"

"In the stores..... I do believe." He twisted his head looking for someone to confirm.

"Yes ...... err yes sir." The ashen face Basil replied through his fingers which still covered his mouth.

"Good for I need them this morning." Jem acknowledged turning back to face the rest of the men.

"Soldiers of the Manchester militia. I promise you this. By the time I have finished with you, you will not only respect the movement of which you represent, but you will also respect yourselves as individuals. When I return in exactly one hour I expect you to either stand with me or against me."

Leaving the men with orders to build up more large fire and boil plenty of water Jem was satisfied with the outcome of the morning's events.

Crossing the boggy field with the haughty De Winter, Jem noticed from a distance that Countess Van Buren had joined the party of observers. He didn't know how long she had been there or how much of the affair she had seen. He wiped his smarting knuckles with a handkerchief De Winter offered him and he tried to brace away the pain which enervated his every muscle.

"Captain Basil. Ask Tebb to prepare and salt linctus and Primrose oil immediately." De Winter ordered his attention now drawn to the Countess. "My dear, decided to join us after all." He added with sarcasm as they re-joined the leaders.

"I don't know why you didn't just hang or shoot the mutinous pig." She snapped back in response with a cold icy glare. She seemed unimpressed with the outcome and even worse, she did not acknowledge or even consider Jem of due worthy or importance to offer him one of her chilling glances. This roused his anger and he couldn't resist faulting her stupidity.

"Because anyone with any common knowledge of human nature would have understood that the society would have lost far more than it could ever have gained."

Jem's rebuke infuriated the woman and she instantly glared hatred as she snapped back.

"How dare you speak to me like this?"

Jem dared to raise his voice above her and cut her off. "How dare you interfere in matters that are no concern to you?"

"And how dare you cast your judgement when you know so very little of which you endeavour to speak." She spat back now fighting to restrain her composure in front of the audience.

"Arrabella! Captain Benedict is correct." De Winter stepped in sensing it was time to end the dispute and preventing the volunteers in the distance becoming aware of the amusing conflict. "The welfare of the men is no longer your concern."

"Forgive me my dear brother-in-law, but may I take this opportunity to remind you that the entire Manchester operation is of my concern." She then gestured with a waving finger. "And you know it."

"Only in the capacity of an observer." He scorned with hurtful pleasure.

"I am an observer because you cannot be trusted even by your own kin and it grieves you so."

"You are an observer because you have no other use."

"Damn you so." Raising her hand quickly she tried to slap De Winter across the face as finally her patience and composure snapped, but De Winter reacted instantly and caught her arm stopping the motion.

"Raise your hand to me again and I will cut it from your wrist and feed it to the pigs." Humiliating her to the full, De Winter refused to release his grip until she submitted a nod of compliance.

"Good now that both of today's exhibitions are over I'm sure we all have pressing matters to attend to."

De Winter finished cruelly, but she had not heard his words. She had already turned to hide her embarrassment and hastened away in the direction Temple house.

With raised eyebrows the group turned away from the macabre scene and began to follow the distant Countess.

"You displayed commendable grace under the pressure Captain." Trevean's praise distracted from the spat as they walked.

Jem had a constructive morning. After he had washed away the signs of combat with Tebb's linctus and applied a cold compress to this forehead he found himself to be almost satisfactory unblemished.

He had returned to the men alone and found them not to be apposing. He ordered them to strip naked, burn their clothes then wash and bath with hot water and lye soap. Confused by and unaccustomed to the new practice the men agreed after Jem explain to them that the soap would rid them of their fleas. Using smuggled soap it was a ritual that worked well during the days of confinement in the Dutch jails.

Whilst half the men were bathing, he had the loiters pack up camp and move all the tents and burn the all rubbish and infestation.

By midday the camp was based on a much firmer and healthier ground and the men were assembled to display their new attire and equipment. Jem was impressed. The standard of weaponry far surpassed any military force he had seen before and he was well aware a great deal of thought and planning had gone into providing the latest muskets, swords, pikes and halberds all of which were the made to the highest quality and all were in plentiful supply.

The men now stood tall and proud adorning their new jackets, trews, tartan slashes, belted plaid and cartridge filled Sporrans.

Knowing he had succeeded in gaining Luc De Winter's confidence and trust he hoped the reduced scrutiny would enable him to find a respite from his fraudulent duties and allow him to revert his attentions back to his priority of finding the secret agent.

After the inspection of the troops, Jem joined De Winter and Trevean for a light meal. The conversation turned out to be interesting and informational.

With Captain Tavish journeying back to Scotland, Captain Basil brooding in his room and Evan Rinold and Countess Van Buren out of the grounds on some hastily arranged business, De Winter spoke openly about his relationship with his sister by virtue of marriage. He revealed that Arrabella Van Buren was married to his half brother, Count Marco Van Buren, whom he despised.

Sipping on brandy his explained that his mother, Erin De Winter had been left a young widow by courtesy of the French invasion of the Spanish Netherlands and using her cunning to avoid poverty and ruin she married a wealthy Dutch nobleman. When Marco was born five years later, young Luc was not favoured by his new father and it was Marco who reaped the financial benefits of having a rich father. Although they grew apart as the years passed they both shared the same desires for lust and power.

Often their paths crossed as they searched for their ultimate goal and several times they found themselves on the same collision course as they both sought power. This occurred again when they were both introduced to the Society of Revolutionary Jacobites by the same man, Walter Rutledge.

Jem recalled the name being mentioned by Edmund Beechey, The Baron of Ripon and he admitted that he knew of the connection from his own informants. De Winter expected as much and he did not view it with either concern or suspicion.

He went on to explain in considerable detail how Rutledge and Marco were financing the supply of troops from Europe and he explained that when Charles Edward Stuart was ready to invade England from the north Rutledge and Marco would transport reinforcements of men and additional supplies from Rotterdam to Dover. With Charles Edward Stuart's army strengthened in the north by the Manchester militia, London would easily fall to the double attack from the north and south.

Jem then carefully persuaded De Winter to reveal more of the vicious Arrabella. He obliged to eagerly tell Jem that she was English and of noble birth. Her father was the late Darius Witton who became a disqualified Tory for supporting the 1715 Jacobite uprising. Fleeing for fear of execution, he died a pauper in France, but not before he had found the right man, Marco De Winter, to marry his only daughter.

De Winter explained how Marco insisted that the Countess and her cousin Felix should be a part of the Manchester connection. There was very little trust and Marco refused to fund the movement unless his brother agreed to the appointment. Although they played a small part with the enlisting of new members her main role was one of an observer and communicator.

Trevean enlightened that it was the Countess who all made the arrangements for his travelling theatre and that she was responsible for hand picking some of the more influential members of the community as new recruits.

De Winter disrespectfully snarled at her duties and blasted her as a mere house keeper and a whore for taking Felix as her lover. Jem sensed jealousy and he suspected that she had more than once had to spurn De Winter's unwanted advances.

His mind was not allowed to conjure up any more conclusions as De Winter coldly boasted he had cut Felix's throat and dispose of his body in the pond beneath Countess Van Buren's bedroom window. He laughed devilishly saying it amused him that all the time the Countess was writing to her acquaintances in Europe for news about her Felix or she was in fact looking down at him every morning when she arose and every evening when she retired. It pleased him even more knowing that she dare not try to contact her lover too hard for fear that she might draw unwanted attention to the society's activities or raise any suspicion upon herself from Marco. He almost choked on his food with laughter as he recalled how every day to no avail, she rushed to the door when a visitor approached hoping for a letter with news. Trevean joined in the humour, but Jem knew as did De Winter, that it was only a gesture to sustain his allegiance.

Jem realised that there was nothing, but hatred animosity and suspicion between De Winter and the Countess and he intended to do his uppermost to widen the rift and increase hostilities.

The luncheon finished with De Winter notifying Jem that he was leaving Temple House until tomorrow afternoon. He said he had some unfinished business to take care of in Lancaster, but he disclosed nothing more.

Trevean revealed, once Luc De Winter had left the room and he was sure he would not return until much later, a horse trader in Lancaster had gone back on his promise to supply and so De Winter intended to kill him. He had admitted that he could have got one of the men or even McCoy to carry out the sentence, but it had become a personal quarrel because the man, who remained nameless had given De Winter his own word of honour. Death was the only solution. The trader had broken his promise for some reason and the Society could not afford to take any risks.

Trevean then left the table boasting to Jem that he would be found at The Plough Inn in Preston if he should need him. A blonde headed whore with a heavy chest had attracted his eye during his last visit there and he admitted that he could not shake her luring temptations from his mind. Leaving with a resurgent stride, he said he could no longer restrain the urge of desire which had teased and tormented him ever since.

With every one of concern engaged in duties away from Temple House for the rest of the afternoon Jem decided to take advantage of the opportunity to search the grounds and buildings of the estate. He briefly returned to his men with the discouraging news that the purging of the camp was not to his satisfaction and so he ordered them to restart the cleansing, then he threatened they would continue with this act until the camp cleanliness suited his approval.

Returning to the house he inconspicuously worked his way throughout it's many rooms of splendour, however disappointedly they revealed nothing more than opulence furnishings with nothing of importance to interest him. In contrast to this many of the outbuildings provided him with intelligence, but no clues to the location of the missing spy. Piles of grain, sugar, salt, flower and every other conceivable provision needed to supply a vast travelling army was stocked ceiling high and Jem was stunned to how well prepared the society was. It was not just a bunch of foreigners trying to stir up disorder as he had originally believed, it was a serious and very dangerous organisation which had every intention of fulfilling it's ambitions.

Considering what to do next he stood in the late afternoon shadows at the end of the stretching courtyard. He was contemplating leaving Temple House whilst he had the opportunity and return to the Baron and inform him of everything he had seen when he noticed a soldier guarding a small uninteresting door at the opposite end of the yard. Suddenly he was alert again his suspicions aroused, the only other building within the compound to be allocated an armed guard was the munitions store.

There was no activity in the courtyard itself or in the stables so he knew that the Countess and Rinold had not yet returned and the house servants were busy preparing for the evening entertainment.

Curious to find out what the soldier was guarding he looked again at the slouching young man. Judging by his weaponry, it seemed to Jem that whatever he was concealing it could be more than just provisions.

Jem was just about to investigate when he caught a glimpse of McCoy crossing the courtyard. He stepped back into the corner shadows unnoticed and watched McCoy passed words with the soldier who unbolted the door and stepped aside.

He waited a few minutes to see to see if McCoy re-emerged and when he did not he moved out from the cover of darkness and confidently strode towards the guard.

"Name? Jem demanded.

"Athelwaite sir." The man saluted.

"You know who I am?"

"Yes. You are Captain Benedict, sir."

"Then where is your dress?" Jem said with condemnation giving the soldier a false conviction he had been approached because he was not wearing the freshly issued uniform.

"I have not been relieved of this duty sir, therefore I have not been able to change." He blurted out displaying a tremble indicating he knew how demanding the new Captain was.

"Then be sure to do so as soon as you get the opportunity."

"Yes sir, I will."

"And straighten yourself up man. You look like an invalid begging for charity." Jem cursed. "And hold your chin up when you address an officer."

"Yes sir." Suddenly the screams of a woman screeched out from beyond the door to splice the lull of the late afternoon.

"What the hell was that?" Jem demanded.

Averting his eyes nervously Athelwaite did not answer. More screams penetrated through the ill-fitting door to pierce near silence and Jem moved forwards to the door.

"Move aside Athelwaite!" The soldier hesitated and stuttered something inaudible and a frowned expression of fear and confusion twisted his face. He deliberated not knowing what action to take.

"This is an order. Move aside at once." Jem growled assuming the young man's indecision was entirely due to his fear of McCoy and the inevitable punishment he would receive by allowing the Captain to gain admittance.

Jem withdrew his pistol and put it up to Athelwaite's face.

"Step aside or die!" This time the trembling youth obliged and sliding his feet he positioned his hand over his crotch which had suddenly become damp.

Bursting into the room and enlightening the dankness with a fat shaft of afternoon illumination Jem's every fibre locked with monolithic hardness by the sight of McCoy brandishing a hot iron to the breasts of a half naked woman.

Blindfolded, she was shackled upon an iron makeshift bed with her limbs stretched to the four corners and secured to the posts. Her flesh bore the fresh scars of torture and a blooded mouth gag hung loose below her neck.

"What do you want Benedict? ... You have no business here." McCoy spat twisting to face the intruder and waving his damaged and bandaged hand dismissively.

"I heard the cries of a woman." Jem admitted his eyes struggling to absorb the savagery in front of him.

"They'll be plenty more of that before I'm finished." Exertion flushed his face and glistened on his forehead. "I'm only just getting started." McCoy inhumanly boasted.

"Benedict?" The woman wheezed turning her head towards Jem's voice.

"Shut up bitch." McCoy ordered driving his fist across the side of the women's blotched face.

Noting the women's interest and recalling what the Baron said Jem announced.

"Captain .... Lazar Benedict to be precise."

Suddenly his mind became overwhelmed, 'A woman? A woman spy?' He lipped silently. He struggled not to show any signs of emotion as all of his perceptions had been shattered and his illusions scrambled into disarray. 'It couldn't be, could it? A woman spy.' He knew he had to take a risk and find out.

Weakened and hurt to the point where her eyes were swollen and half shut with sweat and tears she muttered.

"Benedict? It can't be." A mouthful of blood followed the doubt.

"Yes, it is me. Lazar."

McCoy's face scowled confusion and anger. He sensed something was wrong and he tilted his head and straightened his stance in the direction of the new Captain.

"Release her." Jem ordered.

"Are you mad?" McCoy shouted raising the branding iron in defiance.

"Do as I say immediately!" Jem demanded.

"The woman is a protestant spy, an English traitor and I'm going to torture her last breath out of her." He snarled.

"Put down the irons and release her." Jem increased the tone of his order.

"Never! She is a spy and she deserves to die." Eyes fixed on Jem he stretched the hot iron once again over the women's flesh.

"McCoy! This women works for me!" Jem spat out to halt the Scotsman from burning her again.

"What?" He scowled cynically.

"What have you told him?" Jem said ignoring McCoy's forbidding iron to lean over the woman's feverish face. She shook her head signalling nothing and Jem turned back to face McCoy.

"You are right. She is a spy, but she isn't a traitor." Thinking fast and standing up tall above McCoy he added. "Her name is Rosanna Bonney and she is the greatest female spy in the whole of Europe. Now do as I say and untie her."

"I take my orders from Luc De Winter and only Luc De Winter." He revoked stubbornly. "She stays my prisoner to do with as I like or until he authorises otherwise."

"No, she does not." Jem counted with a raised tone of determination and a fixed a glare of loathing into the Scotsman's eyes. "I'm taking full responsibility for this woman right now. Untie her."

"And on whose authority." McCoy snarled.

"On my authority. Now do as I order and release her." Jem's face neared McCoy's and both men held there nerve and the glare.

"Can't do that. I am responsible for this whore and I have not finished with her." He contemptuously boasted insolence and he challenged Jem's power.

"Release her and do it now." Jem raged remaining upright and close enough to McCoy to feel his rancid breath on his face.

"Works for you, you say?" He questioned with a challenging sneer.

"I did. You heard correct." Their bodies collided.

"Then prove it." McCoy defied, breathing in to expand his chest and raise his size by an inch or two.

Jem feigned an unruffled laugh at the Scotsman to make him appear foolish and inadequate.

"How do you think I already know so much about the society? You said it yourself, you didn't think I was back in the area by chance."

McCoy's facial expression changed from one of confusion to one of anger as Jem insulted.

"You don't actually think you rescued me from the hands of that worthless landlord do you."

McCoy said nothing, but rage began spreading throughout as he realised what was coming next.

"Thought you'd set it up perfectly. Didn't you?" Jem laughed again. "I played you and the rest of your cronies like a fools from the information given to me by this woman."

"You're a liar." The Scotchman accused, his eyes narrowing as he tried to contemplate the assertion.

"When I stopped receiving reports I decided to come and find out why."

"No. You're lying." Using his functioning hand McCoy directed the smouldering iron over the women's exposed breasts again.

"You just want to have these beauties all to yourself. That's what you want. You rascal."

"Insolent fool." Jem insulted. "You have less intelligence than a farm yard dog."

"That so. Well a dog does not give up it's bone so easily." McCoy continued ignoring Jem's words. He grinned dementedly and slowly tormenting to increase the suffering he began to lower the scolding rod towards the struggling woman.

Jem's reasoning and restraint vanished and fearing the bulging eyed maniac would scar the women his reaction was instantaneous. He levelled his pistol at McCoy's head and fired.

A flame erupted from the muzzle and the discharge ball smashed into McCoy's forehead tearing his skull in half and splattering brains, blood and bone across the prostrate women and rear wall. McCoy was dead before his body hit the floor and the iron dropped harmlessly to the stone slabs.

The thunder of the shot echoed throughout the grounds of Temple House and choking smoke bellowed forming an obscuring large cloud beneath the low ceiling.

Jem crouched beside the woman and holding her hand he covered her nakedness with her torn chemise.

"Does the name Edmund Beechey mean anything to you?" He positioned his face next to her cheek. "The Baron of Ripon?" He whispered into her ear.

Only just being able to hear the words because of the deafening blast reverberating within her ear drum she nodded and coughed out a very weak.

"Yes."

"I am here on his behalf."

"Are you who I think you are?" He whispered frowning quizzically into her face knowing that if she answered negatively or with hesitation he would have to kill her also to protect himself from being detected.

"My name is Jacqueline Beechey." She claimed with a dry throated whisper, but before any more words could be spoken the door creaked open and blinding brightness spread through the haze of smoke.

"What in God's name is going on?" Athelwaite shouted entering the room with a gaping mouth and wide eyes he tried to call out an order.

"Nobody move!" He pointed his musket through the doorway.

"McCoy refused to accept his orders." Jem said arising with a ring of keys which he tugged free from the Scotsman's belt. "And he paid the penalty."

Athelwaite gazed down at the almost decapitated man. The colour drained from his face and shakily he lowered the weapon.

"Go and get some fresh water." Jem ordered putting his hand on the guard's shoulders to turn him. "And be quick about it."

Ushering the soldier through the open frame with a hurried push Jem closed the door and ignored the rushing footsteps which could be heard on the cobble as soldiers and servants began to gather in the courtyard to investigate the shot.

A grim relief arose within Jem as with urgency he knelt beside the spy and began to fumble with the locks.

"The Baron of Ripon is my commander." She finally managed to answer angling her head to allow her to examine her saviour.

"Why have they done this to you?" He sighed.

"I was working under cover for the English intelligence when I was betrayed." A bolt of pain suddenly muted her and she coughed as the gun smoke irritated her throat. Jem supported her shoulder as she covered her mouth with the now released hand.

Again a spray of light followed by a cool chill filled the chamber as Athelwaite appeared with a jug and ladle. Jem sprang to meet him and relieving him of the water he peered out to view the gathering crowd of the curious. Closing the door behind him, Jem soon allayed there concerns and had them returning to their duties when two horses entered the courtyard.

It was the Countess and Rinold and their hasty approach and quizzical looks confirmed they had also heard the shot in the distance. Now knowing that an immediate escape was impossible he returned inside to complete the release of the woman's shackles and ease her discomfort with a much needed drink.

With urgency, aware the Countess and her escort would be dismounting outside he eased the women up to her feet and enclosing his arm around her shoulder to slowly guide her towards the doorway.

Ignoring the piercing glare from the Countess, Jem slanted is head to the direction of the now spewing solider and shouted.

"Athelwaite clear up this mess." And pointing with his thumb to the blood splattered wall and red sodden floor he added, "And feed the traitor to the pigs."

Chapter 10

Jem gazed into the blackness of the night through his bedroom window. His mind was active, mixture with ideas, visions and assumptions all of which resulted with him being too uncertain to be at ease or comfort. He had been pacing along the floorboards of his room waiting to see what incidents and experiences the dawn would deliver when he thought he heard movement in the corridor outside his room.

Since the killing of McCoy, Jem had not yet been given the opportunity to talk with the female spy alone.

Arrabella Van Buren and Evan Rinold's untimely arrival at the scene had prevented him from saying anything further to the woman and so together they had been forced to convincingly bluff their way through an explanation of the killing with the pretence the spy worked for him.

An immediate attempt escape from Temple House was considered now impossible by Jem due to the society's increased volume of people, the clandestine depth of it's connections in the surrounding towns and villages and the traumatic state and the poor physical condition of the tortured woman. So for the time being at least Jem decided to continue with his portrayal of Lazar Benedict.

Whether Jacqueline Beechey was able to shake the terrifying ordeal of torture out of her mind and clear her thoughts enough to conceive or fully understand what had happening was doubtable and so Jem turned to his advantage the woman's distress.

He did all the initial talking and explaining to De Winter immediately on his return to Temple House and during the account he insisted upon rest and solace for his associate with no disruption and no exceptions. He did, however suspect that she was feigning her condition and elaborating her ailments in order to create herself some valuable thinking time. From what he had learned from the Baron he expected the spy with her mind set to offer more resistance and be made of sterner substance than she was making out.

Another thought which flashed through his mind was, even if she did fully comprehend what was happening, she would never accept that her liberator was, in the words of Sir Clifford Cornell an insolent vagabond.

Convincing the Countess and Rinold of his alibi's sincerity was unimportant, it would be the angered Luc De Winter whom he had to persuade to consider things in his favour and when the moment arrived earlier that evening it seemed for a while as if De Winter, through his impassive demeanour, suspected the hidden truth and that their performance was not over.

With the woman spy still resting and being bathed and anointed in her room it was Jem, who obliged with a more detailed explanation to all the leaders during the evening meal. Seated perfectly still and remaining deadly silent De Winter listened to every detail intensely and it was only when Jem reached the conclusion of the tale that he demanded to know more.

Jem tirelessly explained the captured woman worked for him, her intelligence informed him of the society and her subsequent disappearance brought him back to England to search for the eventual reunion. McCoy's refusal to accept both the story and the fact that he would not be credited for introducing Benedict to the society was his own condemnation. Jem insisted that he had clarified his account and he refused to enlighten the society with any names of his 'Benedict's' contacts to the protestations of the embarrassed Trevean.

He knew De Winter had memorised and scrutinised in his mind every word of which he had spoken and he was positive, even though De Winter himself apologised for the society's treatment upon his comrade, that he was not yet satisfied with the outcome nor indeed yet willing to fully accept the new member's testimony.

Announcing that McCoy's usefulness within the society had expired and admitting he was to be eventually terminated De Winter formalised that he was satisfied with the outcome and the incident was over and to be forgotten. He said that there would be some more urgent matters needing their consideration very soon and he urged everyone to get an early night's sleep.

Whilst the rest of the leaders seemed indifferent to the whole incident Jem could sense Trevean's hidden anger and humiliation for being duped so easily and risking the exposure of the society.

Jem was the first to accept De Winters encouragement of the early night by saying that he intended to rise early again so that he could work hard with the militia fitness. Leaving the room with doubts concerning his and Jacqueline Beechey's immediate safety Jem reflected on the mood around the table. Like De Winter, Arrabella Van Buren looked sceptical, Captain Basil, Evan Rinold and Tavish bore the expressions of relief and gratification They seemed glad, even though they never had the courage to say it that McCoy was forever out of their way, but Trevean was irked and hurt. He was unnaturally over talkative and he tried to defend his damaged honour and reputation with exaggerated tales of woe and unforeseeable bad luck.

Leaving the sermons and criticisms to the drawing room Jem was positive that he had heard someone stop at his room door and banishing his reflections of the supper he quietly withdrew his dagger from within it's sheath and silently moved across the floor to stand close to the door with his back against the wall. Bracing the knife tight in his hand, he listened carefully and prepared himself to open the door.

Alarm spread throughout his body and caused his eyes to widen when poised to open the he saw the handle began to slowly twist. He decided instantly that it was he who would implement the surprise and so there could be no delay in his actions. Quickly clasping the door handle with his left hand and pulling it inwards within the same movement he swiftly darted forward with the knife leading the way.

Due to Jem himself reacting in just enough time and Jacqueline Beechey being alert enough to slant herself away from the blade just glancing looks of concern and disbelief were exchanged. The silence in the corridor remained undisturbed due to them both of remaining in full control of their faculties and for a long moment they both held their poise.

Beechey glanced over her shoulder to ensure she had not been followed and without waiting for an invite she brushed past Jem and entered into his room. Before following her into the bed room Jem also glanced anxiously in both directions of the dark corridor to confirm they had not been heard or discovered.

"Do you always greet women in such a way?" She whispered turning to face him as he closed the door.

"I've learnt the hard way that a man can never be too careful where women are concerned." Jem answered derisively and with a smile then released the knife onto the dressing table and chided. "Clarify for me. Do you insist upon constantly flirting with death?" He studied the bruising which slightly flawed her striking beauty.

"Only when there are no safer options." She answered quickly.

"Then why are you once again risking death by coming here?" He said in a slight louder tone than a whisper.

"We have to talk." She replied moving closer.

"I couldn't agree more, but I fear this is neither the time nor the place."

Jem was still concerned they would be discovered so he also moved close to the woman so they could whisper and still hear each other clearly.

Ignoring his obvious examination she concerned. "There may never be a time or a place and there are certain things I must know before I cooperate with you."

Intrigued by the woman's statement Jem paused and frowned. He could sense that she was planning something, but he realised too it late and catching him by surprise she snatched the knife before he could react pressing the sharp edge of the blade against his throat.

"Make one move, twitch one muscle and I'll cut off your head." She threatened with a whisper in his ear.

"You have such an unusually pleasant way of showing your gratitude." Jem gritted.

"Hold your tongue and answer only to what I ask." She demanded.

"Press the blade any harder and it will be you left holding my tongue." He felt the cold of the steel pressing deep into his throat.

"Then stop these words of banter and tell me everything you know."

"I will only be too glad to accommodate you. But I'm curious to your need for such force." Jem questioned bewilderingly. He began to arch his back, but the knife followed firm against his skin.

"This is nothing compared to the pain and grief that the society's traitors have inflicted upon me."

"And you consider that reason enough to hold a blade to me? The man who saved you."

"I trust no one." She warned, her face braced with determination.

"Evidently." He slowly inched back more. "I fear McCoy really has scattered your mind."

Again her arm extended to hold firm the press and ignoring Jem's comment she began to reveal her inner doubt.

"Especially a man who has the ability to kill one of Luc De Winters henchmen and has the power or influence to walk free."

"Ahh ..... that I can understand, but"

"There are no buts, Mister Benedict or whoever you are." She cut Jem off forcefully whilst holding the tone of a whisper. "It is not hard for me to believe that all of this is one of Luc De Winters scheming plans."

Jem scowled at her words. "You kill McCoy. Dupe me into your trust and I tell you everything I know." She explained her reasoning.

"You consider me one of the society?" Jem whispered, adding a hint of disgust.

"It is conceivable."

"I was assured that when you heard the name Lazar Benedict you would know immediately whom I represented and that my tendencies are loyal and true."

"Luc De Winter could have easily found out through his sources that I killed Lazar Benedict by now." Her suspicions would not relent.

"You killed Lazar Benedict?" Jem had to repeat her words to believe them.

Even though she held a knife menacingly against his throat he still found it hard to believe that this delicate woman standing before him had the presence of mind and power of build required to kill a man of calibre.

"And you will be joining him very soon unless you convince me of your loyalty." She increased the press. "Now tell me everything you know."

"I'll tell you, but only when you lower the blade." Jem turned the ultimatum.

"Then bleed to death."

Anticipating that the woman would not agree to this proposal Jem was already prepared to nullify her next move and with unstoppable speed he pulled away from the blade and swung his hands up to block the woman's forward action. Then he clasped his right hand tight around her wrist and pulled her forward to toss her over his shoulder and onto the bed.

He was not, however prepared for the woman's trained agility and she defended herself by rolling over onto her shoulder and off the bed still holding the advantage by springing unhurt to her feet with a knife still firmly held in her grasp.

Standing on solid footing with her face displaying a brace of determination it was obvious to Jem that she was prepared to die rather than yield to him and conceding to the only sensible option available he declined upon the opportunity to give the woman the humiliating beating of which he so much wanted and he seated himself defeatedly, but casually on the corner of the bed.

"Very well then. We will do this your way." He complied feeling safer and more at ease now that there was a yard of distance between himself and the blade.

"Your pleasant submission will not affect my judgement." She said looking unimpressed and holding firm her threatening pose.

"I did not expect it would." He admitted. "But if we carry on like this the whole household will be at my door."

He smiled at her purely to incite agitation with his nonchalance before he began.

"My name is Jem Rose. I am a convicted highwayman and a bigot." He bluntly said looking for a change in the woman's expression. She was unmoved and with a change in her expression not forthcoming Jem continued to tell of his most recent adventures.

At first disbelieving then being disgusted Beechey listened without interruption until she began to feel both confused and bewildered.

Noting her frown of concern Jem quickly backed up his story with facts containing information and secret knowledge of the English intelligence which proved beyond all doubt he was indeed actually who he claimed to be.

Beechey seemed stunned, she was muted and numb, but she still holding the knife dangerously firm she knew he spoke liberally of intelligence that the Baron would trust with only his closest associates.

"This is preposterous." She scorned with a sceptical expression borne from her confusion. "A commoner enlisted by the Baron of Ripon"

"Commoner and a thief." Jem corrected still holding the subtle grin.

"The Baron would never lower himself to such a flagrant degradation."

"Seeing how you let him down I do believe your dear Baron had very little alternative."

"I find your whole story impossible to believe. The Baron would not expose himself to such risks." She shook her head.

"Had he not hitherto allowed such a wilder risk?"

Beechey clenched her teeth understanding Jem's hurtful remark was directed towards the Baron, his allegiance with her and their failed scheme which led to her subsequent capture.

Her complexion drained pale and then immediately flushed again as rage incited by her own embarrassment of failure and the criticism inflicted by a common thief gnarled at her every fibre.

She drew breath to damn Jem's opinions, but just as she was about to unleash her wrath upon him there was a knock at the door. Her remarks never reached Jem's ears as silently and unsure of what action to take, they both simply drew breath and stared at one another. The knock was repeated, only this time it was persistently longer with added vigour.

"Captain Benedict. Are you awake?"

Jem was astounded to hear the call from Countess Van Buren. He looked at Beechey for a reaction, but knowing that she was going to have to restrain her anger for the time being she mouthed.

"Just one wrong move and I swear to god I'll take at least you and your friend straight down to hell with me."

She gestured with the knife as if to emphasise her threat.

With equal curiosity and alarm Jem pulled open the door just enough to enable him to peer out. Slouched against the door frame in her bedclothes Countess Van Buren looked unusually at ease with herself.

Her hair was hanging loose and untidy, her makeup was past it's expiry and she had lustre in her eyes, but more importantly to Jem, her low cut gown revealed unashamedly the fullness of her bosom.

Managing to raise his face from the enticing views to reciprocate the smile his nostrils filled with the odour of gin which explained to him the Countess's sultry appearance and unusually friendly smile. He could see she was not drunk, but he assumed she must have needed the strong spirit to strengthen her resolve.

"Countess Van Buren. What can I do for you at this late hour?" He broke the silence, wondering to what devious motives had drawn her to his room.

"Are you always so direct?" She replied with a sultry pout. "And drop the formalities, it's Arrabella if you please."

"It is late." He awkwardly stated the obvious.

"I admire a man that is direct. Directness indicates a strong backbone for ambition."

"I'm sorry to disagree. Tonight my directness only indicates I'm tired." He sighed.

"Nonsense. You're just being polite now move aside and invite me in?" Her remark was more of a statement than a question and when Jem failed to answer and refused to give way she chided. "A strong back bone, ambition but I see I failed to include no manners." She brushed her way past him to enter the room.

A shudder ran down his spine as he turned expecting to see Arrabella Van Buren lying dead with a knife through her heart, but to his surprise the sight of seeing her half lying seductively on his bed transformed his expression and she immediately commented that upon the sudden change.

"I see you are glad to see me after all Captain Benedict." She angled her head back slightly and exposed her slender neck.

"The pleasure of your company excites me beyond any other possible comfort." He clumsily said as he forced his eyes away momentarily from the luring temptation and towards the direction of his wardrobe door which he noticed was not entirely closed.

"Your words are most gratifying to hear Captain Benedict." She said reclaiming his attention.

"Please call me Lazar." He asked, closing the bedroom door behind him and stepping nearer to the bed.

"You must be wondering why I'm here?" She dropped her head back onto his pillow.

"Erm." Bewildered and expecting a knife welding assassin to leap from the wardrobe Jem failed to answer.

"It is my intention of my visit is to consolidate our relationship." She stated with a seductive fluttering of her long eye lashes.

"Baroness Van Buren." He began.

"Arrabella please." She cut in.

"Arrabella. I know we have had our differences of opinion, but they are in my view purely professional and not in the least personnel. I assure you."

His heart was pounding uncontrollably. Since lodging in Temple House he dare not even contemplate womanly comforts for fear of distraction, now of a sudden there was a woman willingly offering herself to him on his bed and he could not respond as he naturally should nor as he knew Benedict would for fear of the knife wielding spy watching from within his wardrobe.

"You are indeed by reputation a professional in everything you undertake, but tonight it is not only the professional, but also the more personal and intimate Lazar Benedict my desire seeks to make the acquaintance of." She admitted as swinging her legs beneath her she arose onto her knees to lock her arms around Jem's neck.

"Redefining the nature of our association is a pleasure that I'm sure we will both appreciate." He managed to say before she forced her lips tight upon his mouth.

The kiss was long, but the Countess pulled herself away before the intense and uncontrollable urges and passion dominated their actions and overcame her before she had been able to reinforce the mutual trust.

Jem had enough experience with women to understand that there was more than just love making on the Countess's mind and he was not in the least bit surprised when she pulled from the embrace.

"You strike me as the kind of man who should be commanding this operation instead of that imbecile Luc De Winter."

"Arrabella your remarks astound me. How could you possibly consider such a notion?" Frowning a feigned disgust Jem knew that his loyalty was being tested and he understood her provocative visitation.

"You think it yourself," she asked slouching back, "don't you?"

"I will not give such deceits consideration. Your comments repel me." He answered sharply, rising from the bed with his mind distracted by the occupant in his wardrobe.

"Your loyalty intrigues me." She admitted.

"My loyalty is honest." He replied without delay.

"Then I wish I could say Luc De Winter was prepared to return your honesty and reward your loyalty."

"What?" He gazed into the blackness of the small gap of the ajar door.

"What I speak of is the truth."

He doubted her. "Then I demand you explain your accusation."

"He doesn't trust you."

Jem knew that her false tenderness and affection were simply a deceitful ploy to manipulate both his trust and confidence, but he decided to beguile the traitor to create a spurious bond until he could escape.

"Great leaders leave no stone unturned in their quest for the truth and it would only be natural for Luc to be alarmed after what I did to one of his loyalist aides."

"Natural enough for him to send Captain Basil out on the road to Yorkshire at this late hour to confirm or contradict your explanations concerning the girl."

Jem saw the pleasure of delivering the revelation glint in the Countess's eyes, however he had only one option available to him and so deciding it was safer for him to continue the false loyalty he dismissed her information.

"I am not Luc De Winters judge, but his servant."

Jem immediately understood what she meant regarding Yorkshire. Even though the spy's messages were sent in code they were addressed to the Baron's home in Ripley. Luc De Winter obviously had some doubts to Jem's story and he must have decided to investigate further. Jem knew that both he and Jacqueline Beechey did not have time on their side.

"Then you are a fool Lazar for it is sure that he will use you and then discard you." The Countess scorned sensing that her lurid scheme was not making the desired impact she hoped for.

"You seem so sure." Jem sided, not wanting to lose the women's interest nor her allegiance.

"It's all he knows and it's all he understands." She criticised breathing in deep to provocatively expand her chest.

"And why are you telling me this."

He now stood with his back to the wardrobe door.

"When all this is over I guarantee you that Luc De Winter will be nothing. He will be nobody without an existence and a nobody with a life not worth living and if you stand loyal with him you will end up in the same ruin." She expelled and allowed her body to recline again on the pillows.

"You confuse me, are we not all allies? In this together for the good of us all." The Countess shook her head negatively to dismiss Jem's opinion.

"My advice to you Lazar Benedict is to re-assess your situation and loyalties then do the same as I." Jem raised his eyebrows noticeable enough to prompt her to finish. "Do not trust him."

"You intrigue me Arrabella. For what purpose do you tell me all of this? What have you to gain or should I say lose?"

"You boast that your loyalty is honest Lazar. So is mine, but not to Luc De Winter. I am loyal to the society and my allegiances are true to only the founding members and I hope for the sake of the society you are also true to your word because I need your help."

"You need my help?" Jem repeated prompting the Countess to elaborate.

"When the new reign begins all of those who helped in the transition will be vested with their deserved rewards of power, wealth and position and as you know Lazar, we have freelancers amongst our inner circle who are only interested with enhancing their fortunes and securing their own self-preservation. These profiteers will stop at nothing to maximise their own wealth at the expense of loyal and true Jacobites and that is why I need your help. I will need you to defend my honour."

"Defend it against what?"

"Against the deriding accusations Luc De Winter will make when he chooses the opportune moment."

"Accusations of what?" Once again Jem pushed for more.

"Towards me, my husband and other prominent members of the hierarchy." She curled her legs beneath her.

"And these are... ill founded accusations?" He scowled.

"Of course." Her hand raised and she stretched her fingers to cast off his question. "He considers me, Felix and especially my husband a threat to his own advancement. He aims to bring dishonour and ruin upon us all by making false claims of illicit liaisons between myself and other members of the society."

"To make these claims of he must have consider himself to have evidence."

"He doesn't need evidence. Just the words of his spineless cohorts like Trevean and Basil. The accusations are damning enough in themselves to satisfy his aims."

"And you trust me to support you and turn coat against Luc?"

"I need more than just support. I need protection until it is safe for Felix to set foot again on English soil." Water began to glisten in her eyes and a solitary tear ran down her cheek. "You are the only man I've ever met who is capable of equalling Luc De Winter. As for the trust I am still forming my opinions."

"You must form your opinions quickly for surely you wouldn't have told me of Luc De Winters suspicions, unless of course you were just putting my loyalty to the test."

"No test I assure you. You have told me of your honesty and I'm telling you of mine. He views you as a threat and behind our backs you and I are viewed with the same suspicious contempt. That is why my dear Lazar we are both in a very dangerous and perilous position."

He narrowed his eyes at her wondering if her words contained a secret meaning.

"A life of danger is a life of excitement." Jem swaggered with pride.

"And excitement is the spice of life." The Countess once again raised her body on the bed to crawl nearer to Jem.

"Once tasted, it can never be refused." He said gazing into her enticing eyes.

"Only to be fully appreciated, it must be tasted immediately." She added kneeling higher and pressing her breasts against his chest she levelled her face to his.

"Life without it is mellow and dull." He complained willingly allowing her lips to close in almost upon his.

"And who knows. Tomorrow the taste maybe sour and the excitement extinguished." She finished locking her arms around his neck and her mouth on his lips then she eased him onto the bed. A click sounded from the wardrobe as falling forwards into her beckoning arms he purposely heeled the door closed.

A spasm of excitement coursed through Jem's loins as the embrace gained in craving and arose into a crescendo of passion and a surge of pure lust.

Pulling their lips apart Jem looked down to the temptation before him. A slow lascivious smile crossed her lips.

He knew she was selling herself cheaply to gain his favour, but he didn't care, normally the seducer tonight it was Jem, who was vulnerable and he readily submitted.

Too long he had been without the comfort and the feel of a woman and tonight his appetite had been tested and he could not at any risk resist his natural instinct. Gone and banished completely were any thoughts of the mission and his safety. There was no romantic delusion and only two things occupied his mind, the tantalising sight in front of him and how make the best of the situation.

Pulling himself away for only the briefest of moments Jem glanced at the wardrobe door and satisfied he was safe he pulled off his boots. Returning to the bed, the Countess detected the sexual ardour in his gaze and in acknowledgement she returned one of her sultry glances. Their lips once again embraced and their tongues entwined as fervently their hands caressed and hugged tightly.

Jem's hands made their way around to the tie pull on her nightgown and pulling the fastening free he watched with delight as a gown fell from her shoulders to reveal to his disbelieving gaze her perfectly formed breasts.

Now kneeling on the bed Jem urged the Countess to undress him so deftly and without hesitation she unhooked his trouser belt and peeled down his trousers, Within a few moments they were both totally naked and systematically writing in untamed ecstasy.

Several hours later they both lay quivering in each other's arms and reflecting how they lost themselves in the arousal of unexpected passion.

Arrabella Van Buren had many passionate encounters with good looking, strong men before, but never before had one man manage to excite her so much and fulfil her yearning desires to leave her skin tingling and her body breathless.

Jem lay numbed and satisfied, he said nothing and he did nothing soon falling asleep with the Countess tickling his hair, neck and spine with her expert relaxing touch.

By the time dawn was edging through the darkness they had made love again, only this time more slowly, savouring and prolonging the sexual intensity until finally after what seemed hours of yearning their fervent longing could no longer be withheld.

When the morning grey began to irritate and wake Jem he found he was alone, Van Buren had left the room without disturbing him. A little disappointed that she had gone, but relieved that he was able to avoid the uncomfortable morning encounter he jumped out from the bed and into his trousers. With a huge smile upon his face he vaulted the bed only to be astonished when he found his wardrobe empty of at least one expected body.

Disappointment replaced the beam of satisfaction on his face as he wondered how much or how little of his performance she had been forced to endure.

Assuming that the woman had scampered to freedom and returned to the Baron of Ripon, Jem turned to the window to gaze out into the murky dark morning whilst he considered his own position.

Concluding quickly making a break for it now whilst the others were asleep was his best option and without the hindrance of a woman to hold him up it was probably the safest.

On his own he could easily sneak past the guard stations at the boundaries of Temple House and he knew he could easily evade the inevitable pursuit of the chasers when his disappearance was eventually discovered.

He put on his boots and threw about him his overcoat. Time was of the essence, the earlier start he made the better his chances of survival.

Explanations to the Baron of Ripon and the lady spy concerning his connection with the female member of the society could be studied once he was safely back in Yorkshire as could the complication of Captain Basil.

He moved once more forwards towards the window and looked out to study his escape in the forming dawn. Heavy rain bearing clouds blurred the skyline and provided the perfect shroud for his escape. Fastening the final button on his coat and firming his hat Jem once again squinted into the bleakness below as something caught his eye.

He gazed hard and wiped must for the pane to reveal a darkened figure scamper out from behind the trees near to the stables and run across the courtyard. Losing sight of the figure as it neared the door beneath his window Jem could not tell who the hooded figure was, but he could tell by the persons gait it was a woman. It had to be just one of two, the Countess or Beechey, but he could not understand why either would be returning to the building.

He decided that he was going to find out and he moved to open his door. Stepping out into the corridor with soundless steps he instinctively glanced in both directions then quietly he stepped back into his room as he heard muted steps in the corridor. Remaining quiet and holding the door fractionally open he waited until the person levelled at his room then he reached out to pull down their hood and reveal the concealed face.

"We need to speak." Jem whispered as he startled Beechey.

"Indeed we do." She panted holding her boots in her arms as to silent her movements and avoid any muddy prints. "Later when it's safe." She finished moving off towards her own room.

It was then as she moved away and back into her room that Jem noticed a dark liquid dripping from his hand. It was too late for him to say anything because she had disappeared behind the closed door.

Returning to his room Jem held out his hand into the yellow hue of his lantern. Changing in colour the substance glistened red upon his fingers. Shocked and dismayed Jem hurriedly wiped his fingers clean of the blood. Beechey was hurt and with the morning now fast encroaching he was powerless to help her.

Contemplating the escalation of recent events he sat and pondered his next action until he could hear movement from downstairs and outside as the servants began to attend to their daily tasks. He was eager to find out what happened to Beechey, but he knew it was now far too dangerous to go near her room and he would be reckless to enter and to try converse with her.

He decided to continue with the original plan and carrying on with the role of Lazar Benedict until the opportunity for him to speak with her and make plans arose. He shook his head assuming that she had been caught by one of the lookouts as she tried to make her escape.

He was still wiping his hands clean on the already bloodied shirt he wore when he fought Elziver Gunn when once again heard footsteps from beyond his door. They stopped and a subtle knock followed. Jem answered the door.

"Would you like a wash this morning sir?" It was one of the house servants.

"Very much so."

Entering the room with a bowl of steaming lavender water and a towel folder across his arm the servant added.

"Mister De Winter requests that you join him for breakfast sir."

"You can tell Mister De Winter that I will be down presently." Jem answered alertly wondering if there were more complications.

"Thank you, sir." The servant finished placing down the bowl and promptly left the room closing the door behind him.

Entering the dining room half an hour later, De Winter, Trevean, Rinold and the Countess were already seated and engaged in deep seemingly jovial conversations. Greetings and the usual polite gestures of acknowledgement were offered and nothing appeared unusual and nobody seemed uneasy. Copious amounts of food were perfectly laid out ready for the predators to demolish.

"Eat and eat well Mister Benedict." De Winter said. "For today is a day of celebration."

"How exiting and may I be as bold to ask the reason for the celebration." Jem asked outright sensing that De Winter had no intention of explaining what he had teased.

"All will be revealed when our last member joins us."

Jem assumed correct and with the lack of an explanation he thought De Winter was referring to Captain Basil. Without drawing attention to himself he watched the buoyant De Winter for a sign which would indicate the reasoning for his excitement, but he saw no clues, only a large piece of roast pork being devoured with zeal.

Helping himself to a selection of meats and egg slices Jem glanced several times at the highly decorated Countess, but on each occasion she deliberately avoided eye contact and continued her pretence of being interested in Trevean's dull exploits and tales regarding his theatrical performances. Nothing in her appearance or demeanour suggested last night's intimacy.

Several minutes later, Jem almost choked on his meat when he heard De Winter suddenly announce.

"Ah Dorathea."

"Rosanna."

"Of course how careless of me."

Looking up in the direction of the door Jem saw that the empty chair at the table was for the female spy and not Captain Basil as he mistakenly expected.

"Join us and eat since I have an announcement to make." De Winter said rising to greet and lead the woman by her hand to the seat next to Jem.

The minutes seemed to crawl ponderously by before De Winter ended the speculation by announcing he wanted to invite Rosanna Bonney into the society that is if Jem offered his blessings to which he had no option, but to smile and nod his affirmation. Trevean added that he needed her back in his show as they had just one more vital performance to play out and it was too late to find an alternative cast member.

Countess Van Buren told how she had checked and conducted investigations into the loyalties of some of the more very influential possible recruits and Trevean said that with just one more show they were sure to gain the support and the financial backing of these people.

When Jem asked how just one show could bias these people's opinions De Winter intervened and informed that the performance will be more than just a show. He said that after the performance had finished, they intended to invite Sir Ramsey Rothsby onto the stage to make a political speech.

With everyone knowing that Rothsby is a prominent Jacobite there would be almost an immediate uprising when he is murdered in full view of the audience.

Everyone would automatically assume that the murderer was loyal to the Hanoverian government and they would flock eagerly to offer their support and make their donations to the Society's cause.

Beechey and Jem recalled the plan from the one which failed in Durham when the society tried to arrest then execute a leading Catholic, Lord Halivard.

Knowing most eyes around the table were fixed on him Jem suspected there was more to come.

"And the murderer is?" He asked.

"You are of course." De Winter confirmed what Jem already feared. "Only a man of your capabilities would have any chance of escaping such an infuriated crowd."

"The son of a Jacobite slaying one of his own?" Jem stated his false concerns.

"You shall not be recognised." Trevean interrupted, "my cast excel with the painting of faces."

"This will not be another Durham." De Winter boasted holding stare directly at Trevean.

"This is to be the Royal Oak Productions grand finale and the precursor for the new rising." Trevean assured.

Leaving the room, De Winter announced that Trevean, Benedict and Rosanna must make their preparations immediately. The show must be ready to go ahead for the following week.

Chapter 11

Following breakfast and the subsequent disintegration from the dining room, Jem assembled the soldiers for training whilst Countess Van Buren revealed yet another surprise in her characteristics by offering to take Jacqueline Beechey alias Rosanna Bonney into Manchester to purchase some much-needed new garments. A long rickety coach journey meant they would not be back until late in the evening.

Rousing the men into an orderly congregation Jem's mind was not concentrating on the duties, he was merely going through the motions of training whilst his mind remained confused by both the behaviour and condition of the English spy.

For her to apparently escape and return suggested to him that something was severely wrong and then the blood implicated more worry and now two hours later she seemed healthy and undisturbed by any concealed wound.

All day long he pushed and pushed the men through many arduous tasks associated with military training and repetitive drilling associated with a crack unit of fighting men until gradually he could sense that his sustained efforts were beginning to yield results.

Instead of guiding, disciplining and organising the men into a solid unfearing fighting unit his aim was to push them so hard with the long bouts of training so that they would become disgruntled, exhausted and too weak to fight. He aimed to break their moral and force many of them to desert and disappear in the night when the realisation that army life was an enduring affliction they could no longer bear. By late that evening the mere mention of the name Lazar Benedict around the camp was considered as foul as the name of King George amongst the grumblings of the soldiers.

Leaving the exhausted men to their campfires and curses Jem returned to the house to clean himself for supper. He had not seen anyone from the hierarchy since breakfast and crossing the semi dark courtyard he paused and waited when he saw the Manchester carriage return. The gave him only the briefest of greetings before disappearing quickly behind the huge door of Temple House, but Beechey deliberated a few moments as she gave instructions to the house servant who arrived to carry her purchases.

Looking more like a woman should in her new clothes and glowing in the female radiance of which they all seem to omit when they put themselves in something new Jacqueline Beechey still failed to show signs of any injury or wound.

They walked intentionally slow together and they spoke cautiously, but with the fear of peering eyes upon them they proceeded nonchalantly across the cobbles and towards the door.

"How delightfully charming you look Miss Bonney." He complimented moving alongside her.

"I'm pleased my appearance agrees with you, Mister Benedict."

"Your transformation is extraordinary. Had I not seen you with my own eyes, I wouldn't have thought such a beautiful woman could exist within the beast I encountered last night and this morning." He whispered.

"Appearances can be so deceptive Mister Benedict. As you well know." She raised her newly painted eyebrows

"Especially with good reason." He nodded.

"Even more so."

"And the reasons to your behaviour Miss Bonney." He enquired.

"Can you elaborate, Mister Benedict?"

"If you want me to be more precise. The sudden change in your attitude and the more rational and calmer approach to our current situation."

"Like you. I too had a little education last night and with the subsequent allowance of time was able to reconsidered my evaluations and position."

"Oh." They delayed their advance to the house for a moment as Jem scraped the mud from his boots. "Maybe you could be so courteous as to elaborate."

"Of course. After you so kindly locked me in your wardrobe and forced me to listen to your affairs and your amorous activities I decided that you may have just been telling me the truth after all, so as soon as an opportunity arose I decided to catch up with this alleged rider of which the bitch bragged about."

"I deduce from the blood that you are an excellent horsewoman."

"After squealing out information like a true traitor I had no option, but to kill the Captain."

"Captain?" Jem speculated, his eyes widening.

"He claimed to be a high and mighty Captain. Captain Basil, but it made no difference to me. He was still a traitorous pig."

"And his confession proved to you my loyalty?"

"Evidently so for I wouldn't be stood here had he not convinced me of your authenticity by informing me he was on a mission to check your credentials. He admitted De Winter has concerns."

"You make the task sound so simple and easy."

"Task? Surely not. A mere child has the ability to catch up and sneak up on an unwary traveller, especially when his conscience is occupied with treachery and his senses are employed with false wisdom."

"A mere child could not however could not detain and force a confession from a skilled man of credibility and loosen his tongue into a confession."

"How astute you are. Let it never be said Mister Benedict that your mind is not as sharp or indeed as equally active as your loins."

Jem found himself unable to rebuff the woman's sarcasm as nearing the house Trevean opened the door and stood before them.

"Ah Captain Benedict, Rosanna how pleasant." He bowed displaying surprise. "I'm pleased to come across you both together. Dinner will be in one hour and afterwards I would like us to discuss the planning for the show.

"I have no problem with that." Jem answered promptly.

"Nor I. I find the chance to finally do something firmly positive quite exhilarating." Beechey followed without concern.

"I'm sure the communication will excite you my dear." Trevean smiled condescendingly at Beechey then he spun on his heels quickly to disappear inside the house leaving them to enter the long hallway together.

Without daring to risk any further comments, Jem bid Beechey good evening politely adding that he was looking forward to dining with her later in the evening. Remaining silent she did not return the compliment nor his smile.

The meal of banquet standards passed relatively unconcernedly for the highwayman and the spy and only when the rather sour De Winter left the room to attend to some private business did Trevean openly speak about his plans for the show.

To avoid scrutiny and criticism he waited deliberately for De Winter to leave the room before he started discussing his plans. During the meal it was obvious to Trevean that De Winter was waiting for him to make the first move.

It was obvious to the inharmonious company around the table that De Winter seemed frustrated and agitated. He bellowed at and humiliated the table servants, his mood seemed pugnacious and pensive, he seemed disturbed about something and he switched his temperament without warning from one of wit to vexation and then from enjoyment to indignation.

Nobody and especially Trevean dare to risk speaking unfavourably for fear of being humiliated by De Winters razor tongue.

Jem and Beechey were the only two present who had any notion of the cause of De Winters grievance.

Now free to speak at will, apart from the inevitable interruptions from the interfering Countess Van Buren, slowly and deliberately, but with increased enthusiasm Trevean revealed the societies plans for the Royal Oak Theatre's production. His aim was to produce and perform one final show at the Coliseum in Manchester, the grand finale was to be the new and very controversial, The Changing Tide by Benjamin Bohunt. Trevean explained that it was a tale of poverty, criminal injustices and political scandal. It's one and only purpose was to spread the mood of rebellion and gain the favour and support of the locals.

Trevean insisted that the show had to be fully rehearsed with new costumes made and fitted, stage set and scenery built, posters printed and displayed. All must be in place and ready for the deadline of the following Friday, in exactly eight days. He boasted that he had reworded the script near to the end so that Sir Ramsey Rothsby could be invited on stage to deliver his condemning views on the current regime as part of the play. Finally he closed by saying he had received confirmation of Rothsby's participation and that he needed both Beechey and the Countess Van Buren to work with Trevean's crew first thing in the morning to begin the alterations of the costumes.

Initially protesting by claiming sewing was beneath her status in the society, Arrabella Van Buren begrudgingly submitted herself to the task after she had reflected on De Winter's agitation.

Leaving for a port and a smoke he turned and added that Jem should confirm with De Winter, when he showed signs of being more amiable for the final details of the assassination.

Passing the next hour or so with large drinks, light-hearted debate and teasing clever word play Jem, the Countess, Rinold and Beechey all soon found themselves being willingly overwhelmed by the powers of the strong spirits. Trevean returned and drank liberally with Rinold at their usual fastest pace. The Countess kept up with them as if to prove she was more than their equal in everything and Jem and Beechey matched their volume to stay clear of any suspicion and increase a bond of trust.

The jovial atmosphere and teasing puns were suddenly drawn to an abrupt halt when Rinold's advances became too unpleasant for Beechey. The laughter and spirited gaiety suddenly seized when Beechey struck out and slapped Rinold so hard across the face her palm left a white imprint on his rosy cheek. Her reaction was drawn after a comment he whispered in her ear concerning the pair of them uniting in his bed.

Unrepentant about the blow she was just about to throw her drink into Rinold's eyes when Jem clasped tight her arm and squeezed until he forced her to drop the drink and then as her superior, Lazar Benedict he ordered her to apologise and leave the room. Her eyes glared of defiance, but she obeyed after a tightening of the grip increased and only for the sake of her mission and her determination for revenge. This was the utmost importance to her and vengeance was deeply set in her mind at all times.

After she had left the room Jem apologised for her behaviour and for any embarrassment she had caused and he bid the company good evening, concluding that he intended to teach his servant some manners on orderly conduct in the presence of leaders and gentlemen.

"Needs a damn good spanking." Rinold advised, ignorant of her combat abilities.

"And wouldn't you like to be the one to doing it." Jem heard the Countess comment as he closed the door behind him.

Angry words of jealousy and sarcasm were exchanged, but uninterested in their views Jem left the muffled barracking behind him as he chased after his comrade.

"Miss Bonney." He called to halt her stride just as she reached the foot of the stairs. "We must talk." He said as she turned to wait for him whilst rubbing her sore arm.

"I sincerely agree with you Mister Benedict." She answered in a soft hush but, with an undertone of anger.

"My room?" Jem offered.

"Not if my life depended on it." She rebuffed with an accusing scowl. "My room where I know the door will not be locked."

"Whatever makes you feel comfortable?" Jem smiled, recalling the previous evening's escapade and the hilarity of Beechey being detained in the wardrobe.

Silently, together they followed the corridor down to Beechey's room where after a discreet look in both directions they entered after a hesitated delay.

Closing the door behind her, but remaining only far enough away from Jem so he could hear her hushed words Beechey began.

"I owe you an apology, Mister Rose."

He titled his head to listen, but her words lacked sincerity. "Then why do I feel as though I'm not going to receive one."

Increasing the flame on the lantern to illuminate a splash yellow across the room Beechey said. "Because the mere idea of being indebted to a man of your standing repulses me."

Beechey was a lady of her time and even though she mixed with the lower classes on a regular basis as part of her duties, she found it challenging to be alone and especially in her private room with someone of a low life social status.

"Forgive me.... Had I known I would have saved you the embarrassment of living." He curtsied, "and as a man of my standing it is obvious to all who care to see that you actually prefer the company of and are more at ease with traitors, all of whom have the lowest standards than your mere lowly, but loyal subject."

"Please lower your voice. I knew my words would disturb you." She conveyed for calmness by expanded her hands.

"No... No my Lady. It is I who speak the words that hurt." He positioned himself nearer to her.

"Please Mister Rose this is neither the time nor the place to try and express one's grievances." She avoided his advance and stepped back until she was stopped by the door.

"Then tell me Lady of the higher social class. What do you consider we, yes we, we do now?"

"We do as De Winter asks. For the time being."

"Leading us to where?.... death for treason or death for spying. For every day we spend here, the more dangerous it will become."

"Play along to his tune and we will be safe." She nodded assertively.

"You sound confident."

"Why shouldn't I be? De Winter is focusing all of his attention on the movements in the borders. He feels he is assured of success here and he is so occupied with joining Charles Stuart that he is blind to the incompetence's of his generals here."

Suddenly and totally unexpected Jem lunged at the woman. He latched his arms tightly around her waist clasping tight her hands by her side and he hauled her backwards over his shoulder to fall on the bed. Landing on top of her he held her resistance firm enough to lock his mouth against hers.

At that moment the door opened and Trevean stood in the doorway. Easing her struggle at once, Beechey realised that Jem must have heard Trevean approaching and now instead of resisting his advances she enthusiastically responded to them.

"Please, please, forgive me and my interruption. I thought I heard voices." Flustered with embarrassment and jealousy Trevean tried to make an apology for the intrusion. He didn't know what to say or how to say it.

"Good god Sir. You probably did. But just who in the name of the Lord did you expect to be in here Charles Edward Stuart himself!" Jem broke from the embrace to feign rage.

Mantling an expression of disappointment rather than anger Trevean stood in the despondent between the frame. He felt as though a he had been robbed of a treasure he had been pursuing for a long time.

His eyes flickered and his jaw dropped. He wanted the women for himself. He had been grooming her and he had been saving his advances until the day of recompense where he had high hopes of forging a long relationship with her, but now he realised it had all built on a false vision and his dream had been shattered.

"Well then? Either join us or take your leave." Beechey challenged reading the embarrassed man's expression perfectly.

"On this occasion I think I will choose to decline your invitation." He quaffed with a distinctive tremor of humiliation which matched his ever reddening cheeks. "Forgive my intrusion." He muttered closing the door behind him.

"Dare to come this close to me again and you'll be heading for one quick journey to hell." Beechey warned pushing Jem from her and rising with haste.

"You've got a fanciful imagination. Why don't we compromise?" Jem said, allowing his good looks to carry the proposition.

"Compromise is for the weak." She confidently spat readjusting her clothing and her hair back to a state of relative comfort.

Jem smiled briefly as he watched the female inside her subconsciously rule her thoughts momentarily and dictate her actions. She immediately saw his reaction and with her face flushing a slight pink she continued.

"If you have finally finished the cynicism and the ogling may we continue with the Kings duties?"

"We?" Jem began to question, "I think the plural is slightly more than optimistic. As far as I am concerned my duty to the King will be repaid in full when I take you back to the Baron of Ripon."

"Take me back?" She questioned.

"Exactly." He pressed an ear to the door, but confidant all was safe he explained. "I've done all I can here. All I need to do now is safely complete your journey home. My duty to the King will be served, my crimes against Society pardoned and I will be once more a free man."

"It's not that simple Mister Rose. Firstly, I need no escort and secondly, and most importantly, I intend not to return home. At least not just yet." She said determinedly.

"I'm sorry to disappoint you, but I'm afraid it is that simple, my sentence has been served and my debt and my conscience cleared."

"Conscience." Beechey snapped. "It seems you have neither a conscience nor loyalty for surely whilst the society remains at large to pose threats and continue with their acts of treason you would not even contemplate your duty as fulfilled."

"My agreement with the Baron was to return you alive to him." Beechey's face stone and her eye bore straight at his face as he spoke. "And that was all."

"Typical of a thief and a vagabond to try and clear himself of any deed which might just need the slightest trait of honour. Your chivalry Mister Rose, sits well within the ranks of the traitors." She cursed insults to provoke his integrity.

"And your remarks, my lady will neither change my opinion nor rouse my conscience for once I have returned you to Ripley and handed you over to the Baron of Ripon my duties will be accomplished and my debts repaid in full. I will once again be a free man again."

"Then you are simply a coward, Mister Rose. At first you hide behind a robbers mask now you are hiding beneath paltry excuses of present terms. I wonder just how far you are from the real Lazar Benedict for at least he was only a traitor and not a coward. I pity you, Mister Rose for being such a hollow form of life." She turned her back on him and walked towards the window to look out into the darkness.

"Your opinions of me do not sway my intentions. I have felt the cold breath of death upon my face too often and once my duty is done my loyalties lie unto myself."

"Then I'm afraid, Mister Rose your duty will never be completed, your sentence never served and your life will not be yours to live again because I do not intend and nor will I allow you to return me to Ripley. I would rather die alone fighting against the traitors in this building than to simply turn my back and give rise to a rebellion. It is not an option I can even consider."

"Then with certainty you will be captured. They will show no you mercy."

"Life itself shows no mercy and I've come to expect no mercy, just as I myself offer no mercy," she spoke with her back to him, but her voice pained signs of disappointment as she tried to change to his mind, "you stay with me, Mister Rose and see out your duty to the King and your country to the full or it all ends here tonight."

Gazing at his reflection in the shadow she tried to interpret his expression. "Either against you or against the society." She now turned her stern countenance to face him directly.

"I certainly haven't come this far to simply report all I know to the Baron." Jem ignored her threat. "If we leave now whilst they suspect nothing we can successfully bring down the Society of Revolutionary Jacobites."

"I'm not prepared to take that risk." Beechey was unwilling to compromise, "the Society has agents everywhere. As soon as we leave here the news will travel fast and De Winter and his accomplices will be free to escape to Europe. I'm not willing to let that happen. I am to remain here and I want you by my side." She held a silence for a moment hoping the highwayman would relent. "Stay with me Mister Rose and do your duty for once." He knew she was deliberating her next action. "Stand and fight by my side or die along with the traitors of the Society." Beechey's hand was obscured from Jem's view underneath her petty coat, but he knew she was holding tight and prepared to unleash at any moment a concealed weapon.

Jem knew his options were limited. If he decided to leave alone, he would have to fight and subdue Beechey without causing any disturbance, noise or alarm. This would be almost impossible with all the society's leaders residing in the large house with the echoing corridors and from what he had seen of Beechey's skills he knew that she would be very difficult to suppress or restrain.

His mind processed scenarios over and over very quickly. He sat on the edge of the bed and sighed as he studied yet again all possibilities.

If he did manage to successfully overcome Beechey and escape, then he feared his freedom would only be short lived for the Baron of Ripon would submit huge resources to have him tracked down and brought back to justice for abandoning the agreement, and then there was one more reason why Jem should not jeopardise the mission. Should he escape the fear of vengeance being taken out on his son's by the Baron's or more likely his associate tormented his mind.

If he left Beechey would be certain to be caught and tortured to death. He didn't believe for one instant she could have any type of success and live without his assistance, cooperation and involvement.

Jem did not want any harm to come to her and when all the options were considered Jem concluded he could not leave Beechey. There was no escape from the mission. He knew, no matter how hard he would try and convince her to leave she would not yield and accept his reasoning. He moved to the bedside chair dropped his body into the seat and began to remove his boots.

"What are you doing?" Her eyebrows raised.

"You win." He said throwing down one boot and tugging on the heel of the other. "We will do this your way. I can't leave, you've made it impossible for me." He answered and then he began to explain in detail why he had decided to stay and fight by her side, but only if she agreed to one condition and that was he must spend the night in her room.

Reacting to her repulsed cold scowl and the immediate and emphatic dismissal he stated he could not leave her room because he knew Trevean would hear the opening and the creaking of the door. His early exit from the bedroom may raise further suspicion on the pair because Trevean would be fully expecting the Captain to have intimate relations with his spy, especially after what he had just witnessed.

Jem displayed an accompanying smile as he explained, but Beechey was not amused. However, she knew he was right agreed and for tonight and tonight only she stipulated Jem could sleep in the chaise until first light under the strict instruction and full agreement that he would not leave the seat. Jem agreed and Beechey lowered the lamp light and slide under the bed sheet fully clothed.

Together cautiously in the dark they discussed and planned out their next moves with Jem insisting they must make contact with the Baron to inform him of everything they knew. They had too much valuable information to risk losing if they were uncovered as enemy agents.

Beechey didn't like the suggestion. She considered it was too risky and she held a suspicion that Jem would not return, she did not trust him. The debate continued, but eventually and together they decided that Beechey would ride to Ripley the following evening and tell the Baron of Ripon everything she knew about the Society of Revolutionary Jacobites, the Royal Oak Theatre company, Temple House and finally after Jem's uncompromising insistence, the actions of Jem Rose, the hero who had saved her life when it was in peril.

Jem doubted Jacqueline Beechey's ability to make the journey, he knew even with his horse mastery and knowledge of the road that it would be a very difficult challenge, but again Beechey was relentless with her firmness.

She insisted she could make the return journey in less than 10 hours and that the Baron would listen to her facts without any doubts whereas, if Jem made the journey she told him without hesitation, she feared that he may decide not to return and also the Baron may not believe Jem until he had sent officers to check out his story. If this occurred the mission would fail because of either Jem's absence or the lengthy delay in verifying his information.

Again Jem had no option, but to agree to Beechey's terms. He would prepare her the best horse in the stables and she would return on a fresh ride provided by the Baron.

As daylight broke through the condensation on the window panes Beechey stretched out and turned towards a vacant chaise where Jem had been slouched. Laid on the bed, still in her evening attire and with her hand tightly holding the concealed dagger she hadn't slept very well, but at some point in the early hours of the morning she had drifted into a light slumber.

In a strange way she had relaxed with Jem's presence in the bedroom. She had not felt overly threatened by the stranger in her room and she even felt at ease for the first time in this lair of deceit and evil. Even though she held the knife for protection she had been sure she would not need to use it and now she was pleased she her assessment of the man's dignity had been proven correct.

Jem wasn't comfortable nor his mind at ease enough for him to sleep. As soon as the opportunity arose he quietly left Beechey's room and laid on his own bed mulling over their conversation trying hard to convince himself he had made the correct decision by agreeing to her plan.

He visualised the route Jacqueline Beechey had to take. He knew most of the roads and tracks well and the difficulties she would encounter at this time of the year and especially during the night when the roads would be muddy and slippery.

Chapter 12

Their 5th day in the garrison passed by without any alarming events or incidents.

Countess Van Buren, Trevean and Jacqueline Beechey read through Trevean's notes for the play and agreed on a few minor changes and then collated the rest of the cast to commence reversals.

Countess Van Buren collected the costumes and set off to Manchester to find a clothier to make the required alterations.

De Winter and Rinold left Temple House early without informing anyone of their plans or movements and Jem spent most of the day on the assembly grounds with the troops to again relentlessly push them hard with drills and routines of parading, marching and charging at targets with their halberds, pikes and swords. Then he made the hours seem eternal by instructing them clean to their equipment repeatedly before loading and reloading practice with muskets numbed their hands and faces in the bitter wind and sideward rains which battered the landscape throughout the entire day.

Evening dinner was subdued due to everyone seemingly exhausted or in Trevean's case disenchanted because of the previous evening's frustration and dismissal.

To Beechey's and Jem's pleasure the leaders all retired to bed early giving Beechey the ideal opportunity to leave Temple House earlier than expected to begin the perilous night ride to Yorkshire in the driving wind and rain.

Before sneaking out into the darkness they hesitated and paused once more to briefly consider the options, complications and considerations for success and failure. For a moment they considered if the early retirement to bed by the leaders was trap laid out by De Winter, but the hesitation was brief and soon dismissed and so quietly and studiously they slowly made their exit from the house, Jem to stealth fully remove the guard who was on look out and Beechey to the stables.

The horse, a large solid 15 hand Percheron was prepped and ready to go and within a few minutes Jem had returned to cover the hoofs with a muslin bag as Beechey secured the saddle and applied her gabardine riding coat.

Jem led the muscled beast to the stable door and as Beechey mounted the Percheron he placed his hand delicately upon hers as she steadied to adjust her non lady like position with the pommel.

At first her reaction was to gaze at Jem with distain, but this soon relented when he wished her luck and thrust into her other hand a route map he had drawn out the previous night. Then as quickly as he had placed his hand upon hers he removed it and stated if she wasn't back by first light he would make his escape from Temple House.

Again Jem did not sleep much that night. As the rain pelted against the glass panes he relived the events of the past months, he was convinced Beechey could not successfully complete the journey in time. Throughout the night he wondered where she was, what point of the journey she had reached. He visualised her progress through the narrow tracks, unforgiving rises and steep drops of the Pennines. The weather was foul and it would hinder her speed, the heavy rain would make the roads treacherously muddy and slippery. Still he doubted she could make the return journey within the time frame.

To distance himself from the uncertainty he collected what few items he possessed and planned over and over his own escape. He had prepared another fine horse and if she had not returned by first light he would make his escape.

As the dawn broke without any sight of the returning rider, he carefully opened his bedroom door and stealthily crept out of Temple House and towards the stables. The damp cobbles displayed residue of recent horse prints. He looked over to the house and specifically at Beechey's room window wanting to see something to give him a sign of hope, a light or a womanly figure at the window, but there was nothing and he dismissed the prints as he continued to enter the stables.

Inside the stables and as he neared his mount he noticed all the bays were occupied. He checked the bay where Beechey's stallion had been tethered. The Percheron wasn't present, but it had been replaced with another steed and it was obvious to Jem the horse had endured a very recent and arduous journey.

It's breathing was still heavy, sweat was sweeping down it's front and mud layered the horse's legs and body. Jem's heart raced and his pulse increased with speculation swirling in his thoughts. As quickly as possible he scurried around for a cloth to wipe down the horse and once complete he made his way to the encampment to nettle the soldiers by arising them to the accompaniment of dawn's birdsong.

At assembly for breakfast back in Temple House, Jem was relieved to see his assumptions were correct. Beechey arrived at the table looking extremely pale, narrow eyed and almost at the point of exhaustion. She informed the group that she did not feel well, she had not slept at all and that she must be suffering from some sort of ailment. Not wanting to spread the virus she instructed the servant to pack her a tray with bread, fruit, cheese and a hot honey and lemon drink and to deliver it to her room.

She informed everyone she was returning to bed for a few hours and that she would re-join the shows preparations just after midday.

Trevean enquired if she would like a doctor, but departing the room, she insisted that she would rest for a few hours and to call a doctor if she felt no improvement.

The day was a pure repeat of the previous day for Jem and most of the group. Beechey appeared at midday and fully recovered she joined Trevean along with the Countess to concentrate on the shows preparation.

De Winter and Rinold were nowhere to be seen and Jem worked exceptionally hard to de-motivate the now disgruntled troops and the hours soon passed by without him being challenged.

The troops were subdued and disillusionment now embittered their thoughts. Gone were their ideals of enlisting for an unchallenging quick profit and by the minute it was becoming more evident to Jem that his plan was working, but still he aimed to be relentless and work them hard until he was convinced they were on the verge of collapse.

The first opportunity for Jem to speak with Beechey arose as the leader's gathered in Temple House for late afternoon tea. Whilst the leaders were preoccupied and in deep discussions regarding Charles Edwards Stuart's movements, Beechey entered Jem's room to enthusiastically explain how she had successfully completed the journey and communicated their knowledge back to the English secret service.

She explained when she reached Ripley the Baron was not at home so rather than trust a servant with the information she exchanged the horse and rode a further five miles to speak with Sir Clifford Cornell. She had explained the details of society's revolutionary plot, her knowledge regarding the position of Charles Edward Stuart, the Society's resources, their ambitions and all their contacts.

At first she disclosed that Cornell seemed perplexed and unsure what actions to take, he seemed to be indecisive and hesitant. It was plain to her that he was aghast with the level of success the spies had achieved, but after venting his temper towards the traitors he thought it would still be advantageous if Beechey and Jem continued with the society's plans right up to the point of the planned assassination of Rothsby. After gathering his thoughts he communicated his thoughts and plan to Beechey by stating in the days which remained before the final show he would communicate to the Baron of Ripon and the English government all the events thus far, the progress and plot all as described by Beechey's report.

He explained the English government would permit him to immediately, but discretely assemble a unit of superior troops capable of eliminating the rebels and also allow him to make full arrangements in unison with the society's plans so that the Baron and some of his troops would surround the theatre and halt proceedings only moments before the assassination was due to take place. This way he told Beechey, the English troops could capture or kill De Winter, Trevean, and the Countess Van Buren whilst they were all assembled in the theatre and at the same time send troops to subdue Tavish, Rinold and the collection of rebels at the grounds of Temple House.

Cornell assured Beechey that this was the best action to take and not to delay her return so not jeopardising the mission. He assured her that he would track down the Baron of Ripon immediately, inform him of all the details and start proceedings to foil the traitor's ambitious plans.

He supplied another fresh horse and gave Beechey a fresh and dry over garment and some re -nourishments all the time urging her to return with haste to Temple House.

She concluded he was excitingly overwhelmed by the news and their plans to thwart the society's mission, but no doubt she concluded with Jem's agreement That Cornell would be simultaneously planning his own self gains within the higher realms of the government officials and maybe even seeking a reward from King George himself for his part in thwarting the treacherous plot.

The final days of preparation passed by without any further incidents or alarm. Everyone was occupied with their assigned duties and by the evening most were exhausted and willingly retreated to their rooms and the comfort of a warm mattress.

It was during these calm periods that Jem and Beechey secretly met to discuss the events of the day. Over a small port and a dimmed lantern they discussed new developments or suspicions and their plans to prevent the assassination and scupper the supply of reinforcements for Charles Edward Stuart.

Over the passing nightly discussions Jem and Beechey's relationship developed endearingly into a bonded trust. Jem did not attempt any unwanted advances and over the nights which followed they began to understand each other's beliefs. Beechey told Jem everything regarding her life, her marriage and how she became to hate De Winter and why she needed to administer revenge and finish the mission to finally close this chapter in her life.

Jem for his part listened carefully as the tale of deceit and hate developed and it enabled him to fully understand Beechey's resilience and the reasons for her cold behaviour and her uncompromising traits and mannerisms.

He was brutally honest when it came to conversing his story. Beechey was compelled furtively to listen to his bold tales of early adventure and the fall from grace into the heinous highway thief, adventurer, widower and the dual life of a scandalous perpetrator.

She found it difficult to understand and relate to the thief, but she refrained from judgment and commented only that his truths could never be described as dull and lame. She admired his boldness, his strength of character and over the passing nights she began to form a fondness and friendship for the Yorkshire man. The mutual friendship and closeness continued as they approached the end of what seemed to be an endless week.

Chapter 13

On the cold autumn Friday the market town of Manchester was a hive of activity. Trevean had warned and enthused with the leaders to expect the show to be a total sell-out.

He had been given a warm welcome in the region weeks earlier and the crowds he assembled with his preaching and pamphlet issuing were receptive to the performances bias messages. He was not wrong.

Outside the theatre hall where the show was to be performed large crowds were gathering, eagerly waiting for the entrance doors to be opened. Masses of people were bustling to ensure they would get inside, the local women were rushing to finish their last minute duties and the men gathered in the ale and gin houses to consume as much pre-show alcohol as they could. After tasting the fervour for himself, like an excited child Trevean headed backstage to pass on the news to the principal entourage hoping to receive some well deserved praise from De Winter or at least the Countess .

His hope of recognition was in vain as the leaders demanded and expected nothing less to his obvious disappointment. Nothing was said and praise was not given.

Inside the show was ready. Inflammatory protestant posters were displayed in the entrance, hallways and leaflets were placed carefully on the benches. The stage sets were newly painted and the scenery positioned as prescribed by Trevean. Candles were lit illuminating the pits and lanterns were burning and positioned along the edge of the stage with the reflectors angled perfectly. Back stage the performers were applying the finer points to their specifics as they donned their costumes, fixed their powdered wigs and faces painted with the palest foundation and the vividest rouge.

Smoke and haze from the burning whale oil provided a thin cloudy veil which speckled in the light at the front of the stage and the smell of burning wax with the fresh paint filled the nostrils of the congregation as they rushed in to take their positions.

Jem and Beechey had been given their final instructions from De Winter and they confirmed they knew exactly what was expected. After the performance had finished and with the assassination complete they were told to flee the chaos and take an indirect, but approved and tested route out of Manchester. They would be met at the boundary of Farnworth by Rinold who would then lead them to safety in an unidentified alternative route back to Temple House.

Unable to discuss De Winter's final instructions both Jem and De Winter explained with assured confidence they were to wait at Temple House for Trevean to arrive with further orders, maps and detailed instructions which would be issued to enable Jem to assemble the troops for a speedy departure to unite with Tavish and the army of Charles Edward Stuart.

Trevean and Beechey would assemble the servants to arrange a thorough and final clear out of Temple House and the surrounding grounds. Trevean objected, he conjectured that as a pivotal leader of the group he should accompany De Winter and Countess Van Buren to the rendezvous point with Edward Stuart, but De Winter immediately berated Trevean and he soon retracted the appeal and the suggestion as De Winter confirmed he would ensure the heroism of the assembled individuals would be communicated directly to Charles Edward Stuart by De Winter personally. Rinold added that Jem would have no problem leading the Manchester troops out of Lancashire to meet up with the forces of Charles Edward Stewart due to the local constabularies being occupied and detained in Manchester and the surrounding towns and villages as they tried to restore calm and order in the communities.

Beechey conceded to Jem quietly this seemed a reasonable plan considering the events which were to unfurl in the raging, inflamed scenes which were sure to develop on the streets of Manchester and subsequently spread to the local districts fast.

The cast were excited, some experiencing last minute pre-show nerves, but the majority of them had no idea of the secret plot and they were ignorant of all treachery concealed within the villainous performance.

Right on time the theatre hall doors opened and the eager crowd began to fill the hall and take to their seats and pews. There was no hesitation, ambling, needless talk or indecisive wondering and looking for the best positions. The audience rapidly filled the whole building, taking up all the available positions, including standing for four rows deep along the side and rear walls.

All the seats were taken except the five which were reserved and guarded for De Winter, the Countess, Rinold, Sir Ramsey Rothsby and his guest.

Jem watch the show performers from the side of the stage. Stood within the darkness and concealed form view behind the scenery he could see the engaged and wide eyed crowd and from his position he had a clear view of six guests of honour as they occupied their seats.

Beechey viewed the performance on the opposite side of the stage to Jem. They could not see each other, but occasionally their concentration subsided to wonder on the thoughts and the whereabouts of their partner. With their gazes focused on the fascinated audience and the surrounding hall they looked keenly for signs of government troops, secret agents and the Baron of Ripon, but they saw nothing as the performers played out their scenes.

Slowly together they became more and more agitated and nervous, their mouths dried and nervously they fidgeted with their fingers and clothing.

Beechey returned backstage for her final costume change, but pulling back the curtain to her changing area she unexpectedly collided straight into Cornell, their faces no more than inches apart.

Both of them instantly responded in a reaction of both shock and took a step back. For an instant neither of them said anything as they stared unexpectedly into each other's eyes. Beechey's mouth gaped as her mind tried to comprehend what Cornell was doing backstage. She quickly glanced in all directions hoping to see the Baron, but only actors crossed her line of sight as they prepared for their next scene. Quickly and very quietly she asked if everything was alright.

Avoid all eye contact, Cornell responded with a nod and replied.

"Yes, my dear." He rested the palms of his hands supportively on her shoulder. "Now please, you must continue with the plan."

Her mind actively wondered what Cornell was doing backstage, she noticed he seemed flustered at seeing her, or was it just her own natural nervousness due to the tension and the approaching conclusion of the plan.

Still, she wondered, he didn't seem his usual confident and arrogant self. As quickly as he had appeared he had disappeared into the dinginess of the backstage corridors.

Again she pondered, but she refused to acknowledge her doubt, reasoning his sweaty nervousness was due to the high risks involved. However she suddenly changed her mind, even though she had only seen Cornell for a few seconds she detected something wasn't right. His expression revealed an uncharacteristic glimpse of which she had not seen or recognised in him before, a glint of treachery. Immediately she set off in the direction which he had disappeared, but there was no time to follow him because one of the stagehands started calling out for Rosanna to take to the stage to perform her final act.

Jem was still watching from the stage side, his nervousness became subdued for the briefest of moments when he watched Beechey step out of her normal comfort zone to perform a humiliating exhibition in a hideous costume. The site of Beechey awkwardly fumbling on stage creased his cheeks, but his pleasure soon expired as the final act began to approach fast without any sign of any intervention.

He began to feel irritated and he gripped hard on the dagger handle which was secured in his belt and under his outer shirt. He watched Beechey completed the scene and depart the stage on the opposite side to him.

He stood motionless, waiting and hoping that at any moment the proceedings would be halted, but bewilderment clouded his thoughts and he sensed betrayal as he watched De Winter arise from his chair to assist Rothsby's assent up the few steps the stage.

Jem's time to act was only seconds away and shaking his head with bile rising from his stomach he watched Rothsby roll out a scroll. After introducing himself he refilled his lungs to recite and hail forth the agitating divines. Every word had it's meaning, every narrative formed a picture, the whole sermon breathed with powerful reverberations aimed to cause dissent and rouse Jacobite support amongst.

Jem felt the presence of someone emerge from the darkness to stand next to him, it was Trevean. Jem's mouth and throat were dry and he began to sweat as his eyes stared and searched the audience and the rear of the theatre for a sign of intrusion. There was nothing, no signs of disturbances with all eyes fixed on Rothsby.

Trevean urged Jem to act. "Now Benedict complete the finale." Jem did not respond. He had heard Trevean but he dismissed his malign enthusiasm. "Go quickly and do your duty."

Trevean sensed Jem's hesitation, his eyes penetrated for a sign of adherence. "Act now before it's too late. Go now and do your duty!"

Jem remained unmoved his eyes searching across the dark figures of the audience for the Baron.

"Damn you!" Trevean shouted as he pushed Jem onto the stage.

Stumbling clumsily out into the light Jem staggered to regain his poise. The calamity caused the audience to laugh and Rothsby to drop his speech as he turned towards the intruder.

Jem was rooted to the spot and he had no time to react as De Winter raced up the steps and lunged forward with his sword to drive it through the back of Rothsby.

Shrieks, yells and screams of anguish and horror bellowed out from down in the pits as blood sprayed out from Rothsby's mouth and nose. His legs disobeyed him and he dropped to his knees with his back towards the assailant, then slowly he fell forwards with his head cracking against the hard surface of the stage floor.

Realising he had been betrayed Jem knew De Winters blade would be coming straight for him next so he withdrew his dagger in a desperate act of self-defence.

"Long live King George!" De Winter shouted to the fleeing crowd as he determinedly lunged his sword towards Jem.

Parring the blade with his dagger Jem winced as he felt the sword scrape deep into the knuckles of his right hand, but with desperate determination, he held firm the dagger and he steadied himself for the following attack. Retracting his sword from the thrust De Winter swung the blade again in the direction of the standing target this time the point of the blade caught and tore into Jem's right shoulder blade.

"You treacherous bastard. I always knew you were an imposter." De Winter yelled as he again drove forward with another strike.

Jem raised his dagger and was prepared to meet the attack, but suddenly a burning spasm of pain shattered through his back and his whole momentum was rocked as he felt the long blade of Trevean's dirk rip straight through his body. Unable to control his actions due the excruciating pain Jem's body defied all control and was thrust from the stage.

Beechey saw the final few moments of the barbaric slaughter. With her feet riveted she witnessed with horror, Trevean run out from behind the curtains and with a demonic rage emblazoned upon his face force his dirk through the back of her partner and continue with the forward thrust until the blade protruded out of the front of Jem's chest. Still driving forward with hate he continued the motion until Jem was pushed from the stage.

Her reaction was to help, but without any noise or warning she felt two arms wrap tightly around her and drag her back into the darkness.

"You must come with me." It was Cornell's voice. She vigorously struggled and forced him to release his grip a little.

"Please it's for your own safety."

Cornell increased the force of the grip and the pair fell backwards taking down with them a part of the scenery.

"The Baron wanted it this way. You must come with me at once."

Beechey was oblivious to his words and her reactions were controlled by fright, disbelief and the revulsion of what she had just witnessed.

The fracas was not noticed by any of the performers. All eyes were animated upon the activities on the stage so Beechey and Cornell wrestled on the floor in the backstage darkness without any intervention.

Beechey bit hard on Cornell's detaining hand and she powerfully jolted her head backwards so that the back of her cranium smashed into Cornell's face cracking his nose and releasing his blood. Forcing him to relinquish his hold and cup his flattened nose with both his hands Beechey had risen up above him and within and instant grabbed a piece of the scenery and smashed it down heavily on the back of his head. Cornell's round went limp and he dropped unconsciously onto his side with blood now pouring from both sides of his head.

To the front of the stage the audience had begun to flee in a revolting and confused panic. As the crowds crushed in the aisles and fought to reach the doorways, pews were knocked over and chairs were thrown in fear and panic.

De Winter held out his hand to pull Countess Van Buren up onto the stage and to lead her away from the frenzied panic below.

Trevean calmly checked to see if Rothsby was dead then cleaning his blade on the discarded scroll he peered down at the motionless body of Lazar Benedict.

In the darkness and mayhem within the theatre Beechey was able to escape backstage and blend into the masses on the street, but behind her as she fled she caught a glance of the Countess leaning low as she tried to revive Cornell.

By her side, De Winter was scowling in the darkened passageway looking for the spy's escape route. He saw nothing, he could not see Beechey in the darkness looking back at him as she fled wiping clear the makeup from her face and cloaking herself in a dark theatrical shawl.

It was very easy for a spy with Beechey's skills to mingle into the fleeing crowds and escape. Taking up a position under a market stall she watched proceedings develop around the theatre kept low as the pursuers, who De Winter had dispatched spread themselves in the wrong direction.

From her position she scrutinised in the distance both the main and the side exit of the building. The throng in the distance were only darkened shadows, but she could deduce from the actions being taken who were just the shows performers and who were the society's leaders.

Two horses were drawn alongside the actors exit for one male and one female to mount and gallop away hastily on the cobbles to the rear, although Beechey could not hear what was being said she could tell by the gestating motion of arms that the male rider was bellowing out orders as he heeled the horse into a charge.

Moments later a cart was driven alongside the door and two males took up the front as three others carried out and tossed into the back of the cart what appeared to be a limp body.

Beechey determined from the silhouetted portly size and by the very tentative movements made by the large male that it was Cornell who had taken up one of the front seats and she assumed the other was Trevean. The cart sped off in the opposite direction to the two horse riders.

Beechey covered in the safety of the shadows whist she composed herself and thought out her next moves. She was hurt from the force of Cornell and the sight of Jem's body being pierced by Trevean's dagger tugged at her stomach. The sight of Jem gasping his last breath of air as he was kicked into the stalls made her sick and now as she witnessed the cowardly traitors bundled his lifeless body onto a cart her fortitude relented and water welled to blur her vision.

Sobbing into her hands she drew in rapid short breaths to try and compose herself. She knew whatever action she decided to take, that she must act decisively and with speed knowing if her father in-law was not already dead then his life was in danger.

She knew the society's plan had not been foiled, although it could not be considered a success either. Sir Ramsey Rothsby had been murdered and an outcry reaction had occurred as intended, however the society knew their highest ranks had been breached by the English spy and the mission was in jeopardy because she had escaped to report back to the Hanoverian government. Beechey also knew the traitors instincts would be for self-preservation and abandoning their associates they would brood only thoughts for their own survival only.

Beechey knew De Winter and his associates would move fast regardless of what action they also decided to take. Rinold would inform De Winter soon the troop's spirit had been broken by Jem and those who had not deserted in their Captain's absence were not fit or suitable to support Charles Edward Stuart offensive assault on England.

Amidst the chaos and confusion on the streets of Manchester, Beechey joined the crowds until she was able to steal an overcoat and then a horse from a coach house. She wasted no time deciding to head back to Temple House for one final scouting mission before returning east to Ripley at full speed to save the life of the Baron and report the facts to the English secret service.

Chapter 14

Although shrouded in darkness, the main gates at Temple House had been spragged open to permit the many hurried exits. From her position of seclusion Beechey could see into the courtyard. The estate had been put on full alert and guards were stationed along the perimeter in pairs. Assembled at the entrance half a dozen soldiers slouched against the railing as they nervously deliberated their new orders.

She could see the building was hastily being emptied of supplies and a convoy of carts rattled passed the soldiers at speed.

After only a few moments of squinting in the dimness Beechey saw a lantern carrying Cornell in discussion with a group of darkened figures in the courtyard. Her eyes followed him as he and an accompanying guard entered a carriage and, only a few yards away from her mounted position in the undergrowth, drove passed het at speed.

Instantly her next action was decided and she motioned her horse towards Temple House. Lowering down into the saddle to swoop in fast on a stationary guard Beechey galloped towards him out of the darkness and grabbed from his unprepared his hands his musket before he could raise the alarm. Continuing to arch without losing any speed Beechey veered away in the same direction of the escaping carriage.

Although the stolen horse was not a thoroughbred it was capable of closing the distance and catch up with the carriage without much exertion.

Beechey composed herself and prepared the musket for action, then drew her horse level with the carriage driver. Raising the musket in his direction she ordered him to halt the carriage. The driver refused to acknowledge the order and ignoring her call he whipped the horses hard to increase their speed. The carriage slid and bounced on the uneven muddy surface alerting Cornell to the danger. Seeing the gun wielding Beechey riding alongside the carriage he pulled down the glass and craned his head out of the window.

"What in the Kings name are you doing woman?" He cussed.

"I'm taking care of the King's business." She shouted holding firm her aim.

"Lower your aim and ride with us to Ripley where the Baron is waiting there for us." He lied.

"Stop the carriage." She ordered.

Cornell knew very well Jacqueline Beechey's abilities and her unrelenting determination. He knew she would never yield and withdraw and shaking his head scathingly he banged hard on the inside roof of the carriage and hailed.

"Faster! Faster damn you."

Within a moment he had disappeared from the window and he was replaced by a guard who began to aim his pistol at the female horse rider. Ignoring his aim and keeping her musket directed at the coachman she pulled hard on the trigger of the musket until orange flame blazed out in the darkness. The force of the blast threw her backwards and out of the saddle of her rearing and frightened mount. However the shot found its target and the velocity of the lead thrust the carriage driver over onto his side, his limp arms releasing control of the reins.

Scared by the explosion, flash of gun powered and the noise of the blast from the musket the carriage horses release a shriek and bolted in a frenzy into darkness ahead. The uncontrolled horses sped into the unlit countryside at full speed dragging the rocking carriage until they had to violently turn for a sharp bend in the track. Pulling the carriage around the curve with an uncontrolled sway it's rear end veered off the track shredding thick undergrowth as it bounced wildly on.

Thudding and the cracking of timber could be heard as the carriage plunged through hedges, bracken and foliage and then it swung back on the mud track it swayed on his axles from side to side. The carriage structure began to creek and bow until the rapid and violent oscillation forced a wheel to give way leaving the carriage to flip uncontrollably over onto it's side. Still panicked the horses continued to pull and drag the carriage for a few more yards until the holding leathers finally snapped releasing the frenzied horses to bolt away unrestrained into the darkness ahead. The carriage slid and bound along the muddy surface for a few more moments until it crashed against a solid tree.

Beechey had regained her composure enough to hear the hideous yell of the horses, the screeching of the dragged carriage and the thud of it's demise as it crashed to a halt.

Cautiously she made her way towards the carriage frowning as she focused hard into the murky darkness ahead.

The lantern on the carriage had spilt it's oil and blue coloured flames were just beginning to rise and scorch the wooden carriage exterior.

She paused her approach to momentarily gaze down at the body of the coachman. He laid face down and motionless in the thick mud and she tapped his body with the side of her foot. When there was no sound or reaction she reached down and grabbed hold of the man's collar and belt to turn him over. For a brief moment she glared at his death grimace and once assured there was no sign of life she reached to his holster and removed his pistol, and then she searched his shoulder pouch for a ball, powder and flint. Once the flintlock was loaded she continued her approach to the carriage.

The only noise to be heard was the rustling of the trees and the popping of the spreading flames. She stopped again, this time by the side of the turned over wreak and ignoring the spread of flames she climbed up and onto the side of the carriage to peer through the broken glass.

The shear blackness made it very difficult to see inside, but after another pause her eyes adjusted enough to allow her to see a bundle of arms and legs belonging to two motionless bodies. She called out Cornell's name and although there was no response she heard wheezing and gurgling as one of the men fought for breath.

She slid the flintlock tightly into her boot and raised herself upwards and onto the carriage door, then she dropped herself inside carefully landing at the side of the mangled bodies. She lowered her face to the wheezing and saw the noise was coming from Cornell.

"We must get you out of here." She warned.

"You stupid bitch. What have you done?" He managed to spit out.

"Save your strength until we get you out of here."

"The Baron wanted it this way." He hissed through his pain.

"I don't believe you." She knew the Baron would never negate a deal and not go back on his word

"It's true."

"You're lying." She began to raise his shoulders, but he resisted as an intense bolt pain spliced his midriff causing him to shout out in pain.

"The Baron didn't want to give the outlaw amnesty." He tried to gather spittle in his dry mouth.

"You're a damn lying maggot. The Baron would never betray anyone." She answered easing him back into a recumbent position.

"Words are nothing." He coughed some blood into his hand. "When the stakes are high." He moaned rubbing his rib cage. "Help me."

"Tell me the truth." She released his shoulders and he winced as his body fell back then she pulled out the pistol and pointed the barrel at his widening eyes. "I know your lying."

"What are you doing?" He pleaded with a throat drying fear then raised his arms in a protective manner to cover his face.

Smoke began to swirl around the window and choke the air.

"You are a lying traitor. I want to know the truth."

"I've told you the truth. The highwayman couldn't be allowed to live." Sweat of fear glistened on his forehead.

"I don't believe you, I know the Baron better than anyone and I know he would never betray anyone. Now if you want to get out of here tell me the truth before it's too late." She gripped tight on his collar and raised his face to the press of the metal barrel. "The truth damn you."

He shook his head and clamped tight his mouth so she pressed the pistol hard until it stopped against the bone in his cheek.

Smoke began to fall thick in the carriage and irritate their throats. They began to feel a shortness of breath and their eyes stung.

"The truth!" She screamed tightening her finger on the trigger.

Cornell began to panic and he spat out. "The Hanoverians are finished. It is time to switch allegiance."

Beechey released his collar and he sagged. She coughed to clear her chest and wrapping her inner forearm around her mouth to act as a screen she repositioned the barrel of the flintlock hard against Cornell's forehead.

"The Jacobites rising will result in the crowning of the true King." He coughed out with a mouthful of more blood. "James will be crowned King when his son Charles Edward Stewart marches into London and captures the throne." He managed to boast of treachery through his pain.

"Where is De Winter?" She demanded ignoring the lung debilitation and the increasing danger.

"He is safe." Covering his mouth and nose with his hand Cornell replied through his fingers. "Now help me. Come with me Jacqueline and assist the rising of the Jacobites. You will not regret aiding the restoration of the King."

The pistol slid into Cornell's eye, but instead of repositioning the barrel the spy pushed even harder and Cornell screamed as unable to retract his head any further the pressure intensified.

"I'm not interested in James Stewart or the Jacobites traitors. My interest lies with only with only one man. Luc De Winter, where is he?"

Beechey gritted tilted her head at an angle as the sound of approaching horses sounded above the crackled of flames.

"I'll ask you one more time. Where is that Dutch bastard?"

Cornell's eyes also shifted towards the carriage window indicating he had also heard the hooves approaching.

"Ah, maybe your fun is over." He smirked and coughing again.

Beechey raised her head through the heavy burning fog to peer out the carriage window at the two approaching riders.

The flames from the burning carriage were now beginning to throw out an orange hue and squinting through watery eyes Beechey could just make out that one of the darkened figure's was fastened to the saddle pommel and he was under the control of the accompanying rider. Blinking to clear her vision she began to climb out of the carriage.

Trevean could clearly see from a distance the woman rising from within the carriage due to the illumination spread from the flames.

He steadied the horses and cast a glance at Jem who was bound tightly with a restricting gag, blindfold and hood. Slowing to a gradual and calm halt, he smiled from the thrill of the unexpected encounter then steadying his mount he withdrew his musket to take aim at his nemesis.

"Out you come Rosanna, Dorathea or is it Jacqueline Beechey." He ordered. "And be quick about it before I blow your head open."

Beechey instantly recognised the voice of the dark figure and with the acknowledgement of her true name she now knew Cornell had told the society everything she had told him.

She glanced down into the smog which was blanketing in layers around the floor of the carriage. Cornell had heard the call and was trying to rise, but before he had the chance to comprehend what was happening beyond the smog Beechey stamped hard on his head with her heel over and over with relentless ferocity until his pulpy head sagged and his body dropped limp beneath the smoke.

She knew that she had little alternative, but to abide by Trevean's order. The carriage was a burning inferno and choking smoke was thick in the air which she was trying to breath. She knew he would not hesitate to discharge his weapon after suffering from the embarrassment and deceit she had inflicted upon him.

"Out now, you traitorous bitch." He bellowed out again. "I won't give you another opportunity."

Trevean's mind was excited by the astonishing invention. Humiliated with the demeaning role of prison guard he was transporting Jem Rose to the docks for shipping to the society's leaders in Europe for torture and interrogation, but now with one of the most distinguished English spies within the sights of his rifle his mind was reinvigorated and he was thriving as he contemplated the gratitude he would receive from the leaders if he presented the renowned spy for interrogation instead of a mere highway man.

Beechey was now beginning to succumb to the effects of the smoke her breathing was laboured and her throat and eyes dry. She knew regardless of the risk she must get out of the carriage. She secured her pistol within her clothing and began to raise herself through the window.

Trevean stared hatred at the woman he once admired, knowing how dangerous she was he took no risks and kept a steady aim upon her as at the same time he slowly withdrew his dirk from within it's sheaf.

With only one shot in the rifle he knew that it would be perilous to use the lead on Jem when faced with the skilled spy of notoriety as Beechey.

"Keep your hands high where I can see them."

Jem was wavering in and out of consciousness as he had done only a few months earlier. The pain, the drowsiness, the hallucinations were all too familiar to him. He could clearly recall what had happened and he understood the current situation, but he was powerless to intervene because his arms were bonded securely to his side with his hands fixed tight to the pommel and his legs bound tightly to the body of his horse. All he could do was helplessly watch the blurry figure against the bright orange glow through his blindfold and listen to the familiar voice of his accomplice shout

"I'm coming out."

Trevean flicked his eyes quickly to Jem as he noticed his head angle slightly towards the call. He knew Jem was listening and trying to understand why the rocking of the horse had stopped.

Confident Beechey was now adhering to his orders Trevean quickly finished removing his knife from it's sheaf and thrust it in the direction of his prisoner.

Releasing a sardonic smile it pleased Trevean that Jem's soul would be forever tormented knowing he went to his grave without being able to help his acquaintance.

Beechey dropped down to the muddy surface and was just rebalancing herself when she witnessed Trevean plunge the knife into the body of the defenceless figure. Her reaction was immediate and in one quick motion she withdrew from her rear to swung around her pistol in the horseman's direction.

"You will pay for this!"

Whilst Trevean performed the unmerciful act he had deliberately not moved his gaze from the spy's movements and when he saw her display the pistol a frown set because disappointedly he knew he had to abandon his plan of capture and shoot. His reactions were moments too late as Beechey's pistol bellowed out flame and noise first.

The sound of shot smacking against and breaking branches was heard beyond the carriage as Trevean's blast went high and skywards as a result of him being struck in the right shoulder by Beechey's pistol ball. He screamed in pain as lead cracked hard into bone and he lost control of his mount as it, along with his prisoner's reared and releasing piercing screeches they both raised high their back legs and began to sprint away in panic.

Trevean had no time to react and he was thrown backwards and out of the saddle releasing both his weapons into the air. The loud crack of his head hitting the mud was stifled by the two spooked horses which disappeared into the corridor of darkness.

Beechey sped towards her assailant who lay still on his back with his head crooked over in an unnatural position.

She touched his arm to feel for any signs of life, but his head dropped limp displaying his twisted death grimace. Knowing his neck was broken she briefly glanced over her shoulder to the orange glow as the now fierce flames fully spread engulfing destruction around the carriage.

Grabbing the knife from Trevean side and wiping the blade clear of bloodied mud on Trevean's lapel Beechey began to run in pursuit of the two scared horses and the captive passenger. She hoped that once away from the smell of gunpowder and the rising ambers the horses would abate from the gallop and ease to refill their lungs with fresh air in the dark and peaceful woodlands.

Her judgement was proved correct after only a few hundred yards she could hear in the darkness ahead the familiar noise of horses rustling in the undergrowth as they pulled, to eat the long damp grass.

Careful not to spook the horses Beechey took her time closing in on the horse until she was within grabbing distance of the reins. Finally holding firm the reins with one hand she pattered the side of the horses with her other hand and she hushed calming reassuring noises to the exhausting beasts.

The man upon the horse was leant over to one side almost in a slumber position, but only as far as the binding would allow. Beechey knew that if she just cut the banding he would probably just fall to his death and so she had to plan carefully how to lower him from the saddle. He was motionless and unresponsive to her call, but she could hear slow and shallow breathing.

She spoke out again to the ailing figure stating that he must remain calm and still whilst she cut him free and lowered him to ground level.

First she loosened and discarded the strapping which was securing the man's legs to the body of the horse, once released she cut the rope which was tight around his body and fixing his arms to his side. Then she slowly untied the leather belt which attached his hands to the pommel. Slowly, carefully and steadily she allowed him to tilt sidewards with his under arm on her shoulder. As he slid from the saddle and on top of her she dug in her feet and straddled her legs to strengthen her position, but it was in vain as she could not hold the man's weight as it shifted from the horse to her shoulders and her legs gave way. They both dropped and collapsed into the foliage. Briefly winded, but unhurt Beechey drew in a few gasps of air before she slowly rolled the man from on top of her and onto his back.

She hauled herself again onto her knees and paused for a second to check if he was still breathing then cradling the back of his head with her palm as she hauled him to a spot where the moonlight could shine full on his injured body. Finally with her left hand she slowly pulled free the hood and released the blind fold.

Beechey jolted back and her eyes opened wide as in the darkness when she saw the beaten face of Jem and not the Baron of Ripon as she had expected. Eliminating her shock, she moved quickly to remove the sodden gag which allowed Jem to draw in one very slow and long breath which prompted him to then cough out violently a mouth full of dark liquid.

Beechey urged him not to speak as she raised up the top half of his body and rummaged in the surroundings for leaves to add padding for comfort. She removed a water bottle from the horse and slowly dripped into Jem's mouth water until she felt he was ready to take a sip.

Slowly Jem started to rouse and his eyelids began to flicker. Using the moon light only Beechey opened up Jem's coat and lightly begin to feel his side area where she saw the knife enter his body. It did not take her long to establish the seriousness of the wound. His vest was sodden with hot blood. She opened up his vest to inspect further the stab wound from the theatre. The large hole in his chest was not patched or treated and although congealed around the edges blood still oozed. Her hand continued to investigate his wounds and they feathered along his side and around his back. She felt her way to the rear wound using the hot tacky liquid as a guide until she found the pierced hole near the centre of his back. She looked around in the surrounding area hoping to find a glimmer of inspiration, but there was nothing except the dark shadows of trees from the silver moon and the rustling of the branches in the light breeze.

Jem was slowly stirring from his unconsciousness and he released a groan as his hand moved to feel the latest wound.

"Hold still, do not move whilst I bind your wounds." Beechey reassuringly said in his ear gently placing her palm on his cold and wet forehead then without any further hesitation she began to remove her outer clothing.

Jem's eyes opened just enough to see a vision of a woman undressing in front of him, but only partially conscious and overwhelmed with pain he quickly dismissed the apparition and his eye lids closed.

Beechey removed her vest and quickly re-dressed in only her outer garment then she cut her vest with her small blade into several strips.

Hauling Jem forward she pulled him more upright until he resisted and yelled out words of anguish.

She urged him to remain quiet and with intrinsic gentleness she poured cold water over the gaping holes, then packing them tight with a compress of grass, mud and leaves she bound the wounds with the strips of her vest. There was just enough water left for her to give Jem one more drink before she made him a comfortable in the resting pad of the foliage. She was convinced he was going to die and she tried to ease his suffering for his final moments.

Unveiling her guard briefly Beechey resistance failed her and she began to cry. Her stern and normally controlled exterior submitted to her grief as she began to explain to Jem what she had seen in the theatre and the events after a show.

At first Jem said nothing and just listened to how Beechey told of Cornell's betrayal and Trevean's demise. She feared for the Baron, but she was still driven by a determined hatred to get revenge on De Winter.

Jem was roused enough to listen in full, at first he found it difficult to comprehend that Trevean 'a singer' could be a cold blooded killer. He expected nothing less from De Winter or Rinold and Cornell's betrayal had not had taken him entirely by surprise either.

Through short bursts of pained words he was able to inform Beechey that he was taken back to Temple House for interrogation, but after only a few minutes of torture by Tavish and Trevean he lost all consciousness. He did however, over hear Tavish and Trevean discussing the society's amended strategy.

He explained that Charles Edward Stuart was nearing Carlisle where he was promised and truly expected the Manchester reinforcements. However De Winter and the Countess could not travel to the Jacobites camp and confess their failings to provide the support of much-needed arms and men, especially since they had just received news that the French were no longer prepared to provide backing for the invasion from the south, and so they decided to close down the whole operation and flee to their headquarters in Holland taking with them all the funds they had raised.

The escaping traitors were to split up and take different routes across England to Whitby where they will secure a passage to Rotterdam. De Winter and the Countess were to journey slightly north and across to Nidderdale whilst Trevean was to travel with Jem direct across the Pennines.

Pausing for breath and fighting against the pain Jem managed to give Beechey all the information she needed to determine the next moves. However, she now faced a major dilemma because Jem also revealed that Tavish had been dispatched to Ripley to kill Edmund Beechey, the Baron of Ripon. This order had been issued directly by Cornell as he had demanded all links to himself must be removed. Tavish was dispatched from Temple House once the clear up was underway, but he was instructed to ride direct to Ripley using the Halifax road.

Beechey paced for a few moments rubbing her hands and twirling into ringlet her long locks as she mulled over what to do next. She could not return to Ripley and then ride on to Whitby or even send troops to Whitby in time to prevent De Winter's and the Countess's departure to safety. Riding to Whitby direct would be her only and her last opportunity to kill De Winter, but it would leave Tavish free to kill the Baron.

Plagued with a dilemma she was gazing out into the moon lit fields and forest when she heard rustling in the foliage to her side. She turned swiftly to see Jem raised on one knee gulping in long deep repeated breaths.

"What are you doing?" She asked as she raced over to kneel by his side, "you must remain still."

"I'll track and catch Tavish." He coughed out with a little blood. "You go after De Winter."

"What? No! It's impossible."

She looked deep into his pain anguished eyes as he continued to rise with one hand pressing firmly to stop the flow of blood from the most recent wound.

"You must." He stated swaying on one knee.

"You'll never make it to Ripley. We need to get you to a surgeon." She shook her head dismissively.

"No! You will never get near to De Winter again if you allow him to leave England now. He can't leave. He must not leave."

"It's too far for you to ride alone in this condition."

"You must get De Winter." He put his hand into hers urging her with an unspoken message to assist him onto his feet. "You can't let him leave England." He pulled hard and she held firm to raise him up to his feet and then lifted his face to look her directly in the eyes.

"I can take Tavish." He told her with gritted determination.

Beechey shook her head but said nothing. She stared in the ground before stating.

"It's impossible. You're too weak." She held out the flat of her hand dismissively. I have encountered too many misguided souls who have given their lives too eagerly."

"I am many things, but I am neither feeble nor delusional."

"Remember at Temple. We promised to trust each other. You can trust me to get Tavish before he kills the Baron."

"It will be suicide."

"I have faced death many times before."

"The ride is long and Tavish is a tough brute."

"Then I die serving my country and saving the Baron, but I promise you this. I will remove Tavish."

She shook her head again, she knew he had once been as strong as a warrior and more than capable of the journey and bringing justice to Tavish, but weakened by the stab wounds and the loss of blood, she feared he would not make the journey and die somewhere on a lonely and dark roadside.

She broke from his strained gaze and turned away as this very slight glimmer of hope encroached into her thoughts. She replayed the word trust over and over in her mind and looked back to see him stumble towards the horse. She felt herself choosing between life and death for either the Baron or Jem.

"He saved me from the noose."

"You have repaid your debt."

"I will not allow the Baron to die. Think about it .... If there is the slightest of chances of getting De Winter you should take it whilst you can."

She shook her head to relinquish the temptation.

"Never again will you get this close to De Winter."

She looked at Jem as he battled through the pain to mount the horse.

"The Baron wants justice for his son's death, doesn't he?"

"More than ever." Beechey couldn't believe that she had allowed herself to succumb to Jem's impossible idea.

The mere notion and slightest hope of saving the Baron and admonishing justice on De Winter biased her better judgement and prevented her from making rational decisions.

"We need weapons." Jem's statement jolted her back from the delusion, but still she could not resist nor deny the opportunity.

"Trevean has a musket and the guard will have a sword." She said quickly.

Within minutes she had searched and stripped Trevean and the guard of their few weapons. A dirk and a musket with ammunition from Trevean and a sword and a knife from the guard.

For a moment they looked at the blazing carriage, resembling an island of light, it's glow and searing heat stretched wide across the track and surrounding woodland. There was no way of retrieving any more weapons from the dead within the furnace.

Beechey issued Jem with the musket, she knew that he would be incapable of slaying Tavish in his condition with a sword, even if he did survive the journey back to Ripley. He objected and tried to insist that Beechey should take the musket, but he knew his plea would be in vain.

"I will take De Winter by complete surprise." She announced. "He will not be expecting a solitary attack."

She moved closer to surprise Jem by wrapping her arms around him. She did not grasp him tight, but tenderly and carefully to kiss him on the side of his swollen face. "Bless you Mister Rose and forgive my misjudged preconceptions."

With those last few words Beechey remounted and healed her horse away into the darkness. She did not look back in the direction of the thrown mud divots, but she had to clench her jaw tight and tense her every fibre to control her misguided feelings and prevent tears from filling her eyes.

"Gods speed Jem." She failed and a solitary bead of water released from her eye and rolled down her face as she acknowledged abandoning the man to die, a man she had grown to admire and trust.

Beechey rode with determined ferocity across the English soil her body in rhythmic sway with the gallop of her horse. She had managed to collect one of the loose carriage horses soon into the journey and so throughout the night she was able to switch her weight from one horse to the other.

Only twice did she stop at coach house and each time it was only for a matter of minutes. Just enough time to water the horses and fill up her water bottle.

Near exhaustion had crept up on Beechey as she calmly rode through the cottage lined tracks which bordered the banks of the River Esk. Not wanting to arouse any suspicion she had slowed down the horse and continued her pursuit at an amble as she encroached upon the unmistakable smell of the sea port and the inimitable North Sea.

Chapter 15

Beechey's body was racked with pain and around her buttocks and inner thighs her skin was raw and the tenderness was exacerbated as the country mud surface developed into hard street cobbles.

Avoiding the main entrance down the hill into the bustling area of Whitby, she used the nooks and snickets for her deliberately careful approach down the hill which led the way to the harbour.

The dawn had risen. Gulls were squawking, cawing and wailing and her nostrils filled with the infusion of salt, fresh fish and smoke houses. The cold breath of autumn howled over the waves of the turbulent North Sea and along the harbour road which paralleled the deep inlet.

Dismounting with a lack of gracefulness to continue down the steep route to the harbour on foot, Beechey had to compose herself to allow her body to become accustomed to being out of the saddle and back on jittery feet. At first her knees buckled and her legs almost gave way as she led her mount passed the White Horse and Griffin then collapsing on to a lobster crate she scouted along Church Street and the wharf.

It was an ordinary autumnal morning, the sky was bright and clear, blowing from the north was the usual cold breeze and to the east the sun had risen slightly above the dark green sea to begin to spread it's warmth and over the chilling breeze which had numbed her cheeks and strained in her lungs.

The night fishermen had returned with their catch and were busy unloading their haul of herring, mackerel, pollock and flounder and as normal the harbour was a hive of activity with sea vessels packed in tight taking every available dock and mooring.

The two largest vessels, the Sea Nymph and the Henry Tudor were in the final stages of embarking to depart, their harpoons confirming whale hunting was their prize, but nothing looked unusual and she could see no sign of the traitors.

An elderly chestnut skinned and pipe smoking man appeared from the rear of the Inn and introduced himself as Samuel. He relieved Beechey of the two horses commenting that they looked like they had endured a tough ride and needed a good watering, feed and rest, then quipped by adding that by her dishevelled appearance and exhausted mannerisms she could do with the same.

As he began to lead the horses away into the stables behind the Inn, she agreed with his assumptions, but she admitted she lacked resources to pay for refreshments until the arrival of her husband later in the day, adding to her tale that upon his arrival in Whitby they are bound for a short business trip to Rotterdam.

A small smile appeared through his thick white beard and he removed his clay pipe to blow out a cloud of grey smoke as he commented.

"Ah that will be the Rode Star.... Or simply the Red Star to us Northerners. Normally sails at noon." He enlightened without looking back. "It's a large coal carrier and it does two round trips every week and takes along a few paying passengers."

He was wily enough not to believe her story and he assumed she was on the run from either a work house or the authorities with plans to abscond on the first available passage.

She had the prettiest face he had seen for months and having no inclination to turn her away he pointed in the direction of the south side of the harbour to indicate where she would find the ship.

"There'll be nothing to see there for an hour or two yet so you can rest up in the saddle room at the back of the stables for a while." He shouted as he led the two horses to the courtyard.

She gladly took up the offer now knowing which ship to look for and it's departure time. Aware she had time to rest she wanted to rebuild her strength for the duty ahead.

After only a short while the stable door rasped open and the pipe smoker entered to the saddle room laden with a tray of bread, lard, smoked kippers and a pail of water.

"I figured you might want a little something to put you on until your husband arrives." He offered and Beechey bolted upright from her slumber.

"Thank you very much Samuel, that's very kind of you."

Her eyes widened and her stomach squeezed.

"Ah... it's nothing. I was getting myself something to eat anyway." He bumped the door with his backside to stop draft. "Coming in on one of the jolly's did you say?"

"I didn't." She replied lifting the tray out of his tobacco stained fingers.

Sensing her lack of willingness to converse he shrugged his shoulders and turned away informing her he would be cleaning out the stalls if she needed anything, anything at all he emphasised.

After thanking him Beechey tucked into the food on the tray with relish and preferring to stand, she ate and drank without a pause.

When the old man returned to the saddle room later to check on his new friend she had gone. The only sign that she had been in the room was the empty tray which was left balanced on a bale of hay. He didn't worry or concern himself with her disappearance, he just shrugged to himself and wondered as to whether to keep or sell the two horses.

Although still very saddle sore Beechey was invigorated and ready to hunt down her prey and enact her vengeance.

Getting onto the Rode Star seemed impossible. The Fluyt was stood at anchor and both entrance boards were raised. Beechey observed the crew, busy with their preparations performing their ritual docked duties of fetching, carrying, scrubbing, folding, rolling, collecting and stacking of crates on the bridge and behind the bulwarks.

She was confident De Winter was not yet aboard and with only one possible approach to the ship and with both boarding ramps still raised she decided to lay in wait and launch into a surprise assault before he had the opportunity to step onto the vessel.

There was lots of morning activity on the North Sea. A few small fishing vessels bobbed in the distance and a constant stream of trade vessels passed by on the curved horizon.

A three mast vessel was towed into the harbour for the unloading of it's coal which was destined for the local Alum factory and from a far Beechey could hear the noise of wood cutting from Jarvis Coates shipyard.

To all around this was going to be just another normal day in Whitby, with the exception of a limited few.

From her advantageous position on the steps of a dark and shadowy stairwell in a steep narrow ginnel, Beechey watched fervently the daily activities and the morning slowly past into noon with the sun rising high above the abbey and glistening on the now calm cyan sea.

Church bells echoed the midday call and just as the steel chimes began to fade Beechey's attention were drawn to the noise of approaching clops of horse hooves and the clanking of carriage wheels on the cobbles.

She half raised clutching tight her hidden sword, but disappointment revealed itself on her face as what seemed to be the Captain of the Fluyt appearing out from within the carriage. He shouted across to the crew giving orders for one of the embarking ramps to be lowered into position and once completed he disappeared from view.

Thirty minutes or so later a tug arrived alongside the Rode Star and the crew began to secure the two vessels with ropes for departure.

Brooding intensely Beechey knew the time for the attack was approaching fast, but no sign of any of the traitors she started to become anxious fearing De Winter used Whitby as a decoy.

Minutes later her apprehension was replaced by alertness because only after a few more glances along the main throughway another carriage drew close, her pulse rate increased.

Beechey watched carefully as the driver lowered himself from the coach and approached the Fluyt's boarding point. She could not hear what was being said, but the coach driver called over a deck orderly and dispatched him back onto the boat with a note. A few moments later the ship's Captain reappeared and approached the driver, Beechey watched the Captain look across and study the stationary carriage. Then after nodding his head the coach driver produced and gave to the Captain what appeared to be a coin purse.

The Captain held out the purse in the flat of his hand, balanced it as if he was studying the weight, then after a quick inspection he deposited the purse within his jacket and again briefly looked in the direction of the carriage. He then shook hands with the driver, turned his back and returned upon his vessel.

Beechey readied herself and she drew a slow long breath to expand her lungs until her hands were tremble free then holding tight all her muscles she slowly released the tension. She swallowed hard with salvia, convinced De Winter would now appear from within the carriage.

Slowly she raised herself and moved down another step and closer to the end of the ginnel to peer out from the shadow. Again she repeated the long breath and the tensing tight of her muscles before slowly exhaling to calm herself. Now braced and ready to attack she concentrated on the carriage, just a few yards away from her.

The driver returned to the carriage and looked around in all directions then he dropped the step and opened the door. He held out his hand to receive a small gloved lady's hand. Gripping the hand with just enough tension to offer a steadying comfort the driver assisted the female out of the carriage and out onto the cobbles of the harbour.

Beechey frowned and squinted hard, but she could not tell who the woman was because she wore a velvet hooded gown which she held in position with her free hand to conceal her identity. Cursing silently Beechey was certain the woman was the Countess, but not yet wanting to reveal herself she deliberately held back in the shadows.

Releasing the woman's hand the driver took a step back and curtsied then opened the carriage door again. This time a man leant forwards and a head appeared, but again Beechey could not identify the man as De Winter because he was looking along the street in the opposite direction to where she was stood, but then as he turned to glance around the opposite side of the harbour to assess the docks Beechey drew a large gulp of salty air, as there stood less than ten yards away was the despised Dutch traitor.

Deliberately timed he stood down from the carriage and whilst he narrowed his eyes to allow them to adjust to the brightness he still looked cautiously in all directions.

He placed his Tricorne upon his head with precision and nodded to the driver then he held out his arm for the Countess to clasp and link as slowly they started walking towards the embarking ramp.

Wiping the damp from her brow with her sleeve Beechey daringly leaped out from the darkness and charged forward without hesitation, sword drawn and held firm.

However, De Winter had an embedded instinct for danger and he had learnt from experience always to be prepared for the unexpected and to stay alert. He reacted with a wry smile as instantly he withdrew his sword and erected his gait to meet the assailant face to face.

His confidence oozed when he recognised the attacker as the English spy and his eyes opened wide with vengeance and fury. As both blades collided and he parried the forceful blow he taunted.

"There you are my dear. I've been expecting you."

The powerful rebuke of steel against steel hurled Beechey sidewards and her loss of balance forced her to collide into the startled Countess.

Beechey fell backwards and hard against the cold solid cobbles but the momentum of the contact resulted with the Countess losing total control of her poise and she screamed as she tumbled backwards and fell over the edge of the harbour wall plummeting into the dark water twenty feet below.

Neither of the combatants had time or an inclination to look at the hopeless woman as immediately they continued with their quest of killing each other.

Beechey was uninjured from the fall and she held firm her sword, but this time it was she who needed to avoid or block a swinging blade as De Winter lunged forward and hissed.

"This time you die! Traitorous Bitch."

"Not by you." She replied as she ducked low to avoid the returning swing. Then from her kneeling position she launched her blade forward. The move was easily counted by De Winter and he stamped on the blade holding it firm against the cobbles, but Beechey did not dwell on the failure and she deftly pulled out a knife from her boot and stabbed it hard into the side of De Winters calf just as a victorious look was setting on his face.

He gritted his teeth hard and clamping tight his jaw so that he did not scream out and release the acknowledgement of severe pain. He was forced to stagger back a few paces releasing the grounded sword.

Seeing her adversary stumble in pain, Beechey arose with regained vigour to seize upon the opportunity to attack the wounded man and in a continuous movement she raised her blade and swung it upwards towards his chest and face.

Although immense spasm bolted through his leg, De Winter was still astute and he read the attack by arching his back away from the flashing blade so that the only contact he felt was the gust of air as the steel passed close by his face.

Quickly he counted the failed attack and securing his feet he drove forwards again this time with his sword held straight at Beechey's chest area.

Beechey's side step was not entirely successful and the edge of De Winters sword sliced through her sleeve and into the flesh at the top of her right arm. She winced, but refused to show that she was hurt and trying to act unaffected she rebalanced herself quickly and held her stance firm as she prepared to counter his next attack.

"Damn your soul to hell!" He cursed.

"Coward!" She baited, but there was no instant reaction, instead De Winter grinned took an intake of breath and limped sidewards to prepare his next at attack.

The noise of swords clashing and the Countess's scream grabbed the attention of workmen and loiters and within a moment a large crowd of bewildered, but excited spectators had circled around the two fighters and they hailed eager for more blood to be spilled.

Attack, evade, attack, block and counter attacks of rapier blows continued for the next few minutes at a ferocious and relentless pace. Occasionally sarcastic and goading comments were passed between De Winter and Beechey as they struck out and parried with their skills being a match of equal excellence and calibre.

Blood flowed from them both where the sharp blades had found success and nicked several times against the flesh of it's target. Beechey's arm and the leg of De Winter were heavily damp with a continuous release of energy sapping blood.

Sweat poured heavily from them both and streaked their foreheads as a result of the effort, the tension and the stakes, but neither of them was prepared to yield or negotiate a truce.

The crowd enthused and in their excitement they occasionally drew in too close around the fighters, enclosing them in a small arena of tight bodies which restricted the fighter's movements, but as the blades swung perilously close to the bloodthirsty onlookers they alarmingly hurled back to put themselves out of the reach of the savage blows.

Some of them jeered and cheered in favour of the woman, but most of them were held in awe and aghast at the level of her skills which she displayed.

They revelled at her attacks and supported her with encouraging banter and at one point a burly figure of a man stepped in between the combatants to halt the duel, but he retreated quickly to disappear back amongst the crowd as De Winter threatened to condemn him to eternity.

"Step aside or die!" De Winter warned swinging his sword close to the man to demonstrate he was prepared to cut him down if he did not stand down.

"The bitch is a traitor and justice must prevail." He shouted at the crowd of encircled bodies to ensure there would be no further interference.

Remaining a silent observer on this occasion Beechey also requested that he moved clear by simply casting a fleeting smile and a nod to indicating the confused man should step aside.

Underfoot the cobbles began to get slippery from dripping fresh blood and red footprints were trodden to denote the macabre fighting arena. De Winter occasionally stumbled due to the wound in his left leg, but it did not deter or weaken his resolve. He was familiar to fighting through pain and he was able to mostly ignore the hindrance.

A handful of seamen on the ship had noticed the Countess fighting for life in the dark cold water. Her frantic splashing arm movements confirmed their thoughts that she was unable to swim. They threw down ropes, nets and fish traps for her to grab. Over and over they shouted and pointed, yelling and screaming instructions of what to do, but shaking their heads they sensed it was going to be in vain as she failed keep a grip on the lifesaving equipment and her head disappeared, protruded again out of the water and disappeared again beneath the sea, this was repeated a few more times until finally all the effort was lost and she totally disappeared quietly beneath the water leaving no trace that there had been any disturbance to the reflecting ripples.

One area where the fighters were not of equal matching was physically and strength. De Winter was a hardened fighting man and, although Beechey had been trained to the highest levels of duelling she had, only a few hours early endured the long and the lung sapping horse journey across the breadth of England and her toil was now becoming evident to all.

The crowd had noticed the decline in her reactions and speed. They frowned concern and regrets as they glanced impending looks of doom to one another, made hushed comments of fading hope, but lacking courage to intervene they gasped and sighed and waited for her life to be taken.

Beechey jaw hung loose as she drew in hard for breath and her sword now seemed too heavy to lift. She could not coordinate her movements and her timing had waned until it was almost non-existent. The fatigue had crept upon her fast.

De Winter began to toy with her and revel in her demise. He tormented her with feigned attacks and she began to lose her balance as she clumsily shifted to dodge the non-existent blade.

He freely stepped forth to humiliate her by slapping her hard across the face then eliminating her last traces of gusto he spat into her eyes.

With her chest rising and falling fast, De Winter grinned and took his time savouring her suffering and waiting for the opportune moment. Confidence beamed across his face as he watched her deterioration rapidly spreading into her arms and legs. She hovered, swaying and gasping for breath, her face purple with blood and her eyes yellow with exhaustion from inadequate refills of air. Her left arm was hanging motionless by her side and blood pouring down her forearm to pool in the cobbles at her feet.

Swaying defencelessly she waited for the final blow.

De Winter swung the tip of his sword diagonally across her body slicing deep into her flesh as he revelled in her torture her.

"Let it be said that you put up more of a fight than your gutless husband."

Some of the members of the crowd begin to show their displeasure and becoming disturbed and distressed at the barbaric display they called for the butchery to end. A few of the braver men fleetingly raised enough courage to challenge De Winter to stop and show mercy, but they coward back into the crowd as De Winter threatened to slice open anyone who dared to interfere. He was in no mood to yield and stop punishing the traitor.

"Your cries will live long in my memory." He sneered kicking Beechey in the chest with the flat of his foot.

Dropping to one knee completely exhausted, Beechey gathered all her last remnants of energy and defiance to summon one final blow at De Winters calf as he reproached the few protesters, but the movement was awkward, slow and laboured and De Winter deftly stepped back to knock away the sword then turn on his heels to launch his boot powerfully against her mouth. Blood sprayed from her mouth as her head snapped back and her exhausted body fell back and crashed flat onto the cobbles.

De Winters demonic eyes circled across the aghast faces of the crowd as he defiantly waved his blade and touted for challengers to stop him. With no heroes stepping forward his gaze bore down on his expiring enemy.

"Time to die. Bitch!" He threatened as he straddled over her.

"My death scream will haunt you forever."

"I'm afraid my dear it will only give great peace every night."

Beechey tried to summon another reply, but only blood came out of her mouth. He slid his feet closer to her side and stood on her hair pining her head to the blooded cobbles and holding her head tight so she was directly facing him as he raised his sword high above his head and prepared to drive the blade down viciously fast and hard into her motionless body.

"Your death will be savoured."

On the verge of collapse Beechey refused to close her eyes, she said no prayers or held thoughts of regrets. She accepted her fate and defiantly fixed her gaze on the face of her killer then clasping tight her jaw she waited for death.

De Winter stood tall above her raising his sword slowly for the death blow. He knew she was completely powerless to act and defend herself. His eyes flickered across the surrounding blanched faces, but no one moved or spoke and silence beset amongst the sickened fevered.

De Winter stood firm, poised smiling with his head at a slight angle he proudly revelled and savoured his moment of victory and execution. He drew a large breath as he prepared to unleash the final savage blow, but suddenly his facial expression changed from a manic grin of supreme confidence to a grimace of perplexed shock and his eyes gaped open in panic as stepping out of the crowd in front of him he recognised immediately the battle battered face of Lazar Benedict, alias the ruffian Jem Rose.

Speculation danced in his probing eyes ,but he had no time to react as the blade of the highwayman plunge hard and deep into his body only stopping when the metal tip struck the against the Dutchman's back bone.

A high pitched scream of pain lanced everyone's ears as De Winter spat out air and a mouthful of blood, but he could find no words and unable to respond in any way other than casting a look of horror he remained stationary and looked on as the highwayman withdrew the blade and savagely stabbed it back into De Winter's body three more times in rapid succession.

De Winter sword was released and clanked against the floor, his legs gave way and he dropped down to his knees toppling over onto his back. Eyes wide open, blood pouring from his mouth and oozing from the body wounds he lay static as his life began to ebb away.

Beechey shot a disbelieving glare at Jem and summoned up all her energy to haul the top half of her body over De Winter. Looking directly into his eyes she felt the warmth of his last breath expel on her face.

"Go to hell bastard!" She screamed as she spat a mouthful of blood and saliva into his vacant greying eyes.

No one moved, spoke or tried to interact. The crowd remained silent and static in shock as a result of the barbaric scene which had developed and concluded in front of their eyes.

Having dropped his sword, Jem firmed his feet and his stance then he lowered down his right hand to grip under Beechey's shoulder before carefully hauling her onto her feet. Leaning on each other for support they steadied themselves. Beechey's mournful demeanour temporary vanished and smiling she looked direct into Jem eyes.

"The Baron?" She whispered.

"He is safe."

"Tavish?"

"In hell."

CPSIA information can be obtained
at www.ICGtesting.com
Printed in the USA
BVHW042336171122
652258BV00003B/53

9 798215 356142